DREAM STALKER

The bird emitted a single, low "whoo," then spread its wings. As the animal dove from its perch, the frightened girl threw down her flashlight and began to run.

She fell once, feeling the wings of the bird brush against her when she did. She fell a second time as she tripped over what was left of the campfire.

Scrambling to her feet, she stumbled toward the car, trying to swat the bird away. As her fingers touched the door handle, she felt a cold darkness envelop her.

Her screams blended with the screeching of the owl to form a single voice, a voice swallowed by the cold chill of the mountain night.

Miles away, a boy heard the screams. He didn't know what they meant and was afraid that if he went back to sleep, the dream would come again. . . .

Also by Micah S. Hackler

LEGEND OF THE DEAD
COYOTE RETURNS

THE
SHADOW
CATCHER

MICAH S. HACKLER

A DELL BOOK

Published by
Dell Publishing
a division of
Bantam Doubleday Dell Publishing Group, Inc.
1540 Broadway
New York, New York 10036

ISBN: 0-440-22339-3

Printed in the United States of America

Published simultaneously in Canada

March 1997

10 9 8 7 6 5 4 3 2 1

OPM

For
Stan and Julie Gutierrez

ACKNOWLEDGMENTS

Continued thanks to George Sewell and Dan Baldwin, my partners in THE FACTORY. We've pushed, cajoled, complimented, and critiqued each other to the point that all of our dreams are coming true.

Special thanks to my dad, Jack, my sister, Jean Iverson, and Stan and Julie Gutierrez, my in-laws. Their continued moral and—sometimes—financial support has helped see us through the bleak times.

Thanks to Bill and Linda Rambin for all the years of support and friendship. Also to the Perreros: Don (for all his pointers on how to write a sex scene) and Robin (who's actually read my manuscripts, followed by great words of encouragement).

Again, thanks to my agent, Nancy Love, for helping me through the final draft. And thanks to Jacob Hoye and his excellent staff. They all make it easy for me to be a writer.

O, ha le
O, ha le!
Through the air
I will fly upon the eagle's wings
To find the Holy Place.
O, ha le
O, ha le!
The One Who Never Dies
Will guide me through the darkness
To find the Holy Place.
O, ha le
O, ha le!
I have no choice! The Owl has called my name
And I must go
To find the Holy Place!
O, ha le
O, ha le!

Apache Death Chant

MARCUS HAD RIDDEN WITH HIS FATHER AND HIS Uncle Dan all the way up from Dulce, sitting between them in the pickup truck. He had found the conversation dull. It mostly centered on who Uncle Dan, a confirmed bachelor, was currently dating.

Marcus really didn't care. School was out for the summer, and he had been invited to go to work with the big guys. It beat being stuck at home doing yard work and chores around the house.

The oil derrick didn't look that impressive at first. But as they got closer it grew bigger and bigger. When they finally came to a stop next to the drilling supervisor's trailer, the derrick looked a hundred feet tall to the boy.

The constant pounding and clanging of the drilling unit was almost deafening, even with the windows of the truck rolled up.

"I think it's time we pulled some more samples," Daniel yelled as he opened the door of the truck.

Marcus's father nodded. "We'll get right on it." He opened the driver's door and got out. Reaching behind the seat, he pulled out an aluminum hard hat and popped it on his head.

"Dad," Marcus yelled, "can I go up to the platform with you?"

"You got your hard hat?"

"It's in the back of the truck."

His father looked at the rig. No new pipe was being swung into place. "Okay," he nodded. "But you know the rules. Stay clear of the pipes. Stay clear of the chains. If somebody tells you to get out of the way, you do it."

"Yes, sir!" Marcus scrambled out behind his uncle and ran to the back of the truck. He found his yellow plastic hard hat buried under a pile of paper cups and dirty rags. A moment later he caught up to his father, who had nearly reached the metal steps leading up to the drilling platform.

Marcus had an innate curiosity about everything in the world. He tended to notice things that seemed unusual or out of place. That morning was no exception. Atop the utility pole next to the trailer sat an owl.

"Look, Dad," Marcus yelled.

His father glanced toward the pole, but seemed disinterested. He started up the metal steps.

Marcus was a little disappointed that his father wasn't more impressed. Then again, Marcus supposed, his father probably saw owls around the rig all the time.

He followed his father up the steps.

Marcus loved the smell of the oil rig. It reminded him of his father. It was the same odor that permeated his father's clothes and the interior of his truck. It was the smell of an honorable man who worked hard for a living. It was an odor Marcus associated with love and security, like the aroma of one of his mother's pot roast dinners.

Once he was on top of the platform Marcus turned to look out over the surrounding terrain. They were ten feet above the ground, but to Marcus it seemed much higher. He could see the roof of the trailer. He was almost eye level with the top of the utility pole, recently vacated by the owl. At the age of twelve he was more impressed with man-made things—like the great pond of drilling mud next to the rig and the towering derrick above him—than he was with the beautiful mountains that surrounded him.

His father and uncle were standing next to the drilling pipe when the rumble started. Marcus held on to the guardrail to steady himself. This was a new experience for him. He was used to the normal vibrations and thumps that occurred around a platform, but he had never felt a rumble before.

The rumble started to grow louder and the deck began to shake. Marcus found himself holding on to the railing with both hands to keep from falling.

His father began barking orders at the half dozen roughnecks working around the platform. Men started scrambling about in response. His father came running over to him. "Get off the rig!" he yelled. "It's not safe!"

"What about you?" Marcus cried.

"I've got to stay here. You get off! Now! And start running! It's not safe! Run!"

Marcus did as his father said. He bounded down the metal stairs two steps at a time. When he hit the ground he started running. He ran for fifty yards before he stopped and turned to see if his father was coming.

His father was still on the rig. He was waving at Marcus to keep running. Marcus couldn't hear him, but he could see his father mouthing the words *Run! It's not safe! Run!*

Marcus watched as the rig exploded. A fireball of flame and smoke shot into the sky, billowing into a mushroom.

Marcus looked back at the platform in horror. His father was engulfed in flames. As he stumbled down the metal steps he kept waving at Marcus and yelling, "Run! Run! It's not safe!"

"Momma! Momma!" Marcus screamed. "He's on fire! We have to help him! Momma! Daddy's on fire!"

"Marcus," his mother yelled, turning on the light in his bedroom. "What's wrong?"

"Daddy! I saw him. He's on fire!" he screamed again. "We have to help him!"

His mother hurried to his bed and took him in her arms. "It's all right, honey. It's just a dream. You had a nightmare."

"It's not a dream. I saw it! I was there. We have to tell him. It's not safe."

She held him tightly in her arms and began to rock him. "It's all right, Marcus. Daddy's fine. There's nothing wrong."

"We have to tell him!" Marcus whimpered. "We have to tell him it's not safe!"

"You wait right here," his mother said, hurrying to the door. "I have to make a phone call. But you don't have a thing to worry about. Daddy's safe. You were just having a bad dream."

"No!" Marcus screamed. "It was not a dream! I saw it. I saw it! I saw it!"

JOHN BALTAZAR STARTED TO CLIMB DOWN FROM the drilling platform when he saw the pickup truck approaching. The winter had been dry and it was still too early for the summer rains, so a cloud of dust chased the truck down the dirt road.

It was a fine June morning, and once he was clear of the compressor's diesel fumes, the drilling supervisor could savor the clean mountain air. Stopping at the bottom of the metal stairs, something caught his eye. Atop the single utility pole that linked the supervisor's trailer to the rig's generator sat a great horned owl.

The bird's presence surprised him. It was almost midmorning. Owls were seldom seen in the open much after dawn, and the nearest tree was a mile away. What was more, the constant racket generated by the oil derrick kept most animals at a great distance. Even coyotes, the most irreverent of creatures when it came to avoiding human activity, did not venture very close.

As the owl watched him cross the dusty field to the trailer, Baltazar couldn't help but feel a little unnerved. He could remember all the stories his grandfather had told him about owls and what their appearance meant. He shook off the uneasiness. He was a grown man now. There wasn't room in his life for bedtime stories.

He gauged his walk, as he had so many times before, so that he reached the trailer at the same time the truck came to a stop.

"You're late, little brother," Baltazar yelled, trying to overcome the incessant metallic pounding coming from the rig behind him.

"Stopped by the hospital," Daniel Baltazar yelled back, then shook his head. He pointed toward the trailer. His older brother nodded, then led the way.

The decibel level dropped significantly once Daniel closed the door. "I said I stopped by the hospital. Thought I'd check on Grandpa."

"How's he doing?" John asked as he poured himself a cup of coffee from a stained glass pot.

"They're releasing him today."

The interior of the trailer had been converted from a comfortable thirty-foot travel home to a functional oil-field office. Along the wall opposite the door was one long, continuous table cluttered with drilling samples, charts, a microscope, a spectrometer, and dozens of spent foam cups. A metal table with four folding chairs served as the conference center at one end of the single room. At the opposite end was a built-in bunk with a thin cotton mattress.

"Already?" John was concerned. "Do they really think he can take care of himself?"

"All he had was a few bruises." Daniel watched as his brother took a sip from his cup. "Coffee any good?"

John gave his brother a sour look. "About as good as drilling mud. Why don't you make us a new pot?"

"The first one in our family to get a college education and look what you make me do."

Daniel was kidding and John knew it. John was proud of his younger brother. And it was true: Daniel was the first one in their family to go to college. He was a geologist. Not just a geologist. He was the consulting geologist to the Jicarilla Apache tribe and the chief geologist for Baltazar Brothers' Drilling and Oil Field Servicing.

The two men contrasted each other drastically. Although they were close to the same height, John, older by four years, was stocky with a thick middle and wide, clumsy hands. Daniel was thin with slender, artistlike fingers. While on the job John wore dark-green dungarees that always seemed grease-stained. Daniel wore tan khaki shirts and pants that never seemed to wrinkle.

John Baltazar had always hoped the two of them could work together when they grew up. School was never John's forte when he was younger. He'd barely graduated from high school. Fortunately, the Jicarilla vocational school had taught him welding, and there was always work for welders in the oil field. It had taken nearly twenty years to work his way up from welder to supervisor, but he had done it.

Now they were partners in their own business. His younger brother picked the spots and he drilled them. John liked that relationship. Not only was Daniel his brother and partner, he was his best friend. He wished his parents had survived to see their success.

"Christina caught me this morning before I left the house."

"Anything wrong?" There was a hint of worry in John's voice. Like most Jicarilla Apaches, he and his brother lived in Dulce at the northern end of the reservation. Their current drilling operation was seventy-five miles southwest of town, and it sometimes took two hours to cover the distance on the mountain roads. As drilling supervisor John felt obligated to stay with the twenty-four-hour-a-day operation as much as possible. He seldom made it home more than once a week.

"There's nothing to worry about," Daniel reassured him. "She just wanted me to tell you she took Marcus in to the doctor again."

"Nightmares?"

Daniel nodded. "She said they've been getting worse the last couple of nights. She needed to get something to help him sleep."

"You didn't say anything to Grandpa, did you?"

"Of course not."

"Good." Trying to take his mind off his son, John poked at a tray containing a clump of crushed rock from the well. "These are the latest samples. Came in about an hour ago."

Daniel glanced over his shoulder as he filled the coffeepot from a thirty-gallon water can. "We through the sandstone yet?"

"You're the expert, Danny. But I'd say we've hit shale."

Daniel smiled as he poured the water into the top of the coffee maker. "I knew we were getting close."

"Did Grandpa bring up the well?"

"Yeah, and he was none too happy."

"He still wants us to shut this thing down?"

Daniel nodded. "He said he had another vision last night. He said we had to stop drilling. Today. Before it was too late."

"Jeez." John shook his head. "We've brought in twenty-five wells together. I don't know what the hell that old man is worried about. I swear he must have smacked his head when he wrecked that truck."

"That had nothing to do with it. He didn't want us to do any drilling a long time before he had his wreck. What's wrong?" Daniel kidded. "You used to believe in his visions."

"Yeah, and I used to believe in the tooth fairy and

Santa Claus. Hector Velarde would just love for us to shut down. Cuartelejo Management would have our tribal contract before we hit the council chamber door."

"Which is why we won't shut down." Daniel walked over and pinched a small amount of crushed shale from the latest well sample. He held the sample to his nose and sniffed. "Damn, big brother! This smells like oil. When did you take this sample?"

"About an hour ago."

"I'm going to get a new one." Daniel grabbed an aluminum hard hat from a peg next to the door. "We've got to be close. You coming?"

"I'm right behind you. Let me get some coffee. I'll be right there."

John moved the glass pot aside so he could fill his cup with fresh coffee. Through the open door he could see his brother trotting toward the drilling rig. When Daniel reached the bottom of the metal steps leading up to the platform, John glanced down to finish filling his cup.

As John stepped from the trailer he noticed the curious dance of an owl's feather being swept along the ground by a breeze. From the top of the metal steps Daniel was yelling at someone: "Hey, you! What the hell do you think you're doing?"

John looked up to see what the commotion was all about.

That was the last thing he remembered before the explosion.

3

THERE WAS NO MOON. AND EVEN THOUGH THE night was cloudless the stars were masked by the thick canopy of forest. Beams from flashlights swept back and forth, searching the steep mountainside for any sign, any track, any hint.

Lansing had spaced out the searchers to either side of him. Five to his left. Six to his right. They had started at the mountain road, just below the Girl Scout camp. That's where the counselor said she had heard the screams.

But that had been hours ago. Just after lights out. Around ten o'clock. It was nearly one before the sheriff had gathered the search party together.

Lansing was placed in charge of the search. He spread the volunteers ten to fifteen yards apart. The slope was relatively clear of underbrush, so he didn't feel they needed to be bunched together. But the sheer grade made for slow progress. And the beams from the flashlights played tricks with shadows. What could have been a torn nightgown turned out to be litter. What might have been a shoe ended up being a lichen-covered rock.

Lansing was distracted by the plaintive hoot from an owl just above him. Instinctively, he shone his light in the direction of the bird.

The great owl spread his wings, and for a moment Lansing thought the animal was going to attack. The fowl bent down and glowered at the intruder. Then suddenly the bird gave a mighty flap of his wings and disappeared into the darkness.

"Deputy Lansing," the closest volunteer yelled. "I think I found something!"

Lansing nearly lost his footing as he scrambled toward the man's light. The searcher was standing over a pile of dead pine-tree branches. He was trying to shine his light through the tangle of needles while holding on to a sapling to maintain his position.

"It looks like there might be something underneath these branches."

Without a word Lansing dropped his own flashlight and started tossing the clutter of branches aside. The deputy could tell the limbs had been stacked intentionally. They were crisscrossed to blanket something underneath. It took only a moment before the light-colored cloth of a child's nightgown was revealed.

Other searchers began converging on the spot, adding their beams to the first man's light.

It took Lansing a moment to realize what he had uncovered.

Three small bodies lay side by side. Each wore a heavy cotton nightgown to stop the chill of the mountain nights. The nightgowns were torn, soiled, and bloody. Lansing forced himself to look at the faces. He heard himself yelling, "No! No! No!"

Sheriff Cliff Lansing sat up in bed. He was covered with sweat and shaking with anger. It was a second or two before he realized he was at home, in his own bed. He ran his fingers through his hair as if the effort would enhance his consciousness. Both hands stopped at the back of his neck. He could feel the knotted weariness in his muscles.

Why that dream? Why that dream now? Tonight?

Lansing was a practical man. He dealt in a world of facts, cause and effect. Everything could be explained, critiqued, analyzed. This wasn't the first time he'd had that dream. It had been a constant nightmare for almost two years.

But as he grew older, and time separated him from the incident, the dreams had become less frequent. Eventually they'd stopped altogether. Now, after all those years, it was back.

Why?

Lansing caught the faint stench of smoke. He smelled his fingers. Despite lathering up well and standing in the shower for nearly thirty minutes, he still smelled like the forest fire he had helped fight for two days. The musty odor of burned leaves and charred timber still oozed through his pores.

The Apache reservation. There had been an oil-rig explosion. The dry grass had caught fire and spread quickly to the pine forest a mile away.

One of the lookout towers in Carson National Forest caught sight of the blaze and sent out the alarm. Firefighters from the national forest joined Apache volunteers. Additional help poured in from Sandoval and San Phillipe Counties.

Lansing and his deputies had abandoned their regular duties to assist their neighbors in the fight. Despite the dry conditions throughout the mountains, the blaze was contained within thirty-six hours of the initial explosion.

There had been a few injuries during the fire, but no fatalities. The explosion had been another matter. At least six men had been killed. That's all Lansing knew.

It was after midnight when Lansing got to Marilyn's

house. Marilyn was the Earth Mother, secretary-receptionist for the San Phillipe County Sheriff's Department. When Lansing told her that he had to help fight the fire, she volunteered to watch his twelve-year-old son, C.J.

The boy was sound asleep when Lansing arrived to pick him up. C.J. tried to ask a dozen different questions about the fire during the fifteen-minute drive to the Lansing ranch, but he kept dozing off. Lansing had to scoop his son into his arms and carry him to bed once they were home.

Was it because he had spent the past two days on the Apache reservation? Was that why he had the dream?

Or was it the peaceful look on his son's face when Lansing put him to bed? Did that remind him of the little girls? They were barely twelve. The same age as his son.

"C.J.!" Lansing said loudly. He threw his covers off. Grabbing his robe, he nearly ran down the hall to his son's room. Throwing the door open, he switched on the light. "C.J.!"

C.J. sat up, startled. "W-what, Dad? What is it?" He shielded his eyes with one hand.

Lansing felt embarrassed, betrayed by his own fear. He walked over and ruffled his son's hair. "Nothing, son. I just wanted to make sure you were all right."

"Yeah. I'm okay."

"Good. You lay back down and go to sleep."

C.J. did as he was told, rolling onto his side so his back was to the door.

Lansing walked over and switched off the light.

"Good night, Dad," C.J. said from the darkness. "I love you."

"I love you too, C.J." Lansing paused at the door for a long moment. "Good night son."

4

THE TRIBAL COUNCIL MEETING WAS GRIM. IT had been three days since the oil-rig explosion. Even though the forest fire had been brought under control, the well fire still hadn't been extinguished.

The experts from Houston had their equipment in place and had been given the all-clear to go in and put out the derrick fire. They were confident everything would be under control in another twenty-four hours.

Despite the seemingly good news, no one on the Jicarilla Apache Reservation was elated. Six men had been killed. Another three had been burned, two severely. With a forest fire to fight there had not yet been time to mourn the losses.

An emergency session of the tribal council had been called. Tribal President Hector Velarde presided. In attendance were the vice president, the eighteen sitting members of the council, and the three tribal judges.

Though most sessions were open to any member of the tribe, Velarde wanted to keep the chaos to a minimum. For this meeting he was allowing only persons who had information directly bearing on the current crisis. There were statements from the fire chief, the chief of police, the land manager, and the chief physician from the clinic. Once all the pertinent reports had been completed along with the associated discussions, one last person was going to address the assembly.

President Velarde almost regretted the fact that he was going to allow Esteban Baltazar to speak. Esteban was old and frail, and many thought he was senile. But Baltazar was the senior medicine man of the tribe. He had the right to speak. He had suffered from the tragedy, as many of the tribe had. Two of his grandsons had been caught in the explosion. One had been killed. He most certainly had the right to speak.

When Velarde indicated it was his turn to talk, Baltazar stood so he could address the council. At ninety, he was not only the oldest medicine man but the oldest member of the tribe. Thin and wrinkled, with long white hair, he stood just under five and a half feet tall. His solemn dark-gray suit hung on him, two sizes too large. In another setting he would have appeared comical. But not now. Not tonight. His hands refused to shake with the palsy of age, and his voice, though thin with years, was firm.

"I come here tonight, as we all do, with a heavy heart. There is nothing I can say that can change what has happened. There is nothing I can do that will stop our pain. But all of that will pass when the grieving time is over.

"None of you remembers when we almost died as a people. None of you was born yet. Over seventy years ago. It was when Cesar TeCube and I were still young men. We watched our sisters and our brothers, our friends and parents die from the tuberculosis. We watched as our grandparents passed away from too little to eat and from exposure because they still lived in tepees.

"For every birth, two would die. Barely five hundred of us still lived. We were a dying people.

"I thought I would die too. It was then that the *Gahe*, the Mountain Spirits, first came to me. They gave me a vision. Though I did not know it and we did not speak of it for many years, it was the night Cesar TeCube had his first vision.

"The *hactcin*, our holy people, blessed us that we would become Shadowcatchers. Able to see into the future.

"Cesar and I both saw that the Jicarilla people would not die. He as an Ollero and I as a Llanero united our tribe. He became keeper of our Holiness Rite, the Bear Dance. I was taught the secret of *hoddentin* and the curing herbs.

"And for many years people came to us because they believed in us and our powers. They believed in our medicine and that our hold to the traditional ways would keep us strong.

"There was a time when Cesar and I sat on this council. We tried to be wise and give good leadership. We always put the welfare of our people foremost. When the time came for younger, better-educated men to manage our affairs, we rightfully stepped down.

"Since that time the Jicarilla people have become prosperous. We are self-sufficient. We raise enough food to feed ourselves. We mine and drill for the riches of the earth and use that prosperity to educate and train our young people. We provide jobs and opportunities for our children so that they remain on the reservation.

"But in all of our success we are failing. On and off the reservation there are three thousand in our tribe now. And even though each one revels in his Apache heritage, no one comes forward to learn the old ways.

"I grieved deeply when Cesar TeCube died. Not only at the loss of a friend and brother, but because there are less than a dozen medicine men in our tribe now. I am one of the few who knows all forty-eight songs to the Holiness Rite.

"We have let jealousies divide us. The Ollero believe they should be keepers of the Bear Dance. When I pass on, let it be so. It should not divide us.

"But what makes my heart cry is that no one believes. Yes, men wear the buckskin hoods of the Mountain Spirits and dance during the festivals, but no one believes. Parents celebrate the *Na Ih Es* when their daughters come of age in the puberty rites, but no one believes. No one truly believes in the *Gahe* or the powers of *Yusun*, the Creator.

"I am a Shadowcatcher. My visions are strong, but no one believes. I came to you, the leaders of our tribe, and said, 'Do not drill this well.' You listened to my words and then turned your backs. Just as you did last fall when three hunters were killed. Just as you did before the mine accident.

"But you will listen to me now and take my warning. There is a darkness descending upon us. An evil medicine. I have seen his shadow, but not his face. His medicine is too strong. The explosion at the oil rig was not his first mischief. It will not be his last. The others were all part of his design. And there will be more.

"I am old. Too old. I cannot stop the darkness. But I have seen the future enough to know there is still one among us who can stop the evil. When he speaks, the council must listen.

"Those are my words. That is what I came to say."

Baltazar solemnly sat back down.

"Who is it we are supposed to listen to, Esteban?" Velarde asked. There was slightest hint of sarcasm in the council president's voice.

"It was not revealed to me," Baltazar admitted.

"Then how will we know when he speaks to us?"

"When the time comes, you will know."

Velarde studied the old man for a moment, then addressed the rest of the assembly. "Does anyone else have any questions?"

A couple of people cleared their throats indicating their discomfort, but said nothing.

Velarde rapped his gavel. "I declare this meeting adjourned."

5

Esteban Baltazar stared quietly out the passenger window, trying to concentrate on the surrounding countryside. It was night, and the forested mountains were lit by stars and the first half of a new moon. Snow still clung to a few of the higher peaks. Even with summer just a few weeks away, the mountain air was still chilly.

He did not think his speech to the council went well. There was a time when his words meant something. It didn't seem that long ago when any discussion he presented ended only after dozens of questions were asked by eager listeners.

Hector Velarde barely thanked him for his appearance. The other members of the council passed him in the hall of the community center avoiding both conversation and eye contact.

Baltazar knew he was old. But he also knew he was neither stupid nor senile. He was sure that's what the council members thought. What he couldn't stand was the idea that they were all taking pity on him because of that thought.

"Grandfather, are you sure you won't spend one more night with us?" Christina asked.

"I can't. I spent a week in the hospital and the last two nights with you. I'm ready for my own bed."

"None of us likes the idea of you being out here by yourself. Especially now that you've lost your truck."

The thought of the truck accident angered Baltazar. Not because it had happened, but because he hadn't foreseen it. As he lay in the hospital he'd realized there was no physical explanation for the accident. He was driving down Highway 14 on a cloudless day. The road was dry. As he approached one of the turns on the mountain road, the truck failed to respond.

Before Baltazar knew it he was plunging down the side of a mountain. If a pine tree hadn't stopped his truck he would have been killed.

Captain Koteen, the chief of the tribal police, said he inspected the truck. Nothing was wrong with the steering. Koteen suggested that Baltazar had probably dozed off and didn't even see the turn. That angered Baltazar as well. He hadn't fallen asleep. He knew what had happened. His medicine was still strong. Stronger than the Dark One's medicine. So far.

He reached into the pocket of his jacket and felt for the pistol. John always kept a .38 handy. Rattlesnakes were frequent visitors to the drilling sites in the summertime, and John hated dealing with medical emergencies. Since John wouldn't be going to work for a while, Baltazar didn't think his grandson would mind him borrowing the gun for a few days.

"I can take care of myself. Besides, you have your hands full taking care of John."

"His burns aren't as bad as they first thought. And Marcus is always a big help."

"Yes. Marcus." Baltazar continued staring out the window. "He is getting to be a young man."

"It's hard to believe he'll be thirteen in two more

months. It seems like just yesterday he was still in diapers."

Baltazar nodded but said nothing. He wanted to ask about his great-grandson's nightmares, but he knew the subject was taboo. He had tried to tell Christina and John there was nothing wrong with their son. That his dreams were nothing to be afraid of, if only Baltazar was allowed to guide him through them. But neither parent wanted his help. They wanted the help of specialists, people who understood such traumas.

The canopy of stars above the lonely mountain road seemed to flicker for a moment, then disappear. The darkness lasted for only a second or two. Then the stars reappeared just as suddenly.

Baltazar looked at his grandson's wife. Her concentration on the winding road seemed total. She obviously hadn't noticed what he had seen. He decided to keep quiet.

Baltazar's small farm was located thirty miles south of Dulce. For years his family had tried to get him to move into town, but he refused. His father had homesteaded the small plot in the 1890s, and Baltazar refused to abandon the only home he had ever known. The house was relatively new, built in 1950. But the land was what he was tied to, and that was what he refused to leave.

Christina turned off the highway and started driving the short distance to Baltazar's house.

"Stop here," the old man ordered.

"Here?" Christina asked, slowing only a little.

"Yes. Stop here!" Baltazar was emphatic.

She brought the truck to an abrupt halt. "Grandfather, it's still a half mile to your house."

Baltazar opened his door. "I must walk from here."

"Why?"

Baltazar couldn't find the right word to use. As a very young boy his first language was Apache. As he grew older most of the people he encountered spoke Spanish, which became his second language. He didn't learn how to speak English until he went to the tribal boarding school in Dulce. Sometimes he still had trouble with the language.

The word he wanted to use was *compelled*. He felt compelled to walk the final half mile to his house, just as he had felt compelled to spend that night in his own home. The word somehow escaped him. When Christina asked him "Why?" he answered the best he could.

"Because I must." He stepped outside the truck and shut the door. Without another word he started walking down the single-lane road that led to his house.

Christina could only watch as the old man disappeared beyond the range of her headlights. Once he was out of sight she shook her head helplessly, then turned the truck around to head back to town.

Baltazar could hear Christina's truck disappear into the night as the dark outline of his house began to take shape ahead of him. The home he had lived in for half of his ninety years suddenly seemed cold and uninviting.

Above him came the flapping of wings, and a dark, menacing object swooped close to his head. The sliver of moon and stars disappeared again, just as they had on the road earlier. The total darkness lasted only a second or two, but Baltazar froze as the winged object brushed against him.

He felt a cold shudder run through him, and he instinctively knew it was because of something more than the chilly mountain air. He reached beneath his jacket and felt for his *jish*, his medicine pouch. For his entire adult life his *jish* had hung from a leather strap around his neck or lay by his side. It held his *hod-*

dentin, a sacred mixture of corn pollen, catkin bark, Apache sage root, and other things. Secret things. Its power had protected him, protected his people, from the darkness, sometimes even death.

The *jish* wasn't there; then he remembered. It was in a safe place. The pouch's power was strong, and it could be used for good or for evil. He could not let it fall into the wrong hands.

He hesitated as he stared at the stone and mortar house in front of him. A voice deep inside him told him to turn and walk away. But he knew he couldn't. The English word he had looked for minutes before suddenly popped into his head. He was *compelled* to go inside. He knew if he didn't, nothing could be resolved.

As he put his foot on the first step leading to his porch, something rustled in the branches of a tree close to the house. Baltazar looked toward the noise. When he did, a great horned owl emitted two low, almost guttural *hoos*.

The omen was clear.

Whatever fears or misgivings Baltazar had before that moment suddenly evaporated. The Angel of Death was upon him and there was nothing he could do.

As he pushed his key against the lock, the front door swung open. He knew he had locked it before he left. Maybe Christina forgot to lock it when she retrieved his suit the day before. Baltazar doubted that. He reached into his jacket and pulled out the .38 he had borrowed.

As Baltazar stepped inside, the great owl issued a final warning, then spread his wings and swooped from his perch.

6

Lansing had been a little surprised at Ned Koteen's request. The San Phillipe sheriff's office seldom got involved in reservation affairs. This would be the second time in a week that he was going onto the reservation on official business.

The Jicarilla Apache Reservation divided the western portion of San Phillipe County in half and ran from the Colorado state line south into Sandoval County. It was impossible to get from one side of the county to the other without passing through the reservation.

Koteen had eight policemen under his command. The small force was strictly responsible for the twenty-five hundred tribe members on the reservation. Each man, however, had multiple responsibilities. At times they were purely law-enforcement officers. Other times they acted as game wardens, forest rangers, even firefighters.

The state of New Mexico maintained one resident highway patrolman on the reservation. It was his duty to ensure that the numerous non-Apache visitors to the reservation obeyed the laws. If any major crimes were committed, federal officers had to be called in.

Lansing and his deputies patrolled Highway 64 on the north, since that was the only access to the west side of the county. The reservation police occasionally apprehended an Anglo DWI suspect for Lansing to round up, but Koteen and his men always handled their own affairs.

Lansing didn't mind being called in on a professional basis. But Koteen had been vague and very abrupt. He had said only that he had a problem and needed the sheriff's help. He couldn't be any more specific.

The sheriff was disappointed he couldn't send one of his deputies. His son, C.J., was in town for his four-week summer visit, and Lansing wanted to spend as much time with him as he could. He had already lost two days helping with the forest fire.

There was no such thing as a "vacation" for Lansing. He would slip away for the occasional long weekend, but he hadn't had more than four days off in a row in over six years.

Koteen had apologized for the inconvenience, but under the circumstances it was important that the sheriff come himself.

Following the captain's directions, Lansing turned his Jeep off the two-lane blacktop onto the gravel road. A half mile further down he could see Koteen's truck parked in front of a ranch house built of stone and rough-hewn timbers. One other truck was parked next to his.

"Hey, Cliff," Koteen called, emerging from the front door.

Lansing put on his Stetson as he stepped from the Jeep. "Hi, Ned. Looks like a used truck convention here."

Koteen tried to force a smile as he approached

his fellow lawman. "Yeah. You need 'em in these mountains. . . ."

"So, what's up?"

"I have a murder on my hands, Cliff." Koteen's expression was grim.

Lansing glanced at the other truck. "Family disturbance?"

"No, I don't think so."

"Who was it?"

"You knew him—Esteban Baltazar."

"The tribe's chief medicine man?"

Koteen nodded.

"Do you need me to go in and take a look?"

"Not yet. Give them a few more minutes. There's family in there right now."

Lansing glanced toward the open front door. A woman emerged with her face buried in her hands. Behind her came a man dressed in a red flannel shirt and faded blue jeans. The man's hands were wrapped in heavy white bandages. A casualty of the recent forest fire, Lansing thought. A boy of about twelve had his arms wrapped around the man's waist, his head buried so no one could see he had been crying.

The woman didn't stop for introductions. She whispered an "Excuse me" as she hurried past the two officers.

Koteen cleared his throat. "John, you know Sheriff Lansing, don't you?"

"Yeah." The man nodded. " 'Lo, Sheriff."

With fewer than twenty thousand people in the county, Lansing knew most of the residents by sight. John Baltazar had been in town many times. He returned the nod. "Sorry to hear about your grandfather."

"Yeah. It's been a bad week."

Lansing could tell the man was saving his emotions for a more private time.

"Do you need anything from us right now, Ned?"

"No. Go on home. I know you have things to take care of. I'll get in touch with you later."

Baltazar led his son to their truck. Neither looked back at the house as they left.

Lansing looked at Koteen. "What did he mean, it's been a bad week?"

"John and his brother, Daniel, were at the rig when it exploded. Daniel was killed. John was the drilling supervisor. I guess he feels responsible for what happened." Koteen nodded toward the house. "Now this." He took a couple of steps toward the door. "I have to admit, it isn't a pretty sight."

Lansing braced himself. He expected a lot of blood. He figured he would be looking at a gunshot wound. Maybe even a blast from a shotgun. Those were the worst. They left gaping holes, missing limbs, missing faces and heads.

The interior was dimly lit, and it took a few seconds for his eyes to adjust. The living room was fairly big. Larger than Lansing had expected. A struggle had taken place, and the house was torn apart as if someone had been making a frantic search.

On the floor in a pool of blood lay the body of an old man. He was wearing a dark suit that looked too big. The shirt and coat were soaked with blood. It was obvious that the man's throat had been cut. Actual cause of death was still a guess. But as a final insult to old Baltazar's humanity, the assailant had scalped him as well.

Lansing could feel a wave of nausea overtaking him. He fought it back as he quickly turned away, almost embarrassed. As a lawman he had seen the many faces of death and it seldom bothered him. But this was someone he knew. He found it much easier to be detached when dealing with strangers.

Koteen was waiting for him near the door. "Seen enough?"

"I've seen too much," Lansing admitted. He continued onto the porch as Koteen bent over to pick up something just inside the door. "What do you have there?"

Koteen held the object up for better inspection. "Nothing. An owl's feather." He crumpled it up and threw it into the yard.

"You've got a real mess on your hands, Ned," Lansing observed.

"I know." Koteen stood next to the sheriff, staring intently at the pine-covered mountains around them. "I called the FBI first thing. They're sending a team up from Santa Fe. Should be here in an hour or so."

"So, if you have the FBI coming in, why'd you call me?"

"Mostly for moral support, Cliff."

"What about Will Cortez?" Lansing was referring to the resident state patrolman. "Isn't he around?"

"He's been reassigned. Until we get a replacement Marty Hernandez will be stopping through." Koteen paused for a moment. "I don't suppose you've seen any suspicious strangers around."

"The usual tourists. Nothing out of the ordinary. Why?"

"Over two thousand people live and work on this reservation. I know every last one of them. There's not a single one who could do something like this." He kicked at an imaginary rock. "Hell, everyone knew Esteban Baltazar. They all loved him. He was everybody's grandfather." Koteen's voice started getting thick. He had to stop and clear his throat. "You knew him, Cliff. You knew what kind of man he was."

Lansing nodded. "Yeah. Got to admit, I liked him too."

"I know you've got your own stuff to worry about,

but would you mind waiting around till the feds show up? I have a hard time dealing with them sometimes."

"Sure. . . ." Lansing glanced at the house. "Is there a phone inside? I need to give my son a call. Tell him I'll be a little late."

"Yeah, go ahead. Be careful about your prints. I'm sure they'll want to dust everything."

Lansing found the writing in the kitchen while looking for a phone. It was in Baltazar's blood, scrawled in block letters across the white wall: SEKALA KA-AMJA.

7

"WE REALLY ARE SORRY ABOUT YOUR LOSS, MR. Jones," Deputy Hanna apologized. "I hope you understand, it's impossible for us to be everywhere. San Philippe's a big county."

"That doesn't do us a whole lot of good," the man named Jones stormed. "We had nearly a thousand dollars worth of camping equipment in the back of that van. Our whole vacation is ruined."

Gabe Hanna didn't mind the irate tourist berating him all that much. He was used to it. Especially if the anger involved some kind of traffic ticket. Gabe felt badly about the man's van being broken into. He could understand Mr. Jones's frustration. He also knew that all the yelling and screaming wouldn't get the man's property back.

The deputy glanced over the man's shoulder at the motel room. Jones's two small children huddled next to their mother in the doorway, crying. He wondered if the tears were for the lost property and the ruined vacation or out of fear of their father's anger. Jones seemed very expert at ranting. Gabe suspected it was the latter.

"I've got your address and phone number," Gabe interrupted. He tore a sheet from his binder. "Here's a copy of the police report so you can file a claim with your insurance. And as far as your property goes, we'll get in touch with you if anything turns up."

Jones almost crumpled the paper in his hand. "Is this the best you can do?"

"We can always get you duplicate reports—but they cost fifteen dollars each. So I'd be careful with that one if I were you." He started toward his patrol Jeep.

"This is the last damned time you'll ever see me in this town and the last time I'm coming to New Mexico."

As the deputy walked away Jones was still muttering about the entire incident. The only words Gabe could catch clearly were "stupid goddamned Indian."

Gabe ignored the remark. He'd already decided Mr. Jones was an ass. Pursuing a confrontation would only prolong his exposure to the man. He glanced at the California plates on the van. The thought crossed his mind to put an APB out on the vehicle as being stolen, but if Sheriff Lansing ever found out Gabe would get his butt chewed for sure. Besides, Mrs. Jones and her kids had been through enough already. Instead, he tipped his ball cap and smiled. "You have a nice day there, Mr. Jones. I hope you enjoy the rest of your vacation."

Gabe knew Sheriff Lansing would not be very happy. This was the second time in two weeks someone had broken into a vehicle parked at the Thunderchief Motel. Lansing had told the deputies to keep a closer watch on the parking lot. Gabe knew they had tried. At least he knew he had tried. But as he had told Mr. Jones, they couldn't be everywhere.

His thoughts were interrupted by a crackle on his radio.

"Patrol Two, Patrol Two. This is dispatch."

Gabe picked up his microphone. "Patrol Two. What's up, Marilyn?"

"Sheriff Lansing's going to be tied up at the Apache reservation for a while. Could you pick up C.J. at the ranch and run him down here?"

"Should I use the siren and lights?"

"Better not. The poor kid will think he's in trouble again."

"Ten-four." Gabe laughed. "We should be down there in about thirty minutes."

8

 THE LANSING HOMESTEAD WAS FIVE MILES south of town, just off Highway 15. Gabe had heard that at one time the ranch covered over a hundred thousand acres, including the area where the town of Las Palmas now sat. Evidently that had been a long time ago. Sheriff Lansing held only about ten thousand acres now. He leased most of the land to other ranchers for grazing, running only a few head of his own cattle.

Gabe wondered how his boss managed to find any time to play cowboy. The sheriff seemed to be on duty twenty-four hours a day, seven days a week. Even with the addition of two deputies in recent months, Lansing didn't seem to let up on his schedule.

The deputy's Jeep bounced across the cattle guard as he turned onto the gravel road leading to the Lansing ranch house. The house and ranch complex sat two miles off the main highway next to the Rio Questa. Grassy, rolling rangeland spread out to either side of the ranch road. Occasionally, a clump of stunted cottonwood trees broke the monotony, but the eastern side of the ranch consisted mostly of grazing land.

From the Rio Questa westward, the Lansing spread stretched into the high meadows of the Rocky Mountains. During the summer the lush green of the meadows made for valuable grazing property. Gabe could understand why Sheriff Lansing held on to it.

Gabe was only beginning to appreciate the beauty of New Mexico. An army brat his entire life, he had moved to a small town near Las Cruces in his late teens. For a long time he considered New Mexico's "Land of Enchantment" motto a bit presumptuous. Where he lived was dusty and hot. Even though he was half Hispanic and could pass for a Mexican, his Spanish wasn't very good at first. That alienated him from half the people his own age. It wasn't until after he had finished the police academy and moved to Las Palmas that he began to understand the real enchantment of the state.

San Phillipe County straddled the Continental Divide and had a little bit of everything. The western side of the county was high desert. The travel brochures called it "Anasazi Country." Chaco Canyon, the hub of the Anasazi culture, lay only twenty miles southwest of the county line.

The Rocky Mountains sat at the edge of the desert, splitting both San Phillipe County and the Jicarilla Apache Reservation. Las Palmas, the county seat, sat in the broad, grassy valley of the Rio Questa. To the east were the Ortega Mountains, marking the boundary with Taos country. Gabe had never lived around mountains before, so he was impressed with the county's two rivers, dozens of streams, and three lakes. He promised himself he would try his hand at skiing the next winter.

Gabe had to admit, part of his enchantment was that for the first time in his life he felt as if he belonged. And it wasn't just San Phillipe County that had accepted him. The people of the Navajo Nation had started to accept him as one of their own. Every couple of weeks he would ride over to the reservation and learn a little bit more about his heritage. That was important to him.

It was also important to him to see Kimberly Tallmountain on those trips. Kim had taken over as the senior conservationist for the eastern sector of the Navajo reservation after her father's death. She was a very busy woman and Gabe tried to mesh his visits with her free time. Gabe wasn't sure how love was supposed to feel, but he knew he felt something whenever he was near her. Something special. Something warm. Something exciting.

Lost in his thoughts about Kim, Gabe nearly forgot he was going to stop at Lansing's ranch house. Fifty yards further down the road he would have found himself crossing the Rio Questa.

He parked his Jeep in front of the house and walked up to the door. Like many homes in the area, the ranch house was built of natural stone. A wide veranda surrounded the entire building, giving it a warm, comfortable look. Two rocking chairs and a porch swing made the place look inviting.

Gabe rang the doorbell and waited. When there was no immediate response he rang the bell again and peered through the glass of the door, trying to see if there was any movement. There was none.

He rang the bell one more time as he tried the doorknob. The door was locked and there was still no response.

"I wonder if he's even out of bed," Gabe mumbled.

Feeling a little impatient, he followed the veranda around to the back of the house. The back door faced the ranch's outbuildings. Besides the large barn, Lansing had a garagelike shed for his vehicles, a toolshed, and an old bunkhouse. (The sheriff kept talking about turning the bunkhouse into guest quarters someday. That day just hadn't happened along yet, Gabe supposed.)

As he rounded the corner Gabe discovered the back door standing open. He warily stuck his head inside. "C.J.? You in here?"

There was no response.

Before venturing inside, the deputy glanced around the grounds for any sign of the boy. Two horses stood idly in the corral next to the barn, swatting flies with their tails. They showed no interest when Gabe cupped his hands around his mouth and yelled, "C.J.! You out here somewhere?"

"I'm in the barn," came the muffled response.

Gabe walked across the grounds to the barn, annoyed at having to round C.J. up. The deputy had met Cliff Junior twice before on a couple of his weekend visits and thought he seemed nice enough. But Gabe had regular rounds to make and this delay just put him behind. He slid the barn door to the side so he could get through.

"C.J., come on. I'm supposed to give you a ride to town."

"Gabe, is that you?"

The deputy looked up at the loft and the sound of the voice. "Yeah, it's me. Come on. We gotta go."

"Could you help me a minute?"

"Do I have to get up in the loft?"

"Yeah, I think so," C.J. called weakly. "I kinda have a problem."

A set of wooden steps at the back of the barn led to the hayloft. Gabe emerged through the floor opening to discover C.J. standing precariously on a stack of five hay bales. The fifth bale was turned on end, giving the boy as much height as possible. C.J., his back to the deputy, stood with his arms outstretched, trying to reach the end of a rope. The rope was stuck in a pulley that hung from the rafters.

The boy's fingertips just brushed the rope. He tried to make himself taller by standing on his toes. Lunging at the rope, he caused the topmost bale to teeter.

That's when Gabe noticed that the boy's makeshift ladder was perched over an open trapdoor. It was a twenty-foot drop to the barn floor below.

"C.J." Gabe tried to sound as calm as possible. "Stand still."

"Wait," the boy responded, oblivious to the danger. "I almost got it that time."

Gabe wasn't about to wait. He began running toward C.J. and his stack of hay. C.J. had already bent his knees. As he jumped for the rope, the top bale tipped, falling through the open door. Gabe grabbed for the boy, latching on to his belt before he followed the hay through the opening.

Giving a mighty tug, Gabe fell backward, pulling C.J. on top of him.

"What the hell were you trying to do?" the deputy wheezed. He could feel his heart racing a hundred miles an hour. "Kill yourself?"

"No," the boy pouted. "I was just trying to get some hay out of the loft." He pointed at the rafters. "But the pulley got stuck. I was just trying to fix it."

Gabe got up, brushing straw off his uniform. "Why can't you just push the bales through the hole?"

"They'll bust open and the hay gets all over the ground. Then the horses won't eat it."

"If they're that picky you ought to let them go hungry," Gabe complained.

"I was just trying to help my dad," the boy responded, frowning. "I was going to surprise him."

Gabe shook his head. He couldn't be mad at the young man for that. "All right. I understand. Let's see what we can do."

With the help of a pitchfork Gabe managed to snag the end of the rope and drag it through the pulley. The opposite end was fixed with bale tongs. Gabe towered the bales from the loft one at a time. C.J. stood on the ground floor, unhooking the tongs for the next bale. It took the two only a few minutes to lower the four bales the boy had been using for a perch.

Gabe tied off the rope so it wouldn't slip through the pulley again, then stepped down from the loft. "Were those bales sitting next to the trapdoor?"

"No," C.J. admitted. "I had to drag them from the far end. They were the only ones left."

Gabe guessed each bale weighed at least fifty pounds. The deputy was impressed with the boy's determination. The bales had not only been dragged half the length of the barn, C.J. had stacked them as well.

"Well, are we finished with the chores?" the deputy asked, glancing at his watch.

"Yeah," C.J. nodded. "For now. We can put the hay in the straw troughs later."

An old joke about the Lone Ranger and Tonto crossed Gabe's mind. The punch line was "What do you mean *we*, White Man?" It seemed like an appropriate response, but Gabe was afraid it might be lost on his young companion. Instead, he said, "Why don't you get cleaned up then? I'm supposed to run you into town."

"Are we meeting my dad there?"

"Yeah, I guess." Gabe had no idea if the sheriff would be there or not. "Hurry up, C.J. I have other things I need to be doing."

The boy trotted toward the house. "All right," he called over his shoulder. "I'll be right out."

9

"LITERALLY TRANSLATED," CAPTAIN KOTEEN explained, "it means 'the one who never dies.'"

Special Agent Sheridan jotted down the words in his notebook. "*Se-ka-la Ka-am-ja.* Is that the way you say it?" Koteen nodded. "'The one who never dies.' What does that mean?"

Koteen shook his head. "I'm not sure."

The photographer took one more picture of the kitchen wall, then turned to the special agent in charge. "That cleans up this roll, Phil. Do you want another series?"

"Check with the forensics team. See if there's anything outside they need shot. Footprints, broken windows, anything like that."

"You got it." The photographer went into the living room, where the rest of the team was meticulously gathering evidence.

Special Agent Sheridan turned to the two local law officers standing in the kitchen corner. "I know you two probably think we're going overboard, but I want to make sure we don't miss a thing."

"We understand," Lansing said.

"It's just that with no witnesses all we have to go on is the physical evidence left behind." Sheridan made the statement, completely ignoring the sheriff's remark. "You'd be surprised how even the smallest clue can break a case."

"Yeah, I'll bet we would," Koteen said under his breath, just loud enough for Lansing to hear.

The sheriff clenched his teeth to stop a chuckle. He could appreciate Captain Koteen's sarcasm. Both men had dealt with the FBI and the State Bureau of Investigation before. Usually, the encounters were brief and professional. There were some special agents, however, who felt they had no use for local law-enforcement officers.

Lansing had already decided that Special Agent Philip Sheridan was probably okay, that he just hadn't had much experience dealing with backwoods cops. Guessing the agent was all of twenty-eight and still plenty wet behind the ears, he decided he would feed the agent the rope, then wait and see if Sheridan was willing to hang himself with it.

"Phil, can you come in here?" one of the men on the forensics team called. "Looks like we found a weapon."

"Excuse me, gentlemen," Sheridan said, leaving the room.

"What do you think?' Koteen asked. "This his first case?"

"Oh, I think it's the first one he's ever been put in charge of," Lansing admitted.

"Would it be all right if we told him we both went to college?" Koteen asked. "That we actually know how to read and write?"

"Naw." Lansing shook his head. "That would take all the fun out of this. Let's keep it our secret."

Ned Koteen was a big man: six feet three, two hundred and fifty pounds. He kept his hair long, so that even in his khaki uniform he looked like a reservation Apache. Lansing suspected Sheridan had pigeonholed Koteen as being a policeman only because he was bigger than anyone else.

They had known each other for more than twenty years. They had played football against each other in high school. Lansing had played halfback and second-string quarterback. His first recollections of Koteen were of the enormous lineman helping him up after flattening him three plays in a row. Koteen had put Lansing's arm over his shoulder and was helping him to the bench.

"Sorry about that," the big man apologized. "You going to be okay?"

"I will be," Lansing remembered saying, "as soon as we punt the ball away."

They had both ended up at the University of New Mexico, Koteen on a full football scholarship. If he hadn't bummed up his back in his junior year, he probably would have gone pro.

Lansing thought it was kind of funny how closely their careers paralleled each other. He had gotten a degree in psychology and ended up on the Albuquerque police force. Koteen had gotten a degree in criminology and ended up with the Santa Fe police. They both had returned to San Phillipe County the same year, Koteen with the tribal police, Lansing as chief deputy. Although they seemed to see each other only while conducting business, Lansing thought of Koteen as a good friend.

Koteen motioned his head toward the living room. "Why don't we go see what the G-men have uncovered?"

Baltazar's body had already been removed from the house for transport to Santa Fe. Once the body had been cleared out, the agents began moving furniture, looking for any more evidence. That's when they found the pistol.

One agent wearing latex gloves held the gun by the pistol guard. He gingerly opened the cylinder to examine the shells. "Four bullets have been fired. This might be the murder weapon."

"I doubt it," Lansing observed. "Why would they have cut his throat?"

"For effect," Sheridan suggested. "They cut his throat for the same reason they scalped him. It was probably some sort of ritual. We'll know for sure after the autopsy."

"It might have been Esteban's gun," Koteen said. "I'd suggest you do a paraffin test to see if he shot the pistol."

"Yeah, I suppose we can do that," Sheridan admitted.

Glancing around the room, Lansing noticed four black dots on the far wall. He walked over for a closer examination.

"Be careful, Sheriff," Sheridan protested. "We're still gathering evidence."

"I'd suggest you gather this, then." He pointed at four holes in the wall. "These look like bullet holes. Pretty tight cluster too. Might be from the four spent shells."

"Thanks for your help, Sheriff," the special agent snapped. "But I think we can manage." He turned to the Apache captain. "Why don't we go outside so they can finish up in here? I want to ask you a few questions. Would you please come along, Sheriff?"

A crowd had already gathered along the highway. Koteen knew that news of the murder would travel fast. He had already called in two of his patrolmen to keep the curious away. One was busy trying to keep traffic flowing smoothly along the highway. The second kept onlookers on the other side of the yellow crime-scene tape.

"You said Baltazar was found by his grandson,"

Sheridan began. "Do you have an address and phone number where I can reach him?"

"I have a directory in my truck, but I think it's advisable if I come along. A lot of people around here are uncomfortable with outsiders. Besides, this has been a pretty traumatic week for the family. John Baltazar lost his only brother in an explosion just a few days ago."

"I'm sorry to hear that." Sheridan thought for a moment, then nodded. "This is your territory. These are your people. I'm sure you know the best way to handle this." He hesitated a moment. "I hope I haven't been too overbearing. . . . This is the first capital murder case I've been in charge of."

Koteen shot Lansing a quick glance. The sheriff gave a little shrug.

"I think you have everything under control, Ned," Lansing observed. "If you don't need me for anything, I think I'll get back to my own territory."

"No, that's fine, Cliff. Thanks for the help."

"Let me know if there's anything else I can do."

Lansing got into his Jeep and backed the vehicle around. The crowd seemed reluctant to let him through. It was several minutes before he could reach the highway and head for Las Palmas.

10

WHEN LANSING ENTERED THE SHERIFF'S OF-
fices in the San Phillipe courthouse, he found
his son deeply engrossed in a comic book, his
back to the door. The sheriff signaled Marilyn to be
quiet as he snuck up behind C.J.

Reaching around the side of the seat, Lansing lightly
dug his fingers into the boy's ribs. "Gotcha!"

C.J. squealed as he jumped from the chair. "Aw,
Dad. You always do that to me." He walked over
and put his arms around his father's waist. "Are you
done for the day? You said we could go riding this
afternoon."

"Almost. I need to make a couple of phone calls first.
I thought we'd grab a bite at the diner, then take off.
How's that sound?"

"Can I have a hamburger and a Coke?"

"I don't know why not." He looked at his receptionist. "Anything going on?"

Marilyn thumbed through her notes. "Officer Hanna
had a report of a robbery at the Thunderchief Motel
this morning. More camping equipment. It's been
pretty quiet. What was going on at the reservation?"

"It looks like somebody killed old Esteban Baltazar."

"The medicine man? What, some sort of accident?"

"Doesn't look that way." He glanced at C.J., who seemed to be too interested in their conversation. "We can talk about it later."

"Aw, Dad," his son protested. "You never talk about your work in front of me."

"Mostly because it would bore you to death. Listen, Marilyn, Chief Deputy C.J and I are taking the horses out this afternoon, so I may be a little scarce. Who's on today besides Gabe?"

"Jack Rivera and Danny Cortez," the receptionist said, checking her duty roster. "Sidney Barns and Paul DeJesus have the night patrols."

"I guess the county can miss me for a few hours." He looked at C.J. "Wait for me out here. I'll make a couple of calls, then we can be on our way."

"Margarite?"

"Oh, it's you, Lansing."

"I know I was supposed to call you sooner, but things got a little hectic."

"Believe it or not, I'm getting used to it. If you called me when you were supposed to, I'd think there was something wrong. Did C.J. make it in?"

"Yeah, he's here. I was wondering if you could make it down to dinner tonight. Thought we might throw a couple of steaks on the grill."

"Can't tonight, Lansing. I'm heading over to San Francisco Pueblo in a few minutes. How about tomorrow night? I can stop off on my way back."

"Is that a promise?"

"Lansing, how many times have I ever stood you up?"

"Well . . ."

"None. That's how many. Besides, I'd like to see C.J. I can see you anytime." She paused for a moment. "Almost anytime."

"What time do you think you'll get here? So I know when to start the grill."

"Probably around six. If something comes up I'll call."

"See you then."

11

"CAN WE SIT AT THE COUNTER?" C.J. ASKED AS they entered the diner.

"Yeah. It looks like there's room," Lansing said, removing his Stetson and hanging it on the rack near the door.

C.J. hurried and jumped on a stool.

Kelly, the senior waitress, emerged from the kitchen carrying two plates of food. "Ah, Sheriff. I was wondering if you were going to bring C.J. around again."

"Hi, Kelly." C.J. waved as he checked out the spin potential of his stool. "Is Velma here too?"

Lansing couldn't help but smile to himself at the question. C.J. had asked enough questions about Velma to ensure he was working on a full-blown crush. Lansing had to admit Velma was an attractive woman, in a dime-store, cosmetic-counter sort of way. But she wore just a touch too much rouge and way too much perfume.

There was nothing subtle about her, even in her approach to men. She was heavily involved of late with John Tanner, the town's physician, although she seemed to want all men to know that that situation could change any minute.

C.J. was coming of age. The hormones of change were taking over his young body, and the opposite sex wasn't nearly as repulsive as it had been just a few years before. The trouble was that, as with most men, his hormones weren't very discerning. He was sure Velma was one of the most beautiful women in the world. Plus, she was aggressive. That made it a lot easier for his fragile masculinity.

Unfortunately, C.J. made the same mistake most men did with Velma. When she flirted it was nothing personal. That was just the way she interacted with men, no matter how big or small, young or old.

"She's in the kitchen, hon. She'll be right out." Kelly balanced the two plates she carried on one arm as she grabbed the coffeepot. "Sheriff Fulton's in the back, Cliff. Did you see him?"

"No, I sure didn't. Save me a seat, C.J. I'll be right back." Lansing followed Kelly to a booth toward the back of the diner.

"What brings you in to town, you old rattlesnake?"

Bill Fulton looked up from the newspaper he was browsing through. "Hey, Cliff. Good to see you." Fulton stood and the two men shook hands. "I was going to stop by your office earlier, but I didn't see your car."

"I had to make a run out to the Jicarilla reservation."

"More trouble with that fire?"

"Not this trip. Somebody killed old Esteban Baltazar."

"The medicine man? Why'd they ask you out there?"

"I think Ned Koteen needed the company. The feds are crawling all over the place now. I'm sure they'll wrap it up in a day."

"Join me for a cup of coffee."

"I've got time for a quick one. My son's in town visiting. He's up at the counter."

"C.J.?" Fulton craned his neck to see. "What is he? Seven, eight?"

Lansing shook his head. "He's twelve, almost thirteen."

"Damn, has it been that long?"

"Yeah. Afraid so."

Lansing liked Bill Fulton. He had been sheriff of San Phillipe County for over thirty years and was the man who brought Lansing in as chief deputy. When Fulton retired six years ago, he insisted Lansing run as his replacement.

Fulton had had a hard time making the transition to civilian life. For the first year he was in the office almost every day. Lansing tried his best to accommodate the former sheriff, but after a while he became a nuisance. It took the efforts of both Lansing and Emily Fulton to convince him that he needed to start a new life. As the years progressed, Lansing saw less and less of his former mentor.

"So what brings you into the big city?"

"Emily's doing spring cleaning and I was in her way. Told her I'd come into town and get some paint so we can start fixing up the place."

"Fixing up the place?"

"Yeah. I think this was the last winter we're going to suffer around here. It's time to move south."

"You're kidding."

"Emily's got a sister down in Corpus Christi. She has a big old place she can't take care of, so we're going to move in with her. Walking distance to the beach. Maybe I can get caught up on my fishing."

"I thought you hated fishing, Bill."

"Yeah, so did I. I think I hated it because I never had time for it. My job was too important. Couldn't put it aside long enough to enjoy things like hunting, fishing, gardening. Now I'm getting too old to enjoy much of anything." He stared at Lansing intently. "And I see you going the same way. No time for anything but the job."

"You're full of crap like you always were, Bill. I'm taking the afternoon off to go riding with C.J."

"One afternoon isn't much, Cliff. You jumped into your job with both feet when I brought you here ten years ago, and I haven't seen you come up for air yet. When was the last time you took a vacation?"

"I take a weekend off here and there."

"Two days off isn't a vacation. It's just two days off."

"You forget I have a ranch to run. Not many ranchers around here get vacations."

"They take more time off than you do, I guarantee." He paused for a moment while he studied the cup of coffee in front of him. "I probably should have said something to you years ago, but I kind of blame myself for you and Carol breaking up."

"You had nothing to do with it."

"I did, in a way. You came back here all excited about being home and out of Albuquerque, off that damned police force. You thought you were the Lone Ranger, and I let you think it. It took a lot of pressure off me."

"It's over and done with, Bill. Let's just forget it."

"No, we can't. At least I can't. I've been thinking about this a long time. So let me have a say while I have the chance.

"I know you had your hands full back then, what with your dad laid up with a stroke and all. But you were young. I figured you could handle it. I guess it was after he died that things started falling apart between you and Carol. I should have put you on a leave of absence so you could straighten things out, but I didn't. I was selfish. You doubled the number of hours you were working, and I let you. I should have kicked your butt out of that office and told you not to come back until things were fixed up."

Lansing stared at his own cup of coffee. He could remember volunteering for the additional shifts. At the time he told himself it was for the extra pay. He thought if he brought more money home Carol would be satisfied. Deep down, even then, he knew better. He avoided going home because he hated the arguments. His wife was unhappy. She didn't like being isolated on a ranch. She didn't like living in the country. She missed her friends and family. And nothing short of moving back to Albuquerque would satisfy her.

Lansing hated Albuquerque. He didn't like big cities and he hated the politics of the police department. There was no way he could go back.

Something eventually had to give, and it ended up being their relationship. One day Carol packed up and took off with C.J. That was six years ago, and that was the end of it.

Lansing thought it was ironic that Fulton referred to him as the Lone Ranger. When his wife left with C.J., that's exactly how he had thought of himself, the Lone Ranger.

It wasn't until he met Margarite Carerra that Lansing began to realize he suffered from the legacy of his failed marriage. He was still a workaholic, and a lot of times he ran his office as if he were still the Lone Ranger. He didn't allow himself much of a life.

Toward the end his marriage was nothing more than a series of painful encounters with Carol. The divorce and the loss of his son were even worse. Lansing had promised himself he would never hurt like that again.

But Margarite had changed that. He wanted to be close to someone again. The trouble was, he had to tear down the wall he had built to protect himself. It had taken him nearly ten years to construct it, and now he was taking it apart one brick at a time. He wondered for a moment how patient Margarite would be.

"I know it's too late for apologies," Fulton continued. "But it's not too late for you, Cliff. Quit being the Lone Ranger. Try having a life again."

Lansing nodded. "Yeah. You're probably right, Bill."

"I've seen that pretty doctor you've been dating. It'd be a shame if you screwed things up with her too."

Lansing laughed. "That's what I like about you, Bill. I can always count on you for moral support." He stood, leaving his cup of coffee untouched. "I need to get back to C.J. Don't be a stranger. And you'd better not move out of town without saying good-bye. Maybe you and Emily can come out to the ranch for a barbecue."

"Sounds good, Cliff. And you take care of that boy of yours."

Lansing returned to the counter to find Velma leaning on her elbows chatting with C.J. Kelly was busy behind her starting a new pot of coffee.

"Sheriff," Velma said sweetly, "I'm just having the best time talking to C.J. here."

Lansing could see his son blush as he took his seat on a stool.

"Have you ever thought that maybe he could use a momma?" Velma jumped when Kelly kicked her leg. "Ouch! What'd you do that for?"

"He has a momma, you twit," Kelly said in her loudest, raspiest whisper.

"Not when he's here!"

Lansing tried to ignore the argument by walking over to the jukebox and looking for a selection.

"I swear, Velma, you can be the dumbest thing. What if Doctor Tanner heard you talk like that?"

"What if he did?" Velma snapped back. "He's not going to marry me. One of these days he's going to up and leave and not take me. A girl has to plan ahead."

"Well, girl, you'd better make plans to pick up your orders in the kitchen or you're going to be losing a day's worth of tips."

"Oh, what do you know about anything?" Velma turned and stomped into the kitchen.

"Cliff," Kelly called. "You ready to order?"

"Yeah, I believe so."

12

"DAD, IS VELMA DATING SOMEONE?" C.J. ASKED from his saddle.

Lansing thought something was bothering his son. C.J. had said practically nothing from the time their hamburgers were placed in front of them until they were finally on the trail.

"Yeah, C.J.," Lansing replied, looking over his shoulder. "I believe she is. Why?"

"I don't know. I was just wondering."

Lansing looked back at his son. He was staring off into the distance, lost in his thoughts.

They had crossed the Rio Questa on the road bridge behind the ranch buildings, then started following a cattle path that led to the higher pastures. It was a beautiful afternoon. Cement Head, Lansing's horse, acted almost frisky at being outside the corral. C.J.'s pony, Milkweed, was even friskier, and he had to rein him back several times before he finally settled into a casual pace.

"I take it you like Velma?"

"Sort of," came the hesitant reply. "And I kind of thought she liked me."

"Oh, I'm sure she does."

"I don't mean just *like*. I mean she makes me feel kind of special. That kind of like."

Lansing tried to keep a straight face. "Don't you think Velma's a little old for you?"

"Not really. I mean, I'm going to be a teenager pretty soon. What is Velma? About twenty-four?"

Lansing's guess was she was twenty-four plus a decade. "Yeah, twenty-four. That sounds about right."

"That means we're only ten years apart. Frank's ten years older than Mom. They get along pretty good."

"I'm glad to hear that, but what does that have to do with you and Velma?"

"Nothing. I was just thinking."

"If you want to know the truth, there's nothing wrong with you being interested in an older woman."

"Really?"

"But to play it safe, if I were you I'd hang back until I got a little older."

"How much older?" The question dripped with disappointment.

"Oh, I'd say, wait until you were at least sixteen."

"Sixteen! That's three years away. More than that even. Why sixteen?"

"You want to be old enough to borrow the car. That way you can take her out on a date."

"Yeah," C.J. said thoughtfully. "I never thought of that.

"By the way," Lansing said, getting his son's mind off his first lost love, "how'd those bales of hay get down from the loft? I thought I told you to stay down from there till I got home."

"I didn't go up there by myself. Gabe was there too. He helped me get them down."

Lansing was pretty sure there was more to the story. "You're sure you didn't go up there by yourself?"

C.J. hesitated before answering. "No." There was

another long pause. "I wanted to surprise you. It seems like you're always busy. I wanted to help."

"Those bales are bigger than you," Lansing replied sternly.

"Yes, sir."

Lansing let the thought sink in before continuing. "Good thing Gabe showed up to help, I suppose."

"Yeah, he was a big help."

"I'll bet he was." Lansing couldn't help but chuckle. He'd check with his deputy to find out what really went on.

The two rode on for another ten minutes without another word passing between them. Finally, C.J. broke the rhythm of the horse's hooves.

"Is Gabe your chief deputy?"

"No, not really." Lansing considered the question further. "I guess I don't have a chief deputy."

"Why not?"

"Because I don't need a chief deputy."

"Well, who's in charge when you're not around?"

"No one. I mean, I'm in charge all the time. I'm the sheriff."

"But you're not at work all the time. Who's in charge when you go out riding like this?"

"My deputies know their jobs. I don't have to be there all the time."

"What if they have a question? Who do they ask?"

Lansing reined in Cement Head, then turned his horse so he could face his son. "What's with all the questions?"

"I just wanted to know."

"You know who the Lone Ranger is. Right?"

"Sure."

"Okay. The Lone Ranger had Tonto. Tonto was kind of like his deputy. Don't you think Tonto was smart enough to figure things out when the Lone Ranger wasn't around?"

"Sure. He was an Indian. Indians are smart. They're supposed to know how to hunt and all sorts of stuff."

"Okay. Gabe is like Tonto. So is Deputy Rivera and Deputy Cortez. They know what to do when I'm not around."

C.J. considered the situation for a moment. "Well, then, who's the head Tonto?"

"Why are you so interested in this?"

"In your office today you said I was Chief Deputy C.J."

"So?"

"So, I'd like to grow up and be your chief deputy. That way we could hang around together all the time."

Lansing couldn't help but smile at the prospect of them hanging around together all the time. "You know what, C.J.? I think I'd like that. I'd like it a lot." He gave Cement Head a gentle kick. "Come on. It's time we headed back down. It'll be dark pretty soon."

C.J. turned his pony and followed his father down the mountain.

13

 THERE WAS ONLY THE SLIGHTEST HINT OF A breeze, but enough to bring out the chill of the night air.

"Put some more wood on the fire," Sheri said as she pulled the sweatshirt over her head. "It's getting cold."

Barbara picked up the last two sticks they had foraged for earlier in the day. Orange-red sparks danced skyward when she tossed them onto the dwindling campfire. "Well, that's it," she announced. "No more firewood." She clutched her arms around her body to keep warm. "I told you we should have picked up more."

"Don't be such a baby," Sheri scolded. "There's plenty of wood lying around."

"I don't know why everyone thinks camping is such a big deal. There are no toilets. No water. No electricity. And we get to sleep on lumpy ground."

"This is the only week we have off before the summer term begins. I wasn't going to stay in the dorm, and I sure as hell wasn't going to spend a week with my brat brother at home. I don't have any money.

You don't have any money. This is the cheapest way to get away from it all."

"Maybe getting away from it all isn't all that hot."

"Did you want to stay on campus so that dork boyfriend of yours would be around all the time?"

"He's not my boyfriend."

"Well, he acts like he is, and you let him get away with it."

"He's not my boyfriend. Can we change the subject?"

"Sure." Sheri looked down the dirt road that had brought them to their camping spot. "You want to go check out that campsite we passed earlier? A couple of those guys looked pretty cute."

"They looked like high-school kids."

"So? Cute is cute."

"If you want to go play with the High School Harrys, it's all right with me. But before you go, help me pick up some more wood for the fire. I'm not going to sit here by myself and freeze to death."

"You're so negative." Sheri picked up her flashlight and switched it on. As if in response, twenty yards away an owl hooted.

"What was that?" Barbara cringed from the sound.

"It's just an owl. It's no big deal."

"So you say."

"Come on. You want some firewood or not?"

Barbara pulled her jacket tightly around her neck. "Why don't we just spend the night in the car? We can keep the engine running."

"Oh, that would be real smart. We'd run out of gas in the middle of the night and have to walk down out of these mountains. If you want firewood, come on." Sheri started for the edge of the woods.

"All right." Barbara felt around on the ground for her flashlight. When she found it she switched it on and pointed it in the direction her friend had gone. "Sheri?"

There was no response.

"All right, girl. This isn't funny. Where are you?"

Barbara panned the beam of light along the edge of the forest. "Sheri! Come on. Joke's over. Where are you?"

She stopped her beam on a pine tree wide enough for a person to hide behind. "Okay, smartass. I know you're hiding there. You can quit playing now."

Barbara started walking toward the tree, but stopped when she heard the owl hoot again. This time the bird was closer, directly in front of her.

She shone her light toward the sound.

On a branch twenty feet above her sat a great horned owl. It seemed to be glaring at her, its eyes glowing iridescent from the beam of the light.

"Sheri!" Barbara whimpered.

The bird emitted a single low *whoo*, then spread its wings. As the animal dove from its perch, the frightened girl threw down her flashlight and began to run.

All she could think of was the safety of the car. She fell once, feeling the wings of the bird brush against her when she did. She fell a second time as she tripped over what was left of the campfire.

Scrambling to her feet, she stumbled toward the car, trying to swat the bird away. As her fingers touched the door handle she felt a cold darkness envelop her.

Her screams blended with the screeching of the owl to form a single voice. A voice swallowed by the cold chill of the mountain night.

Miles away in Dulce, Marcus Baltazar lay alone in his bed staring at the ceiling. He had heard the screams. He didn't know what they meant. He was afraid that if he went back to sleep the dream would come again.

Marcus was ashamed. His great-grandfather would

have told him, "Let the dreams come. They are your destiny. They hold the truth, if you learn how to interpret them."

He wrapped his fingers around the *jish* and closed his eyes. If the dream did come again, maybe he would understand it this time.

14

"GOOD MORNING, MARILYN," GABE CALLED AS he entered the sheriff's offices. "I saw Sheriff Lansing's Jeep out there. Is he around?"

"Morning, Gabe," the receptionist said, smiling. "He's back on the phone, but he said he wanted to see you as soon as you came in."

Gabe stopped in the dayroom to drop off his cap and jacket, then went directly to Lansing's office. He knocked on the closed door.

"Come in."

"You wanted to see me, Sheriff?" Gabe asked once he was inside.

"Yeah. What do you have for me about those car break-ins?"

"Not much. We've had six so far. The M.O. seems to be the thieves are looking for camping equipment. Sometimes they walk away with a few tools, but mostly it's stuff for camping."

"You think it's kids?"

"Could be. I notified all the pawn shops in the county, but they haven't seen anything coming through. My guess is the perps are hauling the stuff down to Santa Fe."

"Well, it sounds like our friends are branching out. A couple of campsites up in Chama Meadows were ransacked while the campers were away. I need for you to contact an Ed Bowers at the Thunderchief. He's one of the victims. After you get his statement go up to the Meadows and take a look, talk to any campers there. Find out if they saw anyone."

"Anything else?"

"Yeah. Take a look at the Comfax and see if any of the other counties have been hit. I think we're probably dealing with transients. They'll hit San Phillipe for a few weeks, then move on when things start getting hot."

"Okay. I'll get started."

"One more thing, Gabe. What went on with those bales of hay yesterday morning?"

"What do you mean?"

"Just tell me what happened."

Gabe provided a quick summary of the events in the barn the day before. "C.J. isn't in trouble, is he?"

"Oh, not really. But I found his version a little sketchy."

"You've got a nice kid there, Sheriff."

"Thanks. I think so."

"I was going to offer to take him out on my motorcycle, but I thought I'd better check with you first."

"I appreciate it. Do you have a helmet for him?"

"Sure."

"Twelve-year-olds love to do stupid things. I'm sure he'd enjoy the hell out of it."

"Is he around?"

"Juan Martín is doing some work for me around the ranch. C.J. wanted to stay and help, earn a couple of bucks for Fourth of July fireworks."

"I don't blame him. I'll get busy on this break-in business."

As soon as Gabe left, Lansing picked up the phone and dialed the number to the police station on the Jicarilla reservation. When the operator answered he asked for Captain Koteen.

"Yeah, Ned. This is Cliff Lansing. I was wondering if you and the G-men were making any progress."

"Not that I can tell, Cliff." Koteen sounded tired. Between the fire earlier in the week and the murder of Baltazar, Lansing suspected Koteen hadn't had much time for any rest. "Sheridan wanted to talk to everyone who had seen Esteban the night he was killed. Trouble is, he addressed the tribal council that evening. Half the people in Dulce saw him that night. I'm trying to get people to cooperate, but it's not doing much good. Nobody saw anything."

"Is there anything I can do?"

"Yeah, as a matter of fact. We have three funerals this afternoon, for some of the guys killed in the rig fire. We have three more scheduled for tomorrow, but I think it's going to end up being four.

"The FBI said they're going to finish up Esteban's autopsy this morning. They'll have his body back to us tonight, which means his funeral will be tomorrow as well. We're going to have a flood of people in here. I could use a couple of your deputies for traffic control."

"Just tell me when you need them. They'll be there."

"Thanks, Cliff. By the way, Agent Sheridan's staying at the Thunderchief Motel. He may be stopping by to ask you a few questions."

"I'll be glad to help, but I don't know anything."

"He said he can't leave a rock unturned. I guess you're one of those rocks."

"Okay. Thanks for the warning. Talk to you later."

When he was finished with Koteen, Lansing had

Marilyn ring Agent Sheridan's room at the Thunderchief Motel.

"Agent Sheridan, Sheriff Lansing."

"Sheriff, you must have ESP. I wanted to talk to you this morning."

"I don't have any special talents like that. Just a good network. I haven't had breakfast yet. Why don't we meet at the Las Palmas Diner? We can kill two birds that way."

"I'll meet you there in fifteen minutes."

Lansing was already waiting in a booth when Sheridan arrived. Velma served up two cups of coffee and took their orders, then left the two lawmen to their business.

"I don't seem to be making a lot of progress on the reservation," Sheridan began. "It's tough getting those people to talk, but everyone claims they liked Baltazar. There haven't been any strangers around. No one saw anything peculiar."

"I know it's a little early, but has your lab come up with anything?"

Sheridan pulled a notepad from his suit jacket for reference. "So far we know Baltazar wasn't shot. Our guess now is that he died from the wound to his throat. We'll know more after the autopsy.

"We ran the paraffin test. He did shoot a gun. We still don't know if it was the same gun we found in his house. We'll have the fingerprint comparison this morning. We'll also have the ballistics information on the bullets found in the wall, see if they came from the gun we found.

"We're running comparisons on every fingerprint we found in the place, but it may be days before we have anything."

"What about the writing on the kitchen wall?"

"We're bringing in a consultant. Our Albuquerque

office contacted a Doctor Victoria Miles at the University of New Mexico. She's with the history department. I guess her expertise is Native American studies, particularly the Apache people."

"Yeah, I've met Doctor Miles." Lansing had encountered the university professor years earlier. It had not been a pleasant experience.

"You don't sound like you care for her much."

"Let's just say we have different opinions on things. Did you know she's also a member of the Jicarilla tribe?"

"No, I didn't know that." Sheridan made a notation in his pad. "I guess that makes sense now. My office said she would be out this way sometime this afternoon. I offered to reserve a room for her at the motel, but they said it wouldn't be necessary. She had other arrangements."

Velma returned with their breakfast orders and a fresh pot of coffee. She left them alone when she was sure they were satisfied with their meals.

"Can I ask you something, Agent Sheridan?"

"Sure."

"You're being awfully open about your evidence. I thought you feds kept everything close hold until you were ready to make an arrest."

"It could be I'm just telling you what I want you to know."

"Yeah. Could be." Lansing doubted that. Sheridan didn't seem seasoned enough to be that cagey.

"Or it could be that if the local law enforcement knows where we stand in the investigation, we won't duplicate any efforts. You can also fill in any blanks we've left open. Like that information about Doctor Miles."

"Don't expect a very long career with the FBI."

"Why?" There was a touch of resentment in Sheridan's voice.

"You're using too much common sense." Lansing smiled at the young agent, trying to assure him the statement was a compliment. "What can I help you with?"

"The Jicarilla reservation is all open land. People can come and go as they wish. I was wondering if anything peculiar had been going on in the rest of the county, or if any suspicious strangers had been seen. Anything that even remotely might be tied into the Baltazar case."

Lansing told Sheridan about the car break-ins and the missing camping equipment. He explained that those kinds of pranks were usually done by teenagers. He also mentioned there was the possibility that transients might be hitting his county before moving on to other areas. Unfortunately, at that point there were no solid leads.

Sheridan made annotations in his pad as he finished his breakfast. "What kind of investigation are you conducting?"

"We've talked to potential witnesses. Contacted pawn shops to see if any equipment has been fenced. One of my deputies is up at one of the campgrounds this morning. A couple of campers had some equipment stolen while they were hiking. I'll share anything he comes up with."

"Thanks." Sheridan stuffed his notepad into a pocket. "I need to get moving. There are a dozen people in Dulce I haven't talked to yet. Plus I want to talk to John Baltazar again."

"Esteban's grandson? The one with the burned hands."

"Yeah. He and his family found the body. I asked him why they had gone out there. He said the old man had been in a car accident a week earlier and that had been his first night back home. They just wanted to check on him and make sure everything was all right."

"You don't believe him?"

"Oh, there's nothing wrong with his story. Captain Koteen verified everything he said. But the way he talked, it's like there was something more to the story, but he didn't want to tell me about it. You ever have that feeling?"

"Yes. I have to admit I have."

The two men promised they would keep in touch, then Sheridan picked up his bill and headed for the register. Lansing checked his watch. There was enough time to finish his weekly paperwork and still be home in time for lunch. He was sure C.J. would be ready for a hearty meal after working all morning.

Ten years earlier, balancing his job with his home life had been a hassle. Now it didn't seem so bad. He had to admit, he actually looked forward to taking time away from his job to be with his son. He regretted the fact that the situation was temporary. In another three weeks he would be the Lone Ranger again.

The prospect of being alone left a sour feeling in his stomach as he paid for his meal and headed back to his office.

What was so hot about being the Lone Ranger anyway?

15

GABE DIDN'T FIND MR. BOWERS AT THE MOTEL very helpful. The former camper had seen nothing, couldn't remember how long he had been away from the camp, couldn't remember exactly where in Chama Meadows he had camped, and never could decide what had actually been taken. The deputy told him if he thought of anything to add to the police report, he could do it at the courthouse.

Chama Meadows was an unimproved camping area in Carson National Forest. Although it was federal property it wasn't patrolled regularly like a national park. A large metal Dumpster sat at the side of the highway next to the entrance to the forest. Campers were encouraged to deposit their refuse in the Dumpster, rather than leaving it strewn around the mountain.

The Meadows had no toilet facilities, no running water, and no designated campsites, although dozens of spots had been cleared away and used numerous times. Gabe had discovered the profiles of regular users. They were college kids out for a weekend bash, yuppie hikers who liked to avoid the tourist meccas, and the occasional writer who needed a taste of nature and an escape from the blinking cursor of his word processor. Retirees in land yachts and families with children avoided places like the Meadows with a vengeance.

The only road leading up to the Meadows was dirt and gravel and was graded usually once a year. Normally midsummer. Users had to suffer whatever damage the winter snows, spring runoffs, and summer deluges meted out. Quite often the campsites in the higher reaches of the Meadows went unused for several months until the road crew had been through to repair washouts.

Gabe found his first occupied site three miles into the forest. A man and a woman in their early thirties were in the process of breaking camp. They had been there for three days and had decided it was time to move to a place equipped with a shower. They had had no trouble with anyone stealing their gear, and they really couldn't say that they saw anything unusual.

He got the same story from the next two sites he visited. Five miles into the forest he stumbled on a campsite occupied by four high-school boys. Two were still sleeping in their tents. The other two were trying to hide dozens of empty beer cans.

"Hi, guys!" Gabe said cheerfully as he stepped out of his Jeep. When he was in high school Gabe didn't see the big deal about having a few beers. Since becoming an officer of the law he had seen the kind of damage a drunk teenager in a car could do. He was glad these boys had restricted their party to a campground. But they could have just as easily tried driving down the mountain to get more.

"Looks like you had a little party last night."

"N-no. Not really," one of the boys stammered. "We were just hanging out."

"Looks like somebody was awfully thirsty."

"We just had a couple," the second boy said.

"Why don't you wake your friends up? It's getting late and they're missing a beautiful day."

"Sure, officer."

The first boy went into the tents and shook his two sleeping friends. It took a moment for them to realize the wake-up call was not a prank. They stumbled from their tents barefoot, still wearing their clothes from the day before. Gabe guessed the oldest couldn't be more than eighteen.

"Where are you guys from?"

"Española," the first boy said. Being the most awake, he had become the group's spokesman.

"I see. Can anybody here take a guess what the drinking age is in New Mexico?" The spokesman started to answer, but Gabe held up his hand. He looked at the last boy to get up. "How about you, fella? You have any idea?"

"Twenty-one," he mumbled.

"Yeah. In fact, you have to be twenty-one before you can possess alcohol. I'm sure you all have driver's licenses that say twenty-one, right?"

The four looked sheepishly at each other with bowed heads.

"Of course, I guess it doesn't matter much since I didn't find anybody drinking." He could see a physical wave of relief pass over their faces. "That's not why I'm up here anyway. We've gotten a report that thieves have been robbing campsites up here. You wouldn't know anything about that, would you?"

The four spoke in unison. "No!" Followed by various expressions of denial: "That wasn't us." "We didn't do it." "We just got here last night." "It must have been somebody else."

It took Gabe a moment to calm them down. "I'm not accusing you. I just want to know if you saw or heard anything."

"No. Not me," one said.

"Me either," another added.

"I thought I heard someone scream last night," the first boy said.

"That was an owl," the second boy corrected, nudging him. "I told you that last night."

Gabe didn't know anything about owls. He thought all they did was hoot. "Are there any other campers around?"

"We saw a couple of girls drive past yesterday afternoon."

"Naw," another corrected. "They took off after midnight. I heard their car go by."

"What kind of car?"

"They were driving a blue Toyota hatchback."

Gabe nodded. "How long do you plan on staying here at the Meadows?"

"We're going back this afternoon. Some of us have to work tomorrow."

"I'm going to tell you right now: This mess better be cleaned up before you leave. And you are going to be stopped by me or one of the other deputies on your way home. If you have anything left in those ice chests, you'd better dump it before you get back in your car. You got one break today. Don't press your luck."

Gabe got back into his Jeep and made a radio call to dispatch. With all four boys watching him he gave Marilyn a description of their car and the license-plate number. He described the four occupants as teenage boys and possible minors in possession. Marilyn asked if the car should be detained when spotted. Gabe replied that only if it looked like they posed a threat to other drivers.

After the radio call he was sure there was no doubt in their minds that he hadn't made an idle threat. He started his Jeep and waved at them as he continued down the road to the next occupied site.

Gabe passed two unoccupied campsites before he found the blue Toyota the high-school kids had mentioned. He parked his Jeep next to the car and got out.

The doors to the Toyota were locked, as if its owner planned on being away for a while.

The campsite itself had been abandoned. There was no tent, sleeping bags, or any other type of equipment. Gabe could see that someone had made a campfire recently in the small clearing. He poked his finger into the middle of the gray ashes and found they were warm, but not hot.

Even though the deputy wasn't an experienced outdoorsman, he didn't see anything out of the ordinary. The warm ashes were probably from the night before. The fact that there was no equipment could mean the campers picked up and moved further into the forest for their next stop.

Gabe made a casual check of the perimeter of the small clearing, but nothing looked out of the ordinary to him. Looking around for anything suspicious, all Gabe could find was a flashlight someone had dropped. He discovered that it still worked, so it hadn't been there very long.

He walked back to his Jeep and jotted down the license-plate number to the Toyota. He followed the road further into the forest until he realized he would find no more campers. He turned around and headed back for the main highway.

Gabe slowed a little when he passed the high-school boys. He saw they were busy stuffing empty cans into a large plastic trash bag. They didn't seem very enthusiastic when they returned his wave. Two of them gave him the finger once his Jeep was past their camp.

"You guys don't know how lucky you were today," he mumbled to himself. "Jack Rivera would have had your hides."

When he reached the highway he headed back to Las Palmas to report everything he hadn't found out.

16

MARGARITE CARERRA'S GREEN PICKUP TRUCK was already parked behind the ranch house when Lansing arrived home. He found her and C.J. shooing the horses into the barn for the night while Juan Martín manned the gate.

Cement Head was his usual stubborn self. He wasn't wearing a halter, so there was no way Margarite could lead him into the barn. And every time she got close enough to grab his mane, he'd nip at her.

Milkweed was being cantankerous as well. C.J. was trying to direct the animal toward the barn. But each time it looked as if the pony was going to go through the gate, he did an abrupt ninety-degree turn and headed for the far end of the corral.

Lansing got out of his Jeep. After retrieving a rawhide lariat from the back end, he walked over to the corral to watch the circus. Margarite was not amused when she noticed her host leaning against the white-washed fence with a big grin on his face.

"What are you laughing at?" she said, blowing a long strand of black hair out of her eyes.

"Not a thing."

"Then why don't you help?"

"All you had to do was ask." Climbing over the corral fence, he untangled the rope and a second later had a lasso twirling over his head.

Cement Head eyed his master cautiously, but before he could react, Lansing had the rope over the horse's head. Cement Head had to jerk violently at the lariat to show his displeasure, but it lasted only a moment. It was all part of the ritual he and Lansing had established years earlier.

Lansing gave the rope a firm tug, and Cement Head snorted with a nod. His way of saying, "All right—this time."

"Here, C.J. You can put this beast in his stall now."

"What about Milkweed?"

"He wouldn't go in the barn because Cement Head was still out here. Don't worry. He'll follow you in."

"Okay." C.J. took the lariat from his father and gave it a gentle tug. "Come on, boy. Come on, Cement Head. Time for supper." The horse obediently followed the boy into the barn. Just behind the bigger horse came the smaller one. Martín closed the gate when all three were inside.

Margarite walked over and put her arms around Lansing's waist. He bent his head down so they could kiss.

"I thought you were going to have dinner ready for me when I got here," Margarite finally said after savoring the moment.

"You weren't supposed to be here till six."

"Check your watch, Sheriff."

Lansing did. It read six fifteen.

"Would you believe me if I told you I forgot to set my watch forward for Daylight Savings Time?"

"No."

"I didn't think so." He put his arm around her shoulder and led her out of the corral.

"So what is your excuse?"

"Gabe Hanna found an abandoned car up in Chama Meadows this morning. It took us all day to track down the owner and make sure it wasn't stolen."

"I take it that it wasn't."

"No. It's owned by some guy down in Albuquerque, but his daughter evidently uses it. She and a friend are on college break. They came up here to the mountains to do some camping. If he's not worried, I won't be either."

"Good. Then you can worry about burning me a steak."

Lansing was in the process of lighting the charcoal in his brick barbecue pit when C.J. and Martín emerged from the barn.

"They're all fed and watered, Dad," C.J. reported as he ran up.

"Good." He looked at Martín. "How was your helper today, Juan?"

"He did a good job." Martín was a short man in his mid-fifties with salt-and-pepper hair. He and his wife made a sustenance living on a small farm next to the Lansing ranch. With two of their six children still living at home, Martín hired himself out to other farmers and ranchers to make ends meet. There was always something that needed to be done on the Lansing ranch, so Martín was guaranteed a steady income. "I could use a man like him every day. I don't suppose he's for sale?"

"Hmm. What kind of price are you talking about?"

C.J. shot his father a worried look. "They can't sell people anymore, can they, Dad?"

"Oh, yeah. I guess you're right."

Lansing knew better. A slavery of sorts still operated in the United States, especially among the thousands of illegal aliens and their sponsors. People were bought and sold all the time. He had stopped hundreds of vehicles over the years laden with illegal human cargo. He knew it wasn't unusual for a family to sell a child to pay for their access to the promised land. Sometimes they even sold themselves, accepting slave wages and subhuman living conditions for the opportunity of one day living free in the land of the free. It usually ended up being a life they never escaped from.

"Sorry, Juan. I guess I have to keep him. Besides, his mother will want him back in a few weeks."

"Just thought I'd ask."

"I'm getting ready to ruin some steaks. Would you care to join us?"

"*Gracias*, but no. Tilly will have my dinner ready for me by now. I'll be back in the morning to finish repairing that fence."

"All right. Good night."

"How much money did I make today?" C.J. asked after Martín had left.

"I don't know. I'll have to talk it over with your boss."

"Oh." He watched for a moment while Lansing fanned the briquettes with his hat. "Where's Margarite?"

"She's inside washing up. And I thought I told you to call her Dr. Carerra."

"I did, but she told me to call her Margarite."

"Oh. Well, in that case . . . " He stepped back to get away from the smoke of the fire.

"What are we having with the steaks?"

"There's some corn on the cob wrapped in foil in the refrigerator. We'll throw those on the coals in a minute. Why don't you watch the fire for me? I'm going to change out of my uniform."

"Did you always take care of the Indians at the pueblos?" C.J. asked as he finished his second ear of corn.

"Not always," Margarite said, wiping the corners of her mouth with a napkin. "Before Burnt Mesa I worked in the emergency room of a hospital in Albuquerque for about eight years."

"Is that where you met my dad?"

"No. We met in San Phillipe County after I started working here. About a year and a half ago."

Seeing that everyone was finished, Lansing stood and began gathering plates. "Why all the questions, C.J.?"

"Sometimes you act like you've known each other a long time."

"Why do you say that?" Margarite asked, helping Lansing clear the table.

"I saw you two kissing. I thought you had to know someone a long time before you did that."

Lansing noticed the faint smile on Margarite's face when he said, "Let's say we've known each other long enough that it's okay if we kiss."

"So does that mean you're in love?"

The plate Lansing was carrying into the kitchen slipped from his fingers and shattered on the floor. He felt himself blush even deeper when Margarite snorted while trying to stop a laugh. "C.J., can you stop the inquisition long enough to help clear the table?"

"Yes, sir."

Lansing was sorry he snapped at his son. He would apologize later. At that moment, enough was enough.

It was after nine when Lansing walked Margarite out to her truck. The last hints of twilight had been erased, leaving a blanket of twinkling diamonds across the cloudless sky. A half-moon pierced the horizon above Taos. In another week it would bathe the landscape with its iridescent glow.

Neither had mentioned C.J.'s questions as they

cleaned the dishes together. Lansing was hoping the entire episode could be forgotten.

Margarite stopped next to her truck, turned, and put her arms around Lansing's neck. She pulled him close and they kissed.

"So," she said softly, "does this mean we're in love?"

Lansing felt his body stiffen. It was an involuntary reaction that he couldn't stop. "Margarite, you know how I feel about you."

Margarite pulled away. "I kid myself that I do, Lansing. Sometimes you're warm and considerate and tender. Sometimes you even remember to call me. Other times you treat me like an afterthought. 'Oh, yeah. Old Margarite Carerra. I feel like being serviced. I ought to give her a call.'"

"It's not like that at all and you know it."

"All I know is how you treat me, Lansing, because you never talk about how you feel or where I stand."

"Margarite, you're the only woman in my life."

"What? Until something better comes along?" She opened the door to her truck and slipped in. Lansing tried to grab the door before she slammed it, but he wasn't quick enough.

"I don't understand what you're upset about."

"And that's your problem, Lansing. You don't understand. You open little windows every once in a while so people can look in, but you never open the door. I see how you act with C.J. You're a different person. You let your guard down just a little. People see that you have feelings.

"But then, you always know that C.J is going to be around only a short time. As soon as he's gone, you slam all the windows and pull the shades. In fact, even tonight with him you closed up when he started talking about feelings."

"I think you're overreacting."

"And I think you like being alone. You're so afraid of

someone hurting you that you won't take a chance and let them in your life. Even somebody that might be in love with you." Margarite started the engine to her truck. "See you around, Lansing."

Before Lansing could protest, she shoved the shift into drive and stomped on the accelerator, leaving him in a cloud of dust. He watched helplessly as her tail-lights disappeared down the road.

C.J. emerged from the house. "Did Margarite leave?"

"Yeah," he said flatly. "She had to go back to the pueblo tonight." He turned and started for the barn. "Come on, let's make sure the horses are bedded down."

From the roof of the barn came the distinctive *hoo-hoot* of a great horned owl. Father and son looked up to see the bird spread its massive wings against the starry backdrop, then, with a single flap, take flight.

"Did you know that in Apache legends the presence of an owl is an omen that someone is about to die?"

"R-really?"

Lansing put a reassuring hand on his son's shoulder. "Don't worry. It's just a legend."

17

LANSING STOOD OUTSIDE THE LARGE REVIVAL tent that had been erected for the funeral services. Reverend Thomas Pakwa of the American Indian Church assured the tribal council that his portable tabernacle could accommodate over three thousand people. The sides of the tent had been raised to allow easy access and to keep a fresh flow of air for the attendees. To Lansing, it appeared that the pavilion was near capacity.

Deputies Hanna and Rivera had accompanied him to the reservation. They were assigned to keep the traffic flowing smoothly through Dulce, while the Apache officers supervised parking and crowd control.

Gabe Hanna had asked if he could stand outside the pavilion during the services. Although he didn't specifically say so, Lansing knew it was because Gabe was trying to absorb as much about Native American culture as he could. By the time the services began there wasn't much traffic to manage, so Lansing didn't see a problem with his deputy being there.

Lansing wondered what it was like for Gabe. His deputy was half Navajo, but didn't understand what it was like to be a Navajo. He was an army brat with no home, no roots, and no point of reference. He was an outsider who wanted to belong.

As Gabe stood solemnly beyond the boundaries of the pavilion watching the ceremony, Lansing couldn't help but think how appropriately that scene mirrored the deputy's very existence.

In a way Lansing did understand what it was like to be an outsider. He had Native American blood in him. Tewa from his father's side. Cherokee from his mother's. But it had been diluted and distilled through intermarriage, and his heritage, slight as it was, had been overwhelmed by the same manifest destiny that had overwhelmed an entire continent.

The Lansing family had been part of New Mexican history for one hundred fifty years, since the Mexican-American war. But in a way Cliff Lansing was considered, as an Anglo, an outsider. Maybe even more poignant, he was considered an intruder.

He wasn't privy to the mysteries of the native cultures, whose traditions and beliefs found their origins in the mists of antiquity. And as a Protestant, he was considered less than Christian by the Catholic Hispanic population. These were the same Hispanics whose ancestors forced unwanted Catholicism on unwilling native converts three hundred years before the arrival of the Americans.

The reason Lansing was welcome on the reservation, at Burnt Mesa Pueblo, or in any household in the county was his fairness and honesty. It was a Lansing family tradition that dated back to 1846, when Lt. Virgil Lansing first came to New Mexico. It was a trait handed down from generation to generation. When Cliff Lansing first ran for Sheriff, he knew he was elected as much on the reputation of his family as on his own merit. That didn't bother him at all. He was proud of his heritage.

But despite the fine reputation the Lansing family name carried, Lansing knew they were, at worst, intruders in this ancient land and, at best, newcomers.

That was perhaps what separated him from Gabe, he thought. He knew he was an outsider and always would be. Gabe Hanna knew he was an outsider too, but refused to settle for that status.

Besides the members of the Jicarilla tribe, in attendance were representatives from several of the pueblos, from the Navajo reservation, and from the Ute reservation in Colorado. (The Ute and the Jicarilla as independent tribes had been very close in the past, both politically and through blood relations. There had even been an attempt by the U.S. government in the 1870s to collocate the two tribes on one reservation. The Jicarillas wanted their own land, although they had to wait two decades before anything happened.)

The governor's office sent a small delegation to offer condolences, and because politicians were around, camera crews from Farmington, Santa Fe, and Albuquerque had been dispatched. The cameramen looked bored, and the reporters looked desperate for anyone to interview. Lansing turned down an offer for an on-camera report. He explained he was there only for traffic control and insisted that he knew nothing about the FBI investigation.

The ceremonies inside the pavilion lasted for almost three hours. Except for one or two mothers with cranky babies, no one left during the solemnities. All of the songs and prayers were conducted in Apache with Pinto Velarde, the eldest of the Ollero medicine men and now the chief medicine man of the tribe, presiding.

Lansing's Spanish was pretty good, but he could understand only a little Apache. He noticed Gabe mouthing the words to several of the songs during the refrains. That's when he remembered that Navajo and

Apache were both Athapaskan languages and for all practical purposes nearly identical.

When the final chant was completed, Velarde encouraged the throng to pass by the four coffins to pay last respects to Esteban Baltazar and the three oil-field workers. The coffins were closed, as it was considered extremely bad luck for the living to look at the countenance of a dead person. Early in the twentieth century it wasn't unusual for the Jicarilla to take the funeral process one step further by burning the dead man's home along with all of his possessions. The Dutch Reform Church had done much to bring the Jicarilla traditions under Western European influence, but the Apaches still held a strong fear and reverence for the dead.

With the formal ceremonies complete, many people started walking toward the community center a mile away, where a sort of wake had been planned. Others simply headed for their cars. Small groups of people started forming beyond the confines of the pavilion, knots of friends and family, visiting, chatting, sometimes consoling one another over the communal loss.

At the far side of the tent FBI Agent Phil Sheridan stood talking with Tribal President Velarde and a well-dressed woman in her early fifties. The woman looked familiar, but it still took Lansing a moment to realize it was Dr. Victoria Miles. It had been ten years since he had seen her last.

Lansing had to admit Dr. Miles was a strikingly handsome woman. She was thin, almost willowy, which helped accentuate her high cheekbones and deep-set eyes. Her skin was the color of red earth, and her long black hair was streaked with strands of silver. She wore a gray pinstriped business suit and had the air of someone who would be comfortable in the most sophisticated of circles.

Despite her appearance Lansing knew she had a

thinly veiled disdain for whites. Especially those whose families had settled on Jicarilla lands. She was a fierce defender of Apache rights, and anyone who disagreed with her was automatically her enemy. That was the category where Lansing found himself.

Gabe approached, breaking his concentration. "Sheriff, I'm heading back to the crossroads. How much longer will the reservation police need us?"

"Let's give it an hour. By then most of the traffic should be gone. I'll contact you if we need to stay longer."

"Sure thing."

While Lansing and Gabe were talking, Velarde and his companions were spotted by several reporters. In a matter of seconds they were surrounded by cameras and microphones. Lansing decided he would keep his distance.

"Cliff!" someone called from behind.

Lansing turned to see Captain Koteen approaching. "Hey there, Ned."

"I just wanted to tell you thanks again for all the help."

"No problem. I'm glad there was something I could do."

"I have one more favor to ask."

"Shoot."

"Agent Sheridan wants to have a meeting of the minds, I guess you could say. He wants to sit down with Dr. Miles, Hector Velarde, and me to talk about the Baltazar case. He said he didn't mind you sitting in if you were interested. To be honest, I wouldn't mind either."

Lansing glanced at his watch. "When did he want to do this?"

Koteen glanced at the knot of reporters. "I imagine as soon as he can escape the news hounds. We'll be meeting at the police station. There will be a lot less traffic over there."

"Yeah, I can sit in. I need to make a couple of phone calls before you get started."

"You can make them from my office," Koteen said. "We'll meet you there as soon as we can."

As Lansing walked toward the far end of the parking area where he had left his Jeep, a man fell in step with him. He glanced at the stranger and said, "Hi."

" 'Lo, Sheriff." The man wore blue jeans, a white shirt, and a leather vest. His long hair was streaked with a single shock of white and his head was bound with a red Apache kerchief. A long white scar nearly two inches wide ran from the shock of white hair, down the right side of the man's face, ending somewhere below the collar. His eyes were hidden by sunglasses. "That's a fine son you got. Handsome young man."

"Thanks." The man looked vaguely familiar, but Lansing knew he would have remembered the scar. "Do I know you?"

"No. I just happened to see you having lunch at the diner."

"You live here on the reservation?"

"Used to." The man started to walk away. "My car's over there. Nice talking to you."

"Yeah." Lansing stopped and watched as the man got into a rusty old Buick. The stranger started the engine, then drove away without once looking back at him.

Lansing quickly forgot about the incident as he got into his Jeep and headed for the tribal-police headquarters.

18

AGENT SHERIDAN CONVENED THE MEETING IN A small conference room adjacent to Koteen's office. In attendance were Dr. Miles, Tribal President Velarde, Lansing, Koteen, and Koteen's most senior officer, Lt. Bram Vicinti. Even though he was acting liaison officer for the highway patrol, Marty Hernandez was absent. He was being spread thin, and his regular patrol duties preempted any meetings.

Sheridan began the meeting by bringing the others up to date on his investigation.

"We now know for certain Baltazar died as a result of the wound to the throat. Sometime around midnight, not long after his granddaughter dropped him at his house. It also appears that he suffered a severe beating before the final wound was inflicted.

"The paraffin test showed that he had fired a gun recently. We assume it was the pistol found at the scene. John Baltazar confirmed that the weapon belonged to him.

"We did a ballistics test on the four slugs found in the living room wall. All four came from that gun. Again, we're making an assumption that they were fired that night, by Baltazar, at his assailant. We think Baltazar must have missed, because the only blood we've been able to find so far is his. The lab is still analyzing the samples, so that issue is still open."

Lansing raised his hand to interrupt. "Were the slugs examined for blood or tissue?"

"I can't imagine anything being left after the bullets dug into the wall, but I'll ask the lab boys to take a look."

Lansing nodded, satisfied with the response.

"We're still filtering through the fingerprints found at the scene," Sheridan continued. "So far, we've identified only prints belonging to Baltazar and his relatives.

"John Baltazar did an inventory of the house. As far as he could tell nothing was missing, so we're ruling out robbery as a motive.

"Except for the writing on the kitchen wall, that pretty much summarizes all the physical evidence."

"If you don't mind," Dr. Miles interrupted, "now might be a good time to discuss the writing you found." She reached into a briefcase sitting on the floor next to her and pulled out a manila envelope. She handed the envelope to Velarde, who passed it on to the FBI agent.

"As Captain Koteen told you," she continued, "the literal translation of *Sekala Ka-amja* is 'the one who never dies.' In Jicarilla mythology he is our great cultural hero. He was the greatest of the *hactcin*, or holy people. He was our Prometheus, Hercules, King Arthur, our Moses and Christ rolled into one being. Like the Christian Jesus he was mortal, but he was also the offspring of *Yusun*, the Supreme Being.

"In other Apache versions he is immortalized as *Naayenezgane*, or the Slayer-of-Enemies. In yet others he's called Born of Thunder or Son-of-Changing-Woman.

"There is a general consensus that King Arthur actually existed. Many Greek scholars believe Hercules was a real person. It's been proven Troy and Jericho were real cities. What actually happened to them has been lost in Greek and Hebrew myth. As in any mythology based on an oral tradition, there in all likelihood was an actual person who became known as *Sekala Ka-amja*."

Lansing glanced at Sheridan. The agent seemed captivated by Dr. Miles's lesson. "But why would someone scrawl that at a murder scene?" Lansing asked, trying to get back to the case at hand.

Dr. Miles shot Lansing an angry look. He couldn't tell if she resented the interruption or if her former animosity still simmered close to the surface.

"It could be a prank of some type," she said. "Or it might be someone with a Christ complex. Our traditions hold that *Sekala Ka-amja* will return one day and walk among us. The Apache version of the Second Coming. I personally hope it's a prank. I wouldn't know how to deal with someone who thinks he's the Son of God."

Sheridan pulled out his ever-present notepad and thumbed through a few pages. "The night Baltazar was murdered, he made a speech to the tribal council. He said that an 'evil' was visiting your reservation. He mentioned two or three incidents, including the oil-rig fire, that he did not believe were accidents. A couple of people I interviewed said that he had even predicted these events."

"He was a *tsanati*," Velarde offered. "A medicine man. But beyond his powers of healing he also considered himself a Shadowcatcher, a person who had visions and could see into the future."

"Could he?" Sheridan asked.

"I would have never said it to his face," Velarde admitted, "but I don't think so. He was an old man who still believed in the old ways. I remember my father talking about how bad it was in the 1920s. Ninety percent of the children either had tuberculosis or had been exposed to it. There wasn't a damned thing the medicine men could do to stop the epidemic.

"It wasn't until the Dutch Reform Church came in that things started to turn around. They brought doctors and nurses and modern medicine. They set up a sanitarium next to the boarding school. They moved the children from tepees to wooden dormitories, where they had clean clothes and warm meals to eat.

"It wasn't an easy transition, but by 1950 tuberculosis had been eradicated and our population had more than doubled, no thanks to the medicine men. Their power and influence has declined steadily over the years, and that's fine with me. I lost my mother because she thought traditional cures were more powerful than modern medicine."

Lansing was surprised at Velarde's statement. There had been a resurgence of Native American culture in recent years. There was a growing pride among the people the white man had called "Indians." They believed that their traditions and values, based on kinship to and respect for the natural world, were altruistic and pure. Before he could resolve Velarde's statement with what he himself had come to believe, Dr. Miles added her comments.

"There's a good deal of truth behind what President Velarde just said. A lot of people don't believe in the old ways anymore. There are fewer than a dozen medicine men and women in our tribe. Not one of them is under the age of forty. We pay lip service to our heritage. We still conduct the Bear Dance. We still hold the puberty rites for our daughters and run the Ceremonial Relay Race every September. We tell ourselves we are deeply religious, then discourage our children from learning the ways of the *hactcin*. It is more important that they get a white man's education so they can survive in the white man's world.

"I've spent my entire adult life recording the ancient stories in our native tongue so they'll be preserved. But in another twenty years, unless something is done, there will be no more *tsanati* and our ceremonies will be conducted by rote, with no understanding of the underlying beliefs that created them."

"I think I can appreciate your concerns over your heritage," Sheridan said. "But I think we're getting away from the issue here. Baltazar talked about a mining accident, a hunting incident, and the rig fire. One week before he was murdered he was almost killed in a car accident. Is there the slightest possibility any of these are related?"

"I investigated the traffic accident," Koteen said. "I think it was a case of someone too old to be driving losing control of his truck. The mining accident had to do with a buildup of methane gas. Three men were killed over a two-day period in separate hunting incidents. A dozen people are killed in New Mexico every year in the same kind of accidents. There's nothing to link one to another.

"Personally, I never heard Esteban predict those events. People told me he had foreseen each of them, but they never said anything until after the accidents had occurred."

"What about the oil fire?" Sheridan asked.

"I have to admit, he did predict that one. He even went to the tribal council and asked them to stop the drilling, didn't he, Hector?"

"Yes. Yes, he did." Velarde sighed. He sounded as if he was tired of talking about the issue. "But one lucky guess does not make him a fortune-teller."

"All right, let's forget about whether he could predict the future," Sheridan said. "The other thing Baltazar mentioned that night was the differences between the Olleros and the Llaneros."

"That's just an old man ranting," Velarde observed. "We're one tribe with one tribal council. We look out for the interests of all our people, Ollero and Llanero alike. Besides, to survive we intermarried. There are no distinct lines anymore."

"Who are these factions?"

"Before we were confined to a reservation, the Jicarilla Apaches lived in two distinct groups," Dr. Miles explained. "The Olleros, or Plains People, and the Llaneros, or Mountain People. Even though they were linked by a common culture and religion, their lifestyles were completely different.

"The Olleros lived east of Raton Pass in what is now the panhandle areas of Texas and Oklahoma. They were nomadic and made their existence by hunting buffalo.

"The Llaneros lived in the mountains and were seminomadic. They did some hunting, but they were chiefly farmers. They learned the skills from the pueblo peoples of Taos and Burnt Mesa. Like the pueblos, the Llaneros also made pottery and wove cloth from the cotton they raised. Unlike the pueblos, though, they didn't settle at a single spot. Each year they moved to a new location, reusing the same spot every five or ten years. Their territory ranged from Raton westward to the Rio Chama.

"The Jicarilla never achieved the vicious reputation of their Apache brothers because they were more interested in commerce. Every September the Olleros and Llaneros met in a great festival. The Plains People traded their excess hides for pottery, cotton blankets, and other necessities they couldn't find on the plains. They also ran the Ceremonial Relay Race. One team from each group. If the Olleros won, it meant the next year there would be an abundance of buffalo. If the

Llaneros won, it meant the next season would yield a bountiful harvest.

"Both groups would even bring their surpluses into Santa Fe to trade for Spanish goods. When the Americans arrived in 1846, the Jicarilla Apaches saw no profit in going to war. They were content with carrying on business as usual.

"In the 1870s the great buffalo herds began to disappear. About the same time the lands the Llaneros had been farming for generations were being scarfed up by white settlers. That's when the United State government insisted the Jicarillas move onto a reservation.

"Needless to say, the Olleros wanted the reservation located on the Plains. The Llaneros wanted the reservation in the mountains. The federal government ignored both of their wishes and stuck them in a corner of the Mescalero Apache Reservation in the southern part of the state.

"It took nearly twenty years, but the Llaneros finally convinced the whites to grant them a parcel of land in the northern part of the state, where they used to live. The government agreed only because the land they were living on could barely support cactus, let alone a farming economy.

"The Olleros still wanted their reservation on the plains. But they could also see that if they didn't go with the Llaneros, they would never have a piece of land they could call their own. This is where one of the great ironies of our tribe began. To replace their dependence on buffalo, the Olleros had become sheep herders. A few of them had become quite wealthy on the Mescalero reservation compared to the Llaneros. The land around here isn't suited for farming, but it's great grazing land.

"When the Jicarilla finally moved to this reservation in 1887, there was a great disparity between the haves and have-nots. The Olleros were bitter about losing their land on the plains, but they were doing quite well as herdsmen. The Llaneros had the land they wanted, but couldn't make a living on their farm plots.

"The disparity lasted for fifty-five years. Things didn't start to even out until oil was found in the 1940s. By that time the Olleros were considered the dominant faction in the tribe. They controlled most of the council seats and Cesar TeCube, an Ollero, succeeded his uncle as chief medicine man. He held that position for over twenty years.

"There was a good deal of resentment on the Ollero side when Esteban Baltazar assumed the status of chief medicine man—"

"That's not true," Velarde protested.

"You didn't see it, Hector," Dr. Miles replied calmly, "because you live here on the reservation. Whatever petty differences there were you saw as normal political events. Whenever I came home to visit I could see the resentment festering under the surface, ever since Cesar died and Esteban assumed his place."

"Was there enough resentment for someone to want to murder him?" Sheridan asked.

"Of course not," Velarde snapped.

Dr. Miles shook her head. "I hope not."

19

ALTHOUGH A LOT OF INFORMATION WAS TRADED during the meeting, not a lot was accomplished. Sheridan was no closer to finding a suspect than he was the day after the murder.

"Were you able to get anything else out of John Baltazar when you went back?" Lansing asked. He, Sheridan, and Koteen were leaving the police station and heading to their respective vehicles.

"No," the agent admitted. "But he seemed upset that I came back."

"You need to give him a break," Koteen said. "On top of everything else, he's now facing a formal inquiry about the well fire. As drilling supervisor, he's held responsible if anything goes wrong. He could lose his business."

"Well, Captain, you were there with me. He sure flew off the handle when he caught his son listening from the kitchen."

"Maybe he was being overprotective. Some parents are like that."

"He told the boy to stay away from us and not talk to anyone."

"We Apache are a very private people," Koteen explained. "Especially in times of tragedy. I think John was just trying to instill in the boy that we keep our grief to ourselves.

"As far as staying away from us, that's just natural Apache aversion to lawmen in general. Even one from their own tribe."

"I suppose you're right." Sheridan stopped at his car and thought for a moment. "The medicine man who conducted the ceremonies this afternoon, what was his name?"

"Velarde," Koteen replied. "Pinto Velarde."

"Is he any relation to the council president?"

"They're cousins."

Sheridan nodded. "Ollero?"

It was Koteen's turn to nod.

"I may need to talk to him." Sheridan opened the door to his car. "There's also an outside chance that there is some sort of a link between Esteban's murder and the rig explosion. I want to sit in when the board of inquiry convenes and see what comes up. For the time being, I have to go back to Santa Fe. I need to brief my boss on what we've found out so far, which isn't much.

"You have my card, Captain Koteen. Please let me know if anything comes up. I'll be back in a few days."

The three said their good-byes, then Sheridan got into his car and drove off.

"So what didn't you want to tell him?" Lansing asked.

"What do you mean?"

"I've known you a long time, Ned. That cover story about Baltazar was pretty flimsy."

"It's all true."

"I'm talking about when Baltazar was talking to his son. It felt like you were leaving something out."

Koteen looked Lansing squarely in the eye. "Just between you and me? It doesn't go any farther?"

"If that's what you want."

"Marcus has a lot of emotional problems."

"Marcus. That's the son?"

Koteen nodded. "John and Christina have had him to specialists a dozen times. Here, down in Santa Fe, Albuquerque. They've been talking about sending him away, someplace where he can get full-time care. John's always out well-sitting and Christina's at her wits' end. Evidently, ever since the well explosion things have gotten worse. I imagine the last thing the Baltazars need is for some green FBI agent to come in and stir things up for them. John's plate is full. He doesn't need any more grief right now."

When the two men reached their patrol Jeeps, Koteen discovered a folded sheet of paper under his windshield wiper. Lansing watched as Koteen unfolded the paper and read it. The reservation policeman seemed to read the note a second time before folding it and stuffing it in his shirt pocket. His expression was grim.

"Something wrong?" Lansing asked.

Koteen shook his head. "You remember I said Apaches like to avoid lawmen? I get a lot of notes under my wiper. Our way of communicating around here. That way no one has to talk to me directly."

"Whatever works." Lansing opened the door to his Jeep. "I'm heading back to Las Palmas. Give me a call in a day or two, let me know how things are going."

"Sure will." Koteen waved as Lansing backed around and headed for the highway.

Lansing was grateful the meeting didn't last any longer than it did. He could still get an hour's worth of paperwork done at his office and be home by dinner. He toyed with the idea of stopping by Burnt Mesa on the way back, but he wasn't sure Margarite was in the mood for one of his visits. She'd left the ranch fairly angry the night before. He thought he'd give her one more day to cool off.

He knew he'd end up apologizing. He wasn't quite sure what he'd be apologizing about, but he knew he would. That's the way their arguments usually ended. He consoled himself with the thought that being on her good side was worth the effort.

Dulce sat on the western side of the continental divide from Las Palmas. Once he was clear of the mountains and pointed south, Lansing radioed dispatch and reported that he would be back to the office in another thirty minutes.

Except for resolving things with Margarite, this was the first time in almost a week Lansing felt he could relax. He leaned back in his seat and tried to enjoy the quiet drive back to town.

20

IT WAS NEARLY MIDNIGHT WHEN KOTEEN WAS finishing the last of his rounds. It had been a hectic day. After the meeting with Sheridan he had to supervise the funeral escort to the cemetery.

Another mourning ceremony was held after sunset. A small cadre of young men had gotten drunk before the ceremony, causing a minor disturbance. They demanded justice for the slain Esteban. Reasoning didn't work, and a half dozen of them ended up in jail. Six others escaped, but Koteen knew who they were. He would round them up in the morning when they would be somewhat subdued by their own hangovers.

There was always the chance a couple of the "warriors" were still lurking about, looking for more libation. Before calling it a night Koteen wanted to make one last pass by the Dulce liquor store. Just because the shop was closed did not mean some after-hours customers wouldn't be looking for a late-night beverage.

The parking lot was well lit. Koteen stopped at the front of the store and got out to check the door. Through the window he could see that the night lights were on. There was no movement inside the building. He checked the door to make sure it was locked.

As soon as he touched the handle of the door, the lights of the parking lot and store flickered, then went out. Koteen froze, engulfed in darkness. The closest light was from a street pole two blocks away. The half-moon provided little illumination.

Koteen looked inside the store, assuming he would see the beam of a flashlight. It was still dark.

He hurried over to his Jeep and shut off the engine. He pulled his flashlight from beneath the seat, then quietly closed the door.

He figured the intruder had broken in through the back door. Not wanting to offer an easy target, he kept the flashlight off as he drew his gun from its holster. He quietly hurried to the side of the building, then, with his back to the wall, edged himself to the back of the store.

He peeked around the corner, expecting to see something. Everything was bathed in darkness. He slipped around the corner and edged his way toward the rear entrance.

From somewhere above came the questioning call of an owl. The officer froze again, listening for any other sound. His patience was rewarded only with another hoot from the owl.

He stepped quickly to the door and tried the handle.

The last two things Koteen noticed were that the door was locked and that he heard the unmistakable flapping of wings.

Then came the crash to his skull and the final darkness.

21

"DEPUTY LANSING! I THINK I FOUND SOME-thing!"

Lansing looked toward the volunteer searcher only thirty yards away. He was waving his flashlight back and forth.

Lansing scrambled toward the light, losing his footing twice on the steep slope. He stopped where the other searcher had his beam pointed. There was a stack of branches piled three feet high. It looked as though someone was getting ready to start a fire.

The deputy began tearing the limbs off the pile layer by layer. The man with the flashlight kept it trained on the spot. Behind them other men were yelling: "You got something?" "What'd you find?" "Hey, what's going on?"

Lansing was oblivious to the commotion, intent on his task. He had cleared two dozen branches before he spotted anything. It appeared to be cloth. He worked frantically to remove the rest of the branches.

As the other searchers gathered around they added the beams of their lights to the first man's, staying clear of the flying limbs.

Lansing stepped back once he tossed the last branch away.

There were three small bodies lying next to each other. Their bedclothes were ripped and bloodstained. The deputy could feel tears well up in his eyes as he forced himself to look at the first face.

It was the face of his son.

In the pitch black of the night someone screamed, "*No!*"

Lansing's eyes sprung open. He was lying on his back, in his own bed. He was soaked with sweat. He jumped when someone tapped on his door.

"Dad?" C.J. said the word softly.

"Yeah, son." Lansing's voice was hoarse. "What is it?"

C.J. opened the door and stuck half his head through the opening. "Are you all right?"

Lansing sat up in bed. "Yeah, I'm fine." He patted the side of the bed. "Why don't you come in for a minute?"

C. J. obeyed, sitting on the bed where his father had indicated. "What happened?"

"I guess I had a bad dream." He put his arms around his son and held him tightly.

"What about?"

"Something that happened a long, long time ago. Something I wish I could forget."

"I guess that means you don't want to talk about it."

He released his son from the hug, then ruffled his hair. "When did you get so smart?"

"You want me to get you a glass of water or something?"

"I think I'll be fine. Thanks anyway."

C.J. reached over and turned on the lamp next to the bed. "Back when I was a kid, Mom used to turn on my light so I wouldn't have nightmares." He patted his

father on the shoulder. "Let me know if you need anything else."

All Lansing could do was shake his head. "I'll do
that."

"Good night, Dad."

"Good night, C.J."

When he heard his son's door click shut, Lansing
reached up and turned off the light. He stared at the
ceiling for a long time before dozing off, but for the
remainder of the night his sleep was anything but
restful.

22

"DAD, WHAT'S THIS?" C.J. ASKED AS LANSING set a plate of fried eggs, bacon, and hash browns on the table in front of him.

"Let me see." He examined the hand and found four hard, yellow bumps at the base of C.J.'s fingers. "Let me see your left hand." That hand had similar bumps, but not as pronounced.

"It looks like Juan's been keeping you pretty busy."

"What do you mean?"

"Those are calluses. You get those from hard work. Do they hurt?"

"Naw, not really."

"We'd better get you some gloves, before you get a blister."

"I've been wearing gloves. I borrowed a pair of yours."

Lansing smiled. "I'll pick you up something in town today that fits a little better."

C.J. started in on his breakfast with a vengeance. He was finished before Lansing was halfway through his own plate.

"Do I need to cook some more?"

"No, that's all right. I'll just have some more milk." C.J. put his plate in the sink for rinsing, then refilled his glass with milk from the refrigerator. He rejoined his father at the table.

"Dad, what was your dream about last night?"

Lansing hesitated. He was embarrassed over the episode, but he knew he couldn't ignore it as if it had never happened. And he certainly didn't want his son carrying home unfavorable stories about him.

He took a sip of coffee, trying to edit the story down to the shortest, least painful version. "It was about ten years ago. You had just turned two. You know the Girl Scout camp up near Chama Meadows?" His son nodded. "The sheriff's office got a call in the middle of the night. I was still a deputy back then."

"Chief Deputy?"

"Yeah. Chief Deputy. Anyway, somebody snuck into the camp and kidnapped three of the girls. I rounded up a bunch of men—"

"A posse?"

"No. A search party. We went out in the dark and had to look for them."

"Did you find them?"

"Yeah. Yeah, we did." He paused for a moment. "Unfortunately, we found them too late. They were dead."

"You mean somebody killed them?"

Lansing nodded. "I was one of the first ones to see them. It was pretty awful. In my dreams sometimes I still see them, like last night."

"Do you have those dreams all the time?"

"Not in a long time." He stood and took his plate to the sink. He started rinsing the small pile of dishes that had accumulated there since the night before, then put them in the dishwasher.

C.J. brought his empty glass to the sink to be rinsed. "Did you catch the guy who did it?"

At that moment Juan Martín pulled into the parking area behind the house and honked his horn. "Your boss is here. You'd better get moving.

"Tell Juan to have you back here by noon. We're going into town for lunch at the diner."

"Great!" C.J. ran into the living room to retrieve his baseball cap. He stopped just before heading out the back door. "You didn't say, Dad. Did you catch the guy?"

Lansing faced the sink as he shook his head. "No. No, I guess we didn't."

"Oh." There was profound disappointment in that one syllable. The disappointment carried over into C.J.'s parting words. "See you at noon."

"Yeah. Noon."

"Dispatch, this is Patrol One," Lansing said as he headed down the highway toward town. "I'm on my way in."

"Patrol One, Dispatch," Marilyn responded. "Thought I'd let you know. Patrolman Hernandez called already from Dulce this morning. He needs you to call him as soon as you're in."

"Ten-four. Anything else?"

"Nothing from the night ledger. I guess things have been quiet."

"That's good to know. I'll be there in about ten minutes."

"Dispatch copies."

"Marty? Cliff here. What's up?"

Marty Hernandez had left a message to reach him at the Jicarilla police station. The resident highway patrolman had an office of his own at the station. As the temporary state representative to the reservation, Hernandez used the small room as his base of operations.

"I've got some bad news, Cliff." There was a brief pause. "Ned Koteen is dead."

"Dead!" Lansing couldn't believe it. "When? What happened? Traffic accident?"

"No, it was no accident. He was murdered sometime last night."

"What do you mean?"

"It looks like the Baltazar incident all over again."

"You're kidding."

"I wish I were. I have to get back to the crime scene. Do you have time to make a run up here?"

"I'll make time. What about the FBI?"

"They've been notified, but it will be a couple of hours before they get here."

"What about the tribal police? Are they going to mind me coming in?"

"Lieutenant Vicinti seemed reluctant to have you around. I reminded him that you'd been helping Koteen with this business all along and that you knew as much as anyone else. He finally agreed to let me call you, but you might want to give him a little space when you get here. There are a lot of upset people on the reservation."

"I'll bet. I'll be there in about forty-five minutes. Where can I find you?"

"Behind the Dulce liquor store, about a half mile from Highway Sixty-four."

"I know where it is. I'll see you there."

Lansing grabbed his jacket and Stetson from the coatrack in his office and headed for the outer door. Deputy Hanna was just coming in.

"Sheriff, do you have a minute?"

"Yeah. What is it?" Lansing couldn't help sounding impatient.

"I made a couple of phone calls yesterday trying to get a lead on the stolen camping gear. The owner of a used-camping-equipment store down in Santa Fe said a couple of guys come in twice a week with a load of stuff to sell. They claim they get the gear from garage sales, but the owner says he's not so sure. What do you think we should do?"

"Call the owner. Get a list of the items that he bought. Also, see if he knows when these guys might be back. Maybe we can send someone down there to get an I.D. You might check and see if he can set up a surveillance camera. If these are our perps it would be great to catch them on tape trying to fence the stuff." Lansing turned to his dispatcher. "Marilyn, I have to go to the Jicarilla reservation. I don't know when I'll be back."

"Anything wrong?"

"Yeah. Ned Koteen was murdered last night."

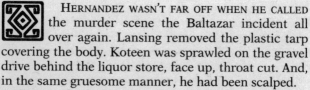

23

HERNANDEZ WASN'T FAR OFF WHEN HE CALLED the murder scene the Baltazar incident all over again. Lansing removed the plastic tarp covering the body. Koteen was sprawled on the gravel drive behind the liquor store, face up, throat cut. And, in the same gruesome manner, he had been scalped.

Next to the body, almost unnoticeable among the bottle caps, beers tabs, and sundry items typical of a service drive, was an owl's feather. Lansing picked it up and looked at it. It was rather unremarkable and he wouldn't have noticed it at all if Koteen hadn't found one at Baltazar's house. He returned it next to the body so it could be included in the forensics photos.

Lansing had tried to prepare himself for the scene, but it wasn't easy. He kept his jaw set and his emotions to himself as he pulled the tarp back over the body.

Across the white-painted back walls of the building were scrawled more Apache words, presumably made with the police chief's blood: NAHWHEESHNII NAAYENEZGANE NI' NIKEEIDLEE.

"It says, 'I came back to life. The Slayer-of-Enemies

has returned to earth.' " Dr. Miles shook her head. "I'm not a psychiatrist, but I think you're dealing with a psychopath here."

"I don't doubt that a bit," Hernandez agreed. "But what does it mean?"

Dr. Miles gave a rehash of her impromptu lecture from the day before; however, trying to fit her explanation of the words into the context of the murders didn't seem to work.

Lansing was surprised that Dr. Miles hadn't returned to Albuquerque. He later found out that she had explained to Agent Sheridan that the summer quarter wouldn't begin for another week. Since she was already there she was taking the opportunity to visit relatives and friends.

Surprisingly, Sheridan arrived by helicopter only minutes after Lansing got there. The rest of the team was following in cars and vans. He quickly convened a meeting with Lt. Vicinti, Hernandez, Lansing, and Dr. Miles. They met in the conference room next to Koteen's office.

"I needed to get here as soon as possible," Sheridan said. "If we're dealing with the same person, and my guess is that we are, we have a serial killer on our hands."

"Plus," Lansing pointed out, "we don't know if these are his first two murders."

"As soon as Officer Hernandez called me this morning and told me what had happened, I contacted Washington. They're going through their crime files to see if there have been any recent murders that fit this scenario."

"And what scenario is that?" Lt. Vicinti asked. There was the slightest hint of animosity in his voice.

"Slit throat, scalping, handwriting on the wall, for starters, Lieutenant." Sheridan wasn't going to be intimidated. "Our computers can cross-reference a hundred cases in a minute. Thousands in an hour. If there's anything that even remotely suggests a connection, we'll take a closer look."

"How far back are you going?" Hernandez asked.

"We've got a loop program that will review data from the last three months, then the three months prior to those, and so on. I asked for a review of everything from the last five years."

"What if nothing turns up?" It was Vicinti again.

"We keep on with what we're doing. Nothing's going to change with that." He pulled out his notepad. "Just to keep the players straight, what did Captain Koteen consider himself, politically?"

"What do you mean?"

"Was he Ollero or Llanero?"

Vicinti shrugged. "I guess Llanero. Most of the Koteens are Llanero. What does that matter?"

"Maybe nothing." He turned to Dr. Miles. "What about the words on the side of the building?"

"They're in keeping with what I told you yesterday. Our cultural hero goes by many names: The One Who Never Dies, Slayer-of-Enemies, Born of Thunder. Just like the titles Christians hang on Jesus: The Christ, Savior, Son of God, Lamb of God. Whoever's doing this just chose an alternate name to use."

"Maybe we need to ignore who is doing this for a moment," Lansing suggested, "and ask why, instead. There could be a thousand reasons why old Esteban was murdered. But Ned Koteen was killed too. There should be a limited number of reasons why both of them were killed. They've got to be linked somehow."

"That's a reasonable assumption," Sheridan said. "On the other hand, the same person could have killed them for only remotely similar reasons. Their only link is that they were killed by the same person."

"Which is something you haven't even established

yet," Vicinti said. "That they even were killed by the same person."

Sheridan nodded. "Unfortunately, Lieutenant, you're absolutely right. We haven't. Could you get me a list of everyone Koteen might have talked to last night?"

"You might as well start with the As in the reservation phone book. Nearly everyone in the tribe showed up for the ceremony last night."

"All right. This is your territory. You tell me where we should start the investigation."

Vicinti seemed to deflate a little. Yes, this was his territory and he did resent the intrusion of the white men, but he was no closer to a solution than any of them. "A dozen or so young men got drunk last night and stirred up a little trouble. Six of them managed to slip away before they could be arrested. We can start with them. I'll have a couple of my officers pick them up for questioning."

"Thanks." Sheridan put his notepad back in his pocket. "I need to get back to the liquor store. The forensics team ought to be arriving any minute.

"Dr. Miles, how much longer are you going to be here?"

"Until Monday. I'll need a day of preparation before classes start on Wednesday. Till then I'm at your disposal."

"I appreciate that."

As they left the police station Sheridan motioned Lansing to one side. "I was just curious how you happened to be out here on the reservation again, Sheriff. I mean, it's not as if Captain Koteen's around to ask you for any help."

"Officer Hernandez called me up and told me about the murder. He got Lieutenant Vicinti's permission before asking me to come up here."

"Why would Hernandez ask you out here? This isn't your jurisdiction."

"For starters, Marty knew Ned and I were friends." Lansing felt himself getting angry over having to explain his actions. He reminded himself to stay calm. "In fact, we were friends back when you were still in kindergarten. I showed up out of respect for our friendship and because he was a fellow officer, killed in the line of duty.

"And I don't know if you've noticed it or not, but we're still in San Phillipe County. This may be Apache land, but there's no big wall separating it from the rest of the county. What happens here can spill over into my jurisdiction at the snap of a finger. I think it's prudent on my part to keep informed." He gave the agent a cold stare, letting the words sink in thoroughly. "Anything else, Agent Sheridan?"

"I just wanted to make sure we all understood our boundaries." Sheridan's statement was made as a matter of fact. There was no hint of resentment or retreat.

"We do." Lansing turned and headed for his Jeep. As a friend he regretted not being involved in solving Koteen's murder. As a law officer he was almost grateful for being pushed away. This Apache business was turning into a real mess.

As Lansing headed south on Highway 15 he had a strong urge to turn off on Burnt Mesa Road. He hadn't talked to Margarite Carerra in two days, and he had to admit that he missed her. His sense of obligation to his job told him he'd better radio in first before allowing himself any personal time.

"Dispatch, this is Patrol One."

"Dispatch here," Marilyn responded. "Go ahead, Patrol One."

"Yeah, you have anything for me?"

"Just one item. We got a call from a George Prentiss in Albuquerque."

Lansing had to think for a moment. "Oh, yeah. The one who said his daughter was camping up in the Meadows."

"Evidently she was supposed to get home last night. He still hasn't heard from her. Wants us to check out the campground. See if she's still up there."

"I'm about thirty minutes from there now."

"I already sent Deputy Hanna. He should be getting there pretty soon."

The speaker on Lansing's radio crackled. Then, "Patrol One, this is Patrol Two. How copy?" The signal was weak, but readable.

"I read you about five by two. What's your twenty?"

"I'm at the Meadows. The blue Toyota's still parked where I found it the other day. No sign of anyone around. What do you want me to do?"

"Scout around the immediate area. See if you can find anything. I'll join you shortly."

"Ten-four. Patrol Two out."

"Dispatch, did you copy that?"

"Dispatch copied."

"Roger. Patrol One out."

24

 LANSING FOUND GABE'S JEEP AND THE ABANdoned Toyota five miles from the main highway. Gabe was emerging from the woods when he parked.

"Well?" the sheriff asked. "Find anything?"

The deputy shook his head. "Sorry, Sheriff. Nothing."

"Have you looked inside the car yet?"

"Thought I'd wait for you. I didn't want to get blamed for anything turning up missing."

"Probably a smart move." Lansing walked around to the back of his Jeep and retrieved a notched strip of metal two and a half feet long. He slid the strip down the window of the car, felt around for a moment, then gave the strip a quick jerk. He heard the door unlatch.

The interior of the car was littered with empty cola cans and candy wrappers. Sliding into the driver's seat, Lansing checked the glove compartment. The registration papers confirmed the car belonged to George A. Prentiss of Albuquerque.

The backseat had been laid down so that the rear bed of the hatchback could accommodate a tent, sleeping bags, and other camping gear. It appeared the car had been cleaned out. The sheriff still popped the hatch lock for a better look.

He and Gabe examined the apparently empty rear of the car. Except for the spare tire in a sunken compartment, there was nothing.

"Evidently they hiked into the woods with all of their gear," Lansing said. "It's possible one or both of them got hurt. We're going to need a search party."

Gabe had been at his job as deputy for less than five months. This was his first exposure to a backwoods search. "Where do we begin?"

"For starters, you stay here. If those girls come stumbling out of the woods, you can radio Marilyn and tell her to call things off. Meanwhile, I'll head back to the office and try rounding up a search party. There might be someone available from the rescue unit. I'll also see if the forest service can spare anyone. This is their territory."

Lansing pointed his Jeep down the rough road, then radioed dispatch as he bounced his way down the mountain. "Dispatch, this is Patrol One."

"Go ahead, Patrol One."

"We need to get a search party organized. Call the forest service office at Los Alamos. Tell them we need trackers for the Carson National Forest, northwest quadrant. Rendezvous point will be Chama Meadows.

"Call the firehouse. See if there are any volunteers. Tell them we're after a couple of good-looking college coeds lost in the woods. That should get a response."

"Dispatch copies. Anything else, Sheriff?"

"Who else is on patrol right now?"

"Deputy Barns."

"If he's close to town have him come in and check our walkie-talkies. Make sure the batteries are recharged. Have him check the flashlight situation as well. Also, get hold of the diner. We'll need sandwiches, coffee, bottled water. Include anything you can think of that we might need."

"Ten-four."

"I'm looking for a George Prentiss," Lansing said into the phone. "Oh, Mrs. Prentiss, this is Sheriff Lansing up in Las Palmas. We found your daughter's car still parked up in the campground. You're positive the two girls were going to return last night?" Lansing paused for her response.

"Okay. In that case I'm afraid we need to organize a search party up this way. Do you have current photos of the two girls? . . . Good. I need you to take them to the nearest police station and have them fax me copies. Include a brief written description of both of them. The sooner you can get that done, the sooner we can get started up here." He paused for a barrage of questions.

"Please calm down, Mrs. Prentiss. Going to pieces isn't going to help you or your daughter. I understand you're upset, but please, I need to get those photos here in the next twenty minutes. Half an hour at the latest. . . . Yes, it's all right if you and your husband drive up. Stop by my office in Las Palmas. We're located on the south side of the courthouse. Somebody can give you directions to the campground. . . . Fine. I'll be looking for those pictures."

Lansing hung up the phone. He hated dealing with upset parents. Irate ones were even worse. They became belligerent. He stepped outside his office.

"How are we doing as far as volunteers go, Marilyn?"

"We've got two from the rescue unit, Carlos Gomez and Willy Sutter. The forest service is sending up three men and a woman from Bandoleer. Counting you and Deputy Hanna, that's eight."

"Make that nine."

Marilyn and Lansing both looked at the entrance

door. Former sheriff Bill Fulton stood there dressed in hiking boots, his old khakis, and his Stetson. His sheepskin jacket was slung over his shoulder.

"What are you doing here?" Lansing was surprised to see his old mentor standing there.

"Do you know how boring painting can get? I heard you on the scanner when I went inside for a drink. There's not much this old dog can do, but I can still walk up and down a mountain pretty good. Could you use another volunteer?"

"One last manhunt before you hang up your spurs for good?"

Fulton shrugged. "Or in this case woman hunt. But sure. Why not? If nothing else I can man the command post at the trailhead. That's where you're going to keep the hot coffee, isn't it?"

Lansing smiled. "Boss, I can use all the help you can give me."

"Good. What do you want me to do?"

"Did you bring your truck?"

Fulton nodded.

"In that case, how about running over to the diner? Kelly's putting thermoses and sack lunches together. You can haul that up the mountain for me. I'm going to be packed down with walkie-talkies, flashlights, and climbing gear, just in case we need it."

"Be back in about fifteen," Fulton said, giving his old deputy a half-salute before leaving.

"You don't think he's too old for this kind of nonsense?" Marilyn asked.

"Aw, like Bill said, he can sit at the trailhead and man the command post. He's in good enough shape for that. I told you he was leaving, didn't I?"

"No, you never did."

"Yeah. He said that he and Emily have had enough of the winters around here. They're moving to Corpus Christi to live with her sister."

"When is all this taking place?"

"Fairly soon, from the sounds of it. Hell, Marilyn. He was sheriff here for thirty-five years. I don't see any problem with him reliving his glory one last time. Do you?"

"No, I guess not."

Lansing went into the dayroom to start hauling gear out to his Jeep.

25

CHRISTINA AND MARCUS BALTAZAR SAT ON HARD wooden chairs across the hallway from the council chamber. Although they held hands, not a word had passed between them in nearly two hours.

Inside the chamber John Baltazar was being grilled by representatives of the State Bureaus of Occupational Safety and of Mining and Drilling. This was one of the few instances where the state of New Mexico could be involved with tribal affairs. Moving oil, coal, or any type of minerals from the reservation was a case of intrastate commerce. As such, the tribe was obligated to adhere to state regulations. Although the board of inquiry did not have any legal standing as a punitive body, it could recommend prosecution in cases of negligence. Only the U.S. Attorney General could bring charges if he so desired. It had happened before.

All of the physical evidence had been gathered from the explosion site and shipped to Albuquerque for reconstruction and analysis. It would be another few days before a preliminary determination as to the cause of the explosion would be announced. Meanwhile, the board of inquiry was interviewing Baltazar and the remaining rig workers to ensure they had followed strict safety measures.

Marcus looked at his mother. She sat with her eyes closed and her lips moving ever so slightly in silent prayer. He couldn't help but wonder which prayers she was saying—the Christian prayers he had been taught in Sunday school or the ancient chants handed down by old Cesar TeCube and his great-grandfather.

He wanted to say something, but he didn't want to break her concentration. His great-grandfather, the man he called *Náhánálí*, had taught him the importance of concentration during prayers and chants. If there was no concentration, then the words were only words and meant nothing.

Náhánálí had taught him that each word had a special meaning. They had been handed down by the *Black Hactcin* to the *diné*—the people—after he had created them. When a *tsanati* said the words they had power. Sometimes even power over life and death.

There were many things Marcus couldn't understand. *Náhánálí* had been very powerful. He could see many things from the future. It was something that he and his great-grandfather shared. It was a gift. The gift of the Shadowcatcher, *Náhánálí* called it. But *Náhánálí* did not see his own death.

Marcus had seen *Náhánálí*'s death the night it happened. He tried to tell his parents, but they wouldn't believe him. Just as he had seen the explosion at the oil rig. He was in hysterics because he saw his own father consumed in flames. But no one would believe him.

He had seen Ned Koteen's impending death. He tried to warn the police captain. He put a note under the windshield wiper. But Captain Koteen didn't believe him either.

Náhánálí would have believed. *Náhánálí* wanted Marcus to follow in his footsteps and become a *tsanati*, a medicine man.

Marcus felt the bulge beneath his shirt. He looked to make sure his mother's eyes were still closed as he unbuttoned his shirt. He reached inside and touched the *jish*. His great-grandfather's *jish*. The smooth, polished leather of the pouch was cool to the touch. *Náhánálí* had told him to keep it safe. If he kept it close to him it would protect him and his family. The *jish* had great powers and could ward off evil.

Náhánálí had warned him that it should be used only for good. Marcus could tell no one about it. If evil men knew about it they would want it for its power, for it could be used for evil as well as good.

"Keep it close to you, little one," *Náhánálí* had said. "With it, one day you will be able to understand your dreams."

His parents were opposed to Marcus becoming a medicine man. He could serve his people better with a college education.

Marcus had been torn between his love for his parents and his desire to follow *Náhánálí*'s wishes. Marcus wanted to follow the ways of the Shadowcatcher and learn how to harness the power of his dreams. With *Náhánálí* dead now, he didn't think that would ever be possible. The only man who could teach him now was Pinto Velarde. But Pinto was Ollero, and his family would never allow that.

At the moment Marcus had only one comforting thought. He had seen the outcome of the board of inquiry in a dream. He squeezed his mother's hand, trying to reassure her that everything was going to be all right.

The doorway across the hall opened. John Baltazar's hands were still bandaged, so someone else had to hold the door for him. Baltazar gave his family a weak smile.

"The board has cleared us of any negligence on the preliminary review," he said. "They think it was probably material failure."

"John, that's wonderful," Christina said, rushing to him and giving him a kiss on the cheek.

"Baltazar Brothers isn't in the clear yet. Hector Velarde wants the council to review everything too. He said I didn't have a thing to worry about. If we lose our contract and Cuartelejo just happens to get it, they would need a good drilling supervisor.

"We can worry about that tomorrow," he said, putting his arms around his family and squeezing them as tightly as he could. "Right now, let's go home."

26

"HOW MUCH LONGER ARE WE SUPPOSED TO JUST wait around here?" Willy Sutter asked. Sutter and Gomez, the two paramedics from the Las Palmas Volunteer Fire Department, were already at the Meadows when Lansing and Fulton arrived. Gabe had seen no sign of the two girls during the sheriff's absence and was grateful to have a little company. He was even more grateful for the sandwiches Fulton brought.

Lansing understood the paramedic's impatience. He wanted to get started too. But it was nearly impossible to conduct a coordinated search unless everyone involved was thoroughly briefed and knew who the other team members were. He glanced at his watch: 12:15 P.M. They'd already been waiting for thirty minutes. "Fifteen more minutes, Willy," Lansing stalled. "The forest service said their people would be here by twelve-thirty."

"Fine, fine." Sutter waved away the comment as if it were a pesky fly. Flicking his cigarette away, he wandered over to where his fellow paramedic, Carlos Gomez, was seated.

Lansing was about to say something to Sutter when Gomez jumped to his feet and hurried over to stomp out the cigarette. "You idiot. You want to start another forest fire?" He ground the butt out with his heel. "We haven't had rain all summer. You stupid, or what?"

"Sorry," Sutter said. The apology was lame. Sutter was a firefighter. He knew better. He sat down with a thud, a little ashamed.

"What if your forestry boys don't show in the next fifteen minutes?" Fulton asked.

"Despite my better judgment I may go ahead and put those two on a trail. If I wait much longer they may get bored and head back to town—or worse, stay here and start a fire."

The small clearing used for a campsite was getting crowded with vehicles. Besides the Toyota and Gabe's Jeep, there were Sutter's truck, Fulton's truck, and Lansing's Jeep. When it arrived, the forestry vehicle would have to park at the next campsite down to keep the road clear.

Lansing had a contour map spread across the hood of his Jeep. Gabe studied the different peaks and valleys intently as he wolfed down a second sandwich.

"So what do you think of this Apache business?" Fulton asked.

Lansing shook his head. "I don't know, Bill. It's some sort of nut case, from what I can tell. The FBI agent they put in charge is awfully green. He keeps bringing up the Olleros and Llaneros like there's some sort of turf war going on. Do you ever remember the Apaches going after each other like that?"

Fulton shook his head. "I've heard of a couple of family feuds that went on for years. But since I can remember I never saw the tribe split in half, one side against the other. Even in the fall when they do their relay race, I've never heard of any fights breaking out. Nothing like that."

"I kind of thought that's the way things were."

"Where'd that agent get an idea like that?"

"Doctor Victoria Miles."

"Oh, her. What brought her down from her ivory tower?"

"The feds. They're using her as a consultant."

"Well, I suppose if she knows anything she knows her own tribe." Fulton studied his younger friend. "You and Koteen were pretty close, weren't you?"

"Yeah, we tipped a few beers together in the past. We had a good working relationship." Lansing shook his head. "I was baffled by why somebody would want to knock off old Baltazar. But I can't figure out *how* someone could take on Ned. He was a big man, and he knew what he was doing. And he was all Apache. You couldn't just sneak up on a man like that."

"Maybe it was someone he knew," Gabe suggested, half-listening to the conversation. "That's how they got in close."

"That has to be what happened," Lansing said, agreeing with the suggestion.

The radio in Lansing's Jeep crackled. "Dispatch to Patrol One. How copy?"

Lansing grabbed the microphone from its cradle. "Patrol One reads you loud and clear. Go ahead, Marilyn."

"We just got a call from C.J. He was looking for you. Said you were supposed to pick him up for lunch."

"Damn!" Lansing swore under his breath. "Yeah, Marilyn. I forgot all about that. Could you call him back and tell him I'm not going to make it? I've got my hands full."

"If that's what you want, Sheriff."

"And listen, Marilyn. After work, if you have time, could you run down to the ranch and make sure he's all right? I don't know what time we'll be wrapping things up around here."

"I'll make sure he's taken care of, Sheriff. Dispatch out."

"Patrol One out."

Lansing stared at the microphone he was holding, trying to convince himself he didn't feel guilty. He was doing his job. Lives were in jeopardy. He had to put his personal life on the back burner. He had explained that to C.J. before. His son understood. But guilt still prodded him.

"Sheriff," Gabe called. "Looks like they're coming."

A forest-green pickup truck with a double cab was rumbling up the mountain road. When it stopped, three of the volunteers got out. Lansing directed the driver to park in a clearing twenty yards further down.

A man named Hall presented himself as the crew chief. When the driver joined them, Hall introduced his entire team. Counting Hall, there were three men and one woman. All four wore dark-green utility uniforms with Department of the Interior Forestry patches on their sleeves and name tags embroidered over the left breast pockets.

"Sorry it took us so long to get here," Hall explained. "We've been up clearing the back trails around Frijole Canyon."

"I'm just glad you could make it." Lansing introduced himself, Gabe, and the two paramedics. "Sheriff Fulton is going to stay here at the campsite and man the command post. He'll be the link between the teams and my office."

He turned to the map spread across his hood. "I want to split up into four two-man teams." He glanced at the female forestry worker. Her name tag read "Petrewski." "Sorry about that."

"Don't worry," she said, smiling. "With these jokers I'm used to it."

"I have maps and a walkie-talkie for each team. I also have photos of both girls. They're fax copies, so they're not very good, but there's a physical description of each of them as well."

There were a dozen well-defined trails that led deeper into Carson National Forest. Lansing decided their best bet would be to stick to those trails initially. Some of the trails made a loop, dumping out somewhere along the Meadows' access road. Others simply wandered deeper into the woods, terminating at some remote campsite. He assigned the loop trails to Hall's people.

Before splitting up he made sure all the radios and flashlights he handed out worked.

"Make sure you have food and water before you leave. It's one o'clock now. If you haven't found anything by five, start heading back this way. On this side of the mountains it starts getting dark an hour before sunset. We can't afford to send out search parties for our search parties."

27

MARGARITE PARKED HER TRUCK IN FRONT OF the Las Palmas Rexall and looked through her rearview mirror. She could see the courthouse parking area from that spot, and there was no sign of Sheriff Lansing's Jeep. She wasn't sure if that made her happy or not.

She grabbed her purse and the shopping list she had thrown together and went into the store.

The pharmacy counter was located along the rear wall. She noted that the front register was closed, which meant the checkout girl was probably at lunch. She'd have to get Alden, the pharmacist, to ring her up in the back. Grabbing a plastic convenience basket, she began a careful search of the aisles for what she needed, usually opting for store-brand items. She could never see the sense in paying inflated prices to cover the advertising budgets of the name brands.

"I thought doctors always got their supplies free."

Margarite glanced up from the package she was studying. "Oh, hi, Marilyn. No. Nothing's free. Some pharmaceuticals will give you a kickback once in a while if you prescribe the right stuff. But that only works if you're in private practice. In public health you use what's on the shelf." She held up her basket. "If there is anything on the shelf.

"What are you doing out of the office?"

Marilyn laughed. "They unchain me from my desk every once in a while. I had to pick up some sewing items for my quilting club."

"So who's minding the mint?"

"Deputy DeJesus is covering for me."

"Where's the sheriff?" Margarite tried to sound casual.

"He's had his hands full today. He had to run up to the Apache reservation this morning. Captain Koteen was killed last night."

"You're kidding! What happened?"

Marilyn shook her head. "I'm not sure. I know he was murdered. But you know how closemouthed Cliff can get. Officer Hernandez asked if he could come up. That's all I know.

"Before I could get anything out of him, he got himself wrapped up in a search-and-rescue."

"Where?"

"Up in Chama Meadows. Two college girls. Gabe Hanna found their car a couple of days ago. One of their parents decided to file a missing-persons report. So the sheriff and Deputy Hanna are up in the mountains with a handful of volunteers looking for them."

"Where's C.J.?"

"At the ranch by himself." Marilyn looked around to make sure no one could hear her. "You know, I love Sheriff Lansing to death and there isn't a thing in the world I wouldn't do for him. But I don't understand why he bothered to have that poor boy come up and stay with him. He doesn't have time for him. He can't take care of him.

"After work I have to go home, feed my animals, feed myself, get ready for my quilting club. And in the middle of all that, the sheriff wants me to run down to his ranch and make sure C.J. is taken care of. That's why I'm trying to get a little shopping done now. I simply won't have time later."

"Can't C.J. take care of himself?"

"Oh, I'm sure he can. I'm only running down there because Cliff asked me to."

"I don't have anything pressing this afternoon. Why don't I run down there?" Margarite suggested.

"Oh, I wasn't complaining," Marilyn protested. "And I certainly wasn't trying to pawn off my responsibilities on you."

"I know that. I wouldn't make the offer if I didn't want to do it. I like C.J. Besides, these aren't your responsibilities. They're Lansing's."

"Amen to that."

28

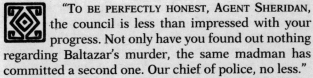 "TO BE PERFECTLY HONEST, AGENT SHERIDAN, the council is less than impressed with your progress. Not only have you found out nothing regarding Baltazar's murder, the same madman has committed a second one. Our chief of police, no less."

Sheridan sat at a table in the council chamber, facing Hector Velarde and a handful of council members. He kept his lips pursed as he impatiently tapped the eraser end of a pencil on the tabletop. "I assure you the FBI is doing its best, President Velarde. We haven't had a lot of hard evidence to go on."

"The people on this reservation are afraid. They're arming themselves. Walking down the streets with loaded weapons. Parents won't let their children outside to play. They're saying, 'If the captain of our police can't protect himself, what are we supposed to do?'

"What is the FBI going to do to protect us?"

"I've already told Lieutenant Vicinti he needs to set up an auxiliary police force. I'll talk to my superiors. Maybe we can come up with some funding to help defray your costs. If you have more patrols out, there's a good chance the assailant will have second thoughts before he tries anything else."

"What you're saying is, our people should quit their regular jobs to make sure their families aren't killed."

"I'm not saying that at all. Surely there are some men around here that need work."

"Few, Mr. Sheridan. Very few. And certainly not enough to patrol every inch of this reservation.

"In the meantime our tourist season is just getting under way. We already have campers and fishermen leaving because they don't think it's safe. When word gets out, no one will want to come here."

"I heard there's talk of closing the reservation to visitors anyway," Sheridan pointed out.

"That's just talk, and we've already put a stop to it. Tourism accounts for thirty percent of our summer income. We can't afford to turn visitors away."

"All I can tell you is the FBI is doing all that can be done. We have neither the charter nor the manpower to patrol your reservation. You're going to have to count on your own people.

"And as far as the investigation goes, I have to rely on the physical evidence, because your people won't talk to me. No one has seen anything. No one has heard anything. No one knows anything. Unless I get some sort of cooperation we're at a stalemate."

"Maybe things would progress better if there were someone in charge with a little experience," Velarde snapped.

Sheridan tapped his pencil too hard, breaking it in two. "There's nothing that says you can't make that request." He stood. Taking out his wallet, he removed a business card and tossed it on the table. "My supervisor's name and phone number. Feel free to contact him."

He walked to the chamber door and stopped. "Until my replacement arrives I'm still in charge of this investigation. If any of you thinks you have information pertinent to these cases, I'm still the one you go through. Now, if you'll excuse me, I have work to do.

"Good afternoon, gentlemen."

Sheridan sat in Ned Koteen's former office. He was using it as his base of operations, since it was already equipped with communications gear and the land lines he required.

The forensics team had come and gone, and the agent felt abandoned. Koteen had been friendly and cooperative and the working relationship was cordial. Vicinti was a whole different matter. He seemed to resent Sheridan's presence and begrudged any request the agent made.

Sheridan picked up the phone and dialed his Santa Fe office. The call was necessary. He needed to find out what progress the forensics boys had made. Plus, he still needed to brief his supervisor on the status of his investigation. He'd been working on the case for four days and he already felt overwhelmed. He wasn't sure what the correct protocol was to request help without sounding incompetent. He halfway wished he hadn't run off Sheriff Lansing. He could use a friendly face.

"Yes, this is Agent Philip Sheridan," he said to the receptionist. "I need to speak to Director Williams." A moment later he was connected.

"Director Williams."

"Yes, sir. Agent Sheridan."

"Are you still up at the Apache reservation?"

"Yes, I'm afraid I am. This is turning into a bucket of worms."

"I'm listening."

Sheridan gave the regional director a synopsis of the events since his initial arrival at the reservation. He described the Baltazar murder scene, the preliminary finding of the forensics lab, and the discussions he'd had with the tribal authorities.

"As you know, I wasn't available to brief you this morning as we had planned. There was another murder on the reservation last night. Captain Ned Koteen, the chief of police. We kept most of the physical evidence for the Baltazar murder under wraps. Nothing was released to the news media.

"Koteen's murder was nearly identical to Baltazar's. There wasn't enough information released for a copycat crime, so we have to be dealing with the same assailant."

"How much cooperation are you getting from the tribal authorities?"

"They've made everything available that I've requested. But nobody up here wants to talk to an outsider. Until I can tie some physical evidence to a name or a face, I basically have nothing. Meanwhile, everyone on the reservation is terrified. They're all wondering who the next victim is going to be. The tribal council is demanding that I provide some sort of protection, but there's not much one person can do."

"They probably want to know who the murderer is as well."

"Basically, yes."

"I'll talk with the Justice Department. If the council really wants protection, we can send in federal marshals. I'm not sure that's what they want. But the FBI is not in the business of carrying on neighborhood watches. I'll let you know what Justice has to say."

"What am I supposed to do about the investigation?"

"At this point, sending in reinforcements isn't going to help. If the tribal members won't talk to you, sending up another two or three agents won't improve things. That's just two or three more people getting the silent treatment.

"Put everything you told me on paper, and fax the

report to my office. Include the lab reports as an appendix. If there's enough there to expand our investigation I'll let you know."

"Thank you, sir."

"Let me know if there's anything else I can help you with."

"I will, sir. Thank you."

Sheridan hung up the phone and shook his head. He really wasn't sure what he was thanking Regional Director Williams for. He picked up the receiver and dialed another number.

"Yes. Forensics lab, please."

29

LANSING HAD TAKEN POINT ON THE TRAIL. THEY hadn't traveled nearly as far as he would have hoped. Of course, he knew search-and-rescue missions were not always a matter of seeing how fast you could travel, unless you already knew your destination.

Lansing scanned the right side of the trail, looking up the mountain. Gabe scanned the left. Every hundred yards one of them would yell "Sheri" or "Barbara." They would stop and listen for a response. When none came, they'd push further into the forest.

Lansing and his deputy had taken the steepest of the trails that day. Although it was not the most difficult trail in the Meadows, he had guessed that two college girls with little backwoods experience would not tackle the tougher Dead Horse Trail or Summit Trace. Even if they had, they would have turned back in an hour or two.

Lansing was a little ashamed of himself. The air was clean and crisp. The temperature was perfect for physical exertion, and the sun-splotched trail, little used since the previous summer, was easy to follow.

He found himself enjoying the exercise and being in the great outdoors. He knew he should have felt more desperate over the situation. Two young ladies were lost in the mountain forest. They could be hurt, even dying. He was doing everything he could do under the circumstances. He was moving along at a sensible pace. He had to keep telling himself he wasn't out there for his own pleasure, no matter how good it made him feel.

At the end of an hour Lansing signaled for a rest.

Gabe gratefully plopped down on the ground. "I used to be in real good shape," he complained.

"One of the worst things about working out of a patrol car is that you get used to driving everywhere. You forget that sooner or later you're going to have to walk farther than just the door to the diner."

"I'm not overweight."

"No. Just out of shape. Do you jog?"

"Not since I left the academy." He looked at the sheriff. Physically, Lansing was in great shape, slim at the waste, flat stomach. Gabe couldn't understand how his boss seemed to work twenty-hour days and still look that good. "Is that what you do? Jog?"

Lansing nodded. "About four times a week. I try to alternate between jogging and weights. I have a weight room in the back of the barn."

"When do you find time?"

Lansing shrugged. "It's just part of my routine. I get up at five-thirty every morning and head out to the barn to take care of my horses. Since I'm up anyway, that's a good time to get in my workout. About forty minutes every morning. One day jogging, the next day my weight routine. By seven I'm showered, shaved, and ready to head into the office."

Gabe crinkled his face in mock pain. "Aren't you too tired to do anything by then?"

"I'm more tired all day if I don't work out. It's like I

never got my heart revved up. And it really ruins my horses' day if I don't work out. They seem to get a real kick out of hearing me grunt and groan."

"I guess I need to get something going. We've been walking only an hour and I'm tired already."

"I guarantee, the longer you wait, the harder it is to get back into shape. Take it from someone who let himself go for almost ten years." Lansing raised his walkie-talkie and pressed the TALK button. "Chama Meadows, this is Searcher One. How do you read me? Over."

"Loud and clear, Cliff," Fulton replied. "All's quiet on this end. Over."

"Copy. Searcher One to Searcher Teams. Radio check by the numbers. Searcher One." He released his button so he could receive the transmissions.

The replies came in sequence: "Searcher Two." "Searcher Three." "Searcher Four."

"Searcher One copies all. Over."

"Command Post copies all. Over."

Lansing slipped the walkie-talkie into the leather carrying case on his belt. "Well, R and R is over, Gabe. Let's hit the dusty trail."

"Yes, sir." Gabe took a quick gulp of water from his canteen, then got to his feet. "Do you want me to take the lead for a while?"

"Can you handle it?"

"Sure."

Lansing stepped aside. "It's all yours."

30

IT MADE SENSE TO MARGARITE THAT CHECKING the house when she got to the ranch was a waste of time. Lansing didn't have cable TV or Super Nintendo, so there was nothing to entertain C.J. inside. After she parked behind the ranch house she went directly to the barn.

"C.J.!" Only Cement Head responded when Margarite called, and that was with a snort. Once inside she noticed the gate to Milkweed's stall was open and the pony was gone. She walked up to Cement Head and rubbed his nose. "That's why you're angry. You didn't get to go out for a ride."

Cement Head snorted again, bobbing his head up and down. After a lifetime around animals, Margarite knew horses weren't the smartest things on four legs, but sometimes she had to wonder about Cement Head. He either knew what was going on and what was being said to him, or he was the biggest phony in the world. She was inclined to believe the latter.

The door at the far end of the barn was open, telling Margarite that was the direction C.J. had taken. She continued through the barn to see if she could catch sight of him anywhere.

The back of the barn faced an open field bordered by a corral, the Rio Questa, and the dirt road leading across the bridge over the river to the back pastures. Margarite was facing west, and the sun was still high enough above the mountains that she had to shield her eyes.

C.J. spotted her first. He was coming down one of the trails from the high meadows. He yelled, "Margarite!" and waved his hat, then put Milkweed into the fastest trot he could handle. It was another five minutes before he crossed the bridge over the river.

"What are you doing here?" C.J. brought his horse to a stop a few yards short of the barn. He sounded as if he was glad to see her.

"I don't know. I thought you might be getting a little lonely trying to run this ranch by yourself."

C.J. swung his leg over the saddle horn and slid from his seat. "Dad showed me how to do that."

"Pretty slick."

"I'm sorry, Margarite, but I don't think he's going to be home for quite a while."

"I knew that. I didn't come out here to see him."

"Oh. You came out to baby-sit me." He took his horse's reins and began leading him into the barn. "I can take care of myself."

"No one said you couldn't," she said, following him. "I just thought you could use the company. I know exactly what it's like sitting around by yourself. I do it all the time. It's not always fun."

"You sure my dad didn't ask you to come over and watch me?"

Margarite held up her hand as if for an oath. "I swear I haven't talked to your father since I was here the other night."

He lifted off the saddle and slung it over a stall railing. "Could you stay for supper?"

"Does your dad's VCR work?"

"Yeah."

"How about Dixie Queen burgers and then we pick up a couple of movies?"

"Great! But I have to curry Milkweed before I put him in the stall."

"No problem. I'll go inside and get us some drinks. We can shoot the breeze while you finish."

"Okay." This was going to be a great evening, C.J. thought. The only thing that might have made it better would have been if Velma had showed up instead.

Margarite quickly realized her own lapse in judgment five minutes into the first movie. She had let C.J. pick the videos. She suffered stoically through his first selection, *Attack of the Cyborg Ninjas*. It was another mutilation of the original Frankenstein story, plastered with Hollywood pretense, served up as a morality story that railed against anything scientific.

"What'd you think of it?" C.J. asked as the ending credits began to roll.

"I'll make you a deal. I'll fix us a batch of popcorn if you let me read a book during your next movie."

"I guess that's fair."

"So how's your visit going so far?" Margarite asked as she moved the pot back and forth over the fire.

"Pretty good, I guess. I just thought my dad would have a little bit more time off."

"Well, he does have a pretty important job."

"Yeah, I know. It's just that I don't get to see him that much. I mean, I really like being here on the ranch and I liked helping Juan, but . . ." The last of his statement trailed off.

"Do you wish your folks were still married?"

C.J. thought about the question before he answered. "All I can remember from when I was little is that they fought all the time. I used to think they were fighting about me or something I had done. I remember I cried a lot when my mom took me away. But when she did, there wasn't any more fighting. No more arguing or yelling.

"I know a lot of kids whose parents got divorced. Sometimes the parents were doing drugs or getting drunk. The dads would beat up the moms. Stuff like that. I know my dad never hit my mom. She told me that. She said he was a good husband, he was just never around."

"Does your dad ever talk about it?"

"Not really. I asked him once why they got divorced. He said he loved Mom very much. He said he always would. He said Mom probably loved him too. The problem was that even though they loved each other, they never became friends." He looked up from the dirty fingernail he had been studying. "Does that make any sense?"

Margarite nodded sadly. "Yes, C.J. Unfortunately, it does."

31

"MARCUS!" CHRISTINA CALLED FROM THE BACK door. "Come wash up for dinner."

Hidden behind his father's toolshed, Marcus hurriedly brushed the *hoddentin* from his palm into the leather pouch, careful not to spill any. He had been studying the mysterious particles of corn pollen and sage root, trying to grasp how something so common could be so powerful. *Náhánáli* had told Marcus that when the time came he would come in a dream and teach him the secret of the *hoddentin*. Until then Marcus had to protect and preserve the little that he had, using it only when he had to.

He pulled the leather strap over his head, then slipped the pouch beneath his shirt so no one could see it. A moment later he was trotting toward the small frame house.

John Baltazar was already seated at the kitchen table. With his hands still wrapped in thick bandages he was having a hard time picking up his fork.

"Can I help?" Christina asked as she poured iced tea.

"I can get it," her husband mumbled.

Marcus washed his hands at the sink and took his

seat. Despite the good news from the board of inquiry earlier, he noticed his father was still in a sullen mood. The week had been a strain on everyone in the family, and Marcus was sure the burns on his father's hands were still painful. He wished there was something he could say or do to brighten things up.

Christina lifted the lid to the cast-iron kettle and began dishing out portions of stewed chicken. Chicken was the summer meat. Marcus had come to realize, even with the availability of beef in the grocery store, each season had its own meat. The Baltazars still followed the traditions, in a way. Whatever meat was cheapest was what Christina put on the table.

In early spring they ate mutton. Lamb, actually. When it was tender and young and very inexpensive. The reservation couldn't support more than ten thousand head. In a good year as many as five thousand lambs might be born. Some of the older sheep would be culled, replaced by the spring lambs. The rest of the lambs were sold to ranchers outside the reservation or slaughtered for the Apaches.

In the summer the most inexpensive source of protein was chicken, and poultry was on the table at least six days a week.

Fall brought the cornucopia. Calves born the previous winter were ready for the packing plant. Plus there was the hunting. The Jicarilla Apache Reservation had its own game preserve. There were elk, antelope, and deer. Each family living on the reservation was automatically issued game tags and permitted two of each animal. (Of course, they had to do their own hunting.) Even with those allowances there was still enough wildlife that off-reservation hunters could purchase hunting permits and game tags when the season opened.

John and Daniel Baltazar were good hunters, and

they always filled their quotas. They shared a rented meat locker in Dulce, and from late summer until early spring there was always red meat on the table.

Marcus stared at the chunk of white chicken meat on his plate and began to realize his uncle would not be around for that year's hunt. He suddenly had a hollow feeling in his stomach that he knew couldn't be filled with food.

"I'll be thirteen before the end of the summer," Marcus said. "Maybe I can go hunting with you this year, Dad."

Baltazar had been lost in his own thoughts. He looked at his son. "I'm sorry. What did you say?"

"I said, I'll be thirteen this fall. Since Uncle Dan's not around now, I thought maybe I could go hunting with you this year."

A painful expression passed over Baltazar's face. Marcus couldn't tell if it had to do with Daniel or something else. Baltazar looked at his wife. She reached over and patted his forearm.

"I'm not sure about that," Baltazar said.

"Some of the other guys got to go out when they were twelve," Marcus said, hoping he didn't sound like a whiner.

"That's not what I mean," Baltazar said, wiping his mouth with a napkin. "Your mother and I have been talking. We've decided that it's time for you to go away to school."

"Go away! Where?"

"To the Indian School, in Santa Fe."

"Why?"

"Because it's safer there," his father explained.

"I'm safe here. With you."

"No one's safe around here, Marcus. I'm not. Your mother's not. Even your great-grandfather wasn't safe, and he was the most powerful man I knew."

"But I can't go away. I have to be here with you. I can help."

"I know you want to help," Baltazar said. "But there's nothing you can do. The best thing for us is knowing you're in a safe place."

Marcus could feel the *jish* against his skin. With his great-grandfather's pouch next to him, he knew he would be safe no matter where he went. "Dad, Mom, please. I don't want to go."

"Marcus," Christina pleaded. "You have to go. It's a good school. There are lots of sports. It's good preparation for going to college. And there are people there who can help you."

"You mean my dreams?"

"Your nightmares. Yes. They can help you. There are doctors there who can make them go away."

"They can't go away. I don't want them to go away. *Náhánálí* told me they were important. He was going to help me understand them."

"Well, *Náhánálí* is not here now, is he?" Baltazar exploded, pounding his fist on the table. The sudden flash of pain tore through his arm, and he squeezed his eyes shut to control it and his anger. "He was a foolish old man with foolish ideas, and now he's dead. Enough is enough. A son does not argue with his parents."

Marcus controlled his fear. He had seldom seen his father's anger, but he knew it was something to be respected and avoided.

"Yes, sir," Marcus said quietly.

The three of them sat solemnly at the table watching their plates. Finally, Marcus ventured to break the silence. "May I be excused?"

"You may go to your room," Baltazar said without looking up.

Marcus took his dish over to the sink, then left the

room. Behind him his parents began a whispered conversation that he couldn't hear. He wanted to hide around the corner and listen, but he knew he didn't dare. He had incurred his father's wrath once that night, and once was enough. He hurried to his room to contemplate the mystery of the *jish*.

32

"CHAMA MEADOWS, SEARCH ONE, HOW MANY teams are still out? Over."

"You're the last one, Cliff. What's your ETA? Over."

"I'd guess we're still a half mile out. Should be there in the next ten minutes. Are Mr. and Mrs. Prentiss still around? Over."

"Yeah. They wanted to talk with you when you got in. Over."

"Be there as soon as I can. Over and out."

At five o'clock Lansing had announced over his walkie-talkie that the search teams should start working their way back to the rendezvous point. The message had to be relayed. By that time the trail he and Gabe were following had taken them into a valley and they were cut off from the command post.

"Are you sure we need to head back this early?" Gabe had asked. "We still have a couple of hours of daylight."

"We'll need it for finding our way home. Besides, we're on the eastern side of the mountains. Things start getting dark around here pretty early."

Lansing hunted around and found two long tree branches that had fallen during the winter. He crossed them over the path to mark their turnaround point. "If we come back to this trail tomorrow, we'll know exactly where we left off."

It took nearly four hours to get back to the rendezvous point. It was nine o'clock and well past dark. The two paramedics, Sutter and Gomez, had already headed back to town. They left a message with Sheriff Fulton that they would be back in the morning.

Hall and his crew were finishing off the last of the coffee when Lansing and Gabe tromped into the clearing.

"No luck either?" Hall asked.

Lansing shook his head. "Not a thing." He checked the coffee thermos.

"Sorry," Hall apologized. "We beat you to it."

"No problem. That's what it was there for. I don't suppose you and your crew are up for another round tomorrow?"

"Believe it or not, Sheriff, yes, we are. After clearing back trails for two weeks this is like a picnic." The other three team members nodded in agreement. "We reserved rooms back in Las Palmas just in case. You want us back here at eight?"

"That's what I told Willie and Carlos," Fulton explained. "We'd meet up here in the morning around eight."

Lansing nodded. "Eight o'clock is good. That will give us time to round up provisions before we get started."

As Lansing said his good-byes and thanks, a man and woman approached him from behind his Jeep. The woman looked depleted from crying and had to be supported by her companion.

"Oh, Cliff," Fulton said. "This is Mr. and Mrs. Prentiss."

Lansing extended his hand. "Mr. Prentiss. Mrs. Prentiss. I'm sorry we have to meet under these circumstances."

"Likewise," Prentiss said, shaking hands. Mrs. Prentiss only nodded.

"I'm sorry, but we have nothing to report. I kept the teams out as long as I dared today, but you can see how dark these woods get at night. I couldn't afford to lose one of my search parties."

"We understand." Prentiss reached inside his shirt pocket and pulled out a piece of paper. "I don't know if it will help, but while we were waiting I jotted down a list of the camping items the girls brought with them." He handed the list to Lansing. "If something turns up in the woods, you'll know you're on the right track."

"What are these numbers along the top?" the sheriff asked.

"I got ripped off a few years ago. Somebody broke into my garage and cleaned me out. Whenever I buy anything now, I put my last name and the last six digits of my social security number on it."

"I wish everybody did that," Lansing admitted. He folded the paper and put it in his own pocket. "Right now we only have two bits of information regarding your daughter, Sheri, and the other girl. One is that we found Sheri's car right over there. The other is that a car was heard going down the road, leaving the Meadows, sometime that night. We don't have a description of that car, and we don't know if there's a connection between it and the missing girls.

"We'll keep the search going until we come up with something. Right now that's the only assurance I can offer you."

"Is there anything we can do?" Prentiss asked.

"Yes. I need an address for Sheri's friend, Barbara. My office needs to get in touch with her relatives."

"I hope you don't mind, Sheriff, but we talked

to Barbara's parents this afternoon. They know all about it."

"I'll still need their address and phone number, but would you mind calling them tonight and letting them know how things are going?"

"Sure. We can do that." Prentiss hesitated a moment "Sheriff, would you mind if I helped with the search tomorrow? I'm in pretty good shape, and just sitting around waiting is about to drive me nuts."

Prentiss looked to be in his late-forties and reasonably fit. Lansing couldn't see that it would hurt anything. "It's up to you and Mrs. Prentiss, but we can always use the manpower."

"Don't worry. I'll be fine by myself." Mrs. Prentiss nodded. "At least I'll know one of us is out there doing something."

"Fine. Then I'll see you here in the morning. We'll start at eight."

"I'll see you then," Prentiss said, leading his wife away.

Lansing slipped into the seat of his Jeep and picked up his microphone. "Dispatch. This is Patrol One."

"Patrol One, Dispatch," Deputy Larry Peters responded. "Go ahead."

"Yeah. Contact Deputy Cortez. We're pulling him off patrol. I need him up here at Chama Meadows for a night watch. Tell him to bring some coffee and food. He'll be here till the morning search parties form up."

"Dispatch copies."

"Ten-four." Lansing tossed the mike onto his seat and got out. "Bill, are you game for another day?"

"Absolutely, though I think I'm going to bring a lawn chair and a book tomorrow."

"Sounds reasonable." He turned to his deputy. "How are you holding up, Gabe?"

"So far, so good."

"Sheriff Fulton and I are going to head back to town. I need you to stay put until Danny Cortez shows up. I doubt if those girls are going to show up tonight. But if they do I don't want to miss them."

"You got it. Do you want me back out here in the morning?"

"Yes. I wouldn't want you to miss all of this fun."

"Yes, sir."

Lansing caught Fulton as he was getting into his truck. "Bill, parking's getting to be a problem around here. Why don't you leave your truck at home tomorrow? I'll swing by and pick you up."

"Whatever you say, Cliff. You're the sheriff."

Lansing passed through Las Palmas on the way to his ranch. As much as he dreaded it, he knew he had to stop by his office. It didn't matter how many murder investigations, domestic disturbances, traffic violations, or search-and-rescue missions his office had to contend with, the paperwork had to flow. On top of all of the investigation reports and citations he had to review, Lansing still had to handle time sheets; requisition orders; vehicle maintenance and repair; auxiliary training; federal, state, and county regulatory compliance; and vacation requests.

Marilyn did an outstanding job of keeping the paperwork flowing. Surprisingly, what she couldn't complete during the day shift, Deputy Larry Peters finished at night. Lansing had to admit, Peters was not cut out to be a patrol officer, but he made up for it by being an exceptional clerk and office manager. Plus, he preferred the night desk, which meant the sheriff could leave him in the office and rotate his other deputies for the night patrols.

"Hello, Sheriff," Peters said, closing the drawer to a file cabinet. "I didn't think you'd be coming in tonight."

"I just need to see what I missed today."

"I was trying to prioritize your paperwork for the

morning. It's still on my desk. Should I bring it into your office?"

"Yeah. And is there any coffee?"

"I made some about an hour ago. It shouldn't be too strong."

"Good." Lansing went into his office. He put his jacket and hat on the coatrack, then grabbed his coffee mug. The coffeepot was in the deputies' dayroom. Peters was already in Lansing's office with a stack of papers when he returned with his coffee.

"The only papers that need your signature are the crime statistics going to the state and the requisition forms for office supplies. I included replacement batteries for the walkie-talkies in that requisition, even though they fall under field equipment. I figured we'd get them sooner that way, plus we have more money to work with in our office-supply account."

"I'm proud of you, Larry."

"Sir?"

"You're finally showing a little flexibility and initiative." A year earlier Peters would have fought tooth and nail to put a battery requisition under field equipment because that's what batteries were listed as. It had taken Lansing nearly four years to convince the deputy that getting the job done was the bottom line. The minutia would take care of itself in the long run.

Peters blushed. "Thank you, sir."

"Did we get any interesting calls today?"

"Just one. It was for Deputy Hanna." Peters produced a copy of the telephone log from the bottom of his stack. "A place called The Sporting Life in Santa Fe." He handed the copy to Lansing.

The memo was from Marilyn. The call was taken at 3:05 P.M.

LaPlaya, Stephen. The Sporting Life, Santa Fe. The two men returned with more camping equipment to sell. The equipment was marked with previous owner's name and

I.D. numbers. Mr. LaPlaya was also able to obtain the sellers' names and addresses. Please call after 9:00 A.M.

"Damn, I wonder if that's anything," Lansing mumbled.

"Something wrong?"

"No. Not really." He handed the paper back to Peters. "Neither Deputy Hanna nor I are going to be around tomorrow. We have to get back to the search up in Chama Meadows. Put a note on that log for Marilyn to do a follow-up call. Get all the information Mr. LaPlaya has. We'll see what we can do with it."

"Yes, sir."

"Anything interesting on the Comfax?"

"Not really. It's posted in the dayroom. Would you like to see it?"

"Yeah. Let me see the rest of that paperwork while you're getting it."

Peters handed him the stack he was holding and left the room. Lansing glanced at his watch. It was ten-thirty. C.J. would be in bed already. He decided he didn't want to call and wake him. Besides, he'd be finished with the paperwork in another fifteen minutes.

"Anything else?" Peters asked when he returned with the Comfax printouts.

Lansing leaned back in his seat with his cup of coffee in one hand, the Comfax data in the other. "I'm good for now. I'll let you get back to work."

Lansing flipped through the statewide reports, looking for anything interesting. The only report that caught his eye was a sketchy account of Ned Koteen's murder, and he already knew about that. He just wished there was something he could do about it.

Taking another sip of coffee, he started filtering through the paperwork his deputy had left for him.

33

 THE OWL WATCHED THE TWO DEPUTIES FROM his perch. The new arrival offered a cigarette, but the man who had been watching the small clearing declined.

They talked for a few minutes, then the first deputy walked over to his Jeep. Getting inside, he started his engine, then waved at his replacement. A moment later the lights of the Jeep disappeared down the dark mountain road.

A kerosene lantern sat in the middle of the clearing, dimly illuminating the woods for yards in every direction. The new deputy walked over and pumped up the pressure on the lantern. The mantle began to glow more intensely, changing color from a dull yellow to a bright white.

The deputy walked back to his Jeep and leaned against the grillwork, puffing on his cigarette.

The owl was not particularly interested in the deputy. He had stopped by the clearing out of mild curiosity. It was unusual to see such a large gathering of people on the mountain that late at night. As the number of people dwindled, so did the owl's curiosity.

Now with only one man left—and a new arrival at that—the owl remembered he had something to do. He was on a mission. There was someplace he had to be, and soon.

Spreading his wings, the owl gave one mighty flap, sending himself soaring silently into the night sky.

If at that moment Deputy Cortez had looked up, he would have seen the moon and all of the stars disappear. But it would have lasted only a second or two, and as the shadow moved on he would have convinced himself that his eyes were playing tricks on him.

What Deputy Cortez did notice was the waft of cold air that enveloped him, chilling him to the bone. It was a chill that stayed with him the rest of the night.

Marcus Baltazar dropped to the ground from his bedroom window. He had seen the owl in his dreams. He knew it was miles away and wasn't looking for him.

He had spent the entire evening contemplating his nightmares, while he held his great-grandfather's medicine pouch. He knew his dreams had power. He knew they had meaning. He also knew they amounted to nothing if someone didn't believe him.

Neighborhood dogs barked as he began running through the darkness toward the foothills east of Dulce. He had to find someone who would believe in his dreams. And the only way he could do that was to prove that they were true.

34

LANSING WAS NOT EXPECTING TO FIND MAR-
garite's truck parked behind the ranch house
when he arrived. When he went inside he
found her curled up on the living room sofa, asleep.
The book she was reading had fallen to the floor next
to her discarded boots. She was in her standard uniform, blue jeans and a long-sleeved western shirt. Her
bare feet were buried in the quilt normally draped
across the back of the couch.

He quietly went to the back of the large ranch house
and found C.J. asleep in his room.

On the way back to the living room Lansing stopped
by his own bedroom and turned down the covers. It
was eleven-thirty, and Lansing had no intention of letting Margarite drive back to the pueblo that night.

Going back to the living room, he gently removed the
quilt she was using, then scooped her up in his arms.
She seemed to weigh practically nothing as he carried
her back to his room and laid her on the bed.

She mumbled something as he covered her, but she
never woke.

As Lansing sat on the opposite side of the bed he

suddenly realized how tired he was. He was normally in bed by ten, ten-thirty at the latest. It was nearly midnight, and his body ached from the eight-hour hike.

He pulled off his boots, then laid back on the bed next to Margarite. It felt good to stretch out. He told himself he would close his eyes for just a moment. He still needed to take off his uniform.

The thought that he still needed to remove his uniform was the first thing that crossed Lansing's mind when his alarm sounded.

It was five-thirty. He was in his own house and he had almost forgotten how he got there. He looked at Margarite sleeping on the opposite side of the bed. She truly was beautiful.

Grabbing a set of sweats from his dresser, he quietly went into the bathroom to brush his teeth, change, and take care of other morning business. Ten minutes later he was in the barn getting oats and water for the horses.

Cement Head was his usual cranky self.

"I'd take you for a jog, horse," Lansing said, "but I know you'd run off just to make my day difficult. We'll go out sometime tomorrow." Cement Head whinnied in protest. "Don't worry. I'll put you in the pasture before I leave."

Lansing closed the barn door behind him as he stepped outside to do some stretching. The morning air was cool and crisp. Perfect for running.

Old routines were hard to break. He had already jogged a half mile before he realized he would be tromping along mountain trails again that morning— probably all day. His morning run certainly wasn't mandatory. He'd be getting plenty of exercise. He decided he could go half his normal distance. However, by the time he had finished his first mile, he felt so good that he decided to finish all three miles.

When he got back to the house he put on a pot of coffee, then went back to his room to shower.

Margarite was still asleep.

He thought he was being quiet while he cleaned up, but when he emerged from the bathroom Margarite was gone. He slipped on a pair of trousers and hurried down the hall. He found her sitting at the kitchen table, nursing a cup of coffee.

"You're still here!"

"You sound disappointed." Margarite sounded as if she was still half-asleep.

"I'm not. I mean, I'm glad you're still here."

"I didn't even hear you come in last night," she confessed. "How did I end up in your bedroom?"

"I carried you back there."

"You didn't take advantage of me, did you?"

"I don't think so," Lansing admitted. "In fact, we both ended up sleeping with our clothes on."

Margarite took a sip of her coffee. "What a waste." She glanced at her watch. "What time is it anyway?"

"Six-thirty."

Margarite yawned. "I have to have the clinic open by eight-thirty."

"You have plenty of time," Lansing said, pouring himself a cup of coffee. "I'll be right back. I need to finish dressing."

He headed back to his bedroom, taking the coffee with him. When he returned five minutes later, Margarite was pouring herself a second cup. She held up the pot.

"More?"

"Please."

She filled the cup, then sat back down at the table.

Lansing studied his cup for a moment. "Listen, Margarite. I really appreciate you stopping by to see C.J. last night."

"You don't have to thank me for anything, Lansing. I

came out here because I like C.J. That, and I thought he could use a little company."

"Yeah. I guess he could. This hasn't been much of a visit for him. Things have been a little busy."

"Don't you think you could make a little time for him?"

"I've tried. I wrap things up down at work as quickly as I can, but every time I stomp out one fire, literally, two more pop up. And I'm running out of ideas on how to keep him busy while I'm occupied."

"Why does he have to be entertained?"

"Hell, he's twelve years old, Margarite. Kids have to be kept busy so they don't get bored."

"C.J.'s smart enough to entertain himself. He was out riding his horse when I got here yesterday. He knows what to do when he's bored. Boredom isn't the problem. It could be he's just lonely."

"How am I supposed to fix that?"

"Lansing, does it dawn on you that maybe he's spending his summer vacation with you because he wants to be with you?"

"Well, yeah. Sure."

"Then let him be with you."

"What do you mean?"

"Take him to work with you."

"That's ridiculous. He'd be bored to tears."

"When you were growing up, did your dad ever take you out when he rode the fence?"

"Sure. My older brother and I both went. Of course, I was almost too young to be of any use."

"Did it matter to you that you got bored?"

"No. I was hanging out with the big guys."

"Why would it be any different for C.J.? He came up to see you, and he would be thrilled to death to hang out with the big guys."

"You think he'd like that?"

"Lansing, he mentioned two or three times last night

that he was going to grow up and be your chief deputy. Sounds like he would like nothing better than to hang out with you."

Lansing pondered the idea. "All we're doing is tromping through woods today. He might not mind that so much."

"He'll like it better than sitting around shooing flies all day."

"You're right." He set his cup down. "I'll be right back. I need to roust my most junior deputy out of bed."

A few minutes later he returned with a smile on his face. "Guess who nearly knocked me down getting out of bed when I asked him to go to work with me."

"I'm not so stupid."

"No one's ever accused you of that." Lansing thought for a moment. "I don't know what I said wrong the other night. I've been trying to figure it out for the last two days."

"Don't worry about it, Lansing. You were simply being you." She got up from the table and walked over to him, putting her arms around his waist. "I've had a couple of days to think too, and I need to ask you a question."

"Shoot."

"Would you say we're friends?"

"Sure."

"Forget the fact that we've made love. Am I a friend? Someone you would come to if you had a problem. Someone you would ask advice from because you respect them."

"I considered you that before we went on our first date."

Margarite stood on her toes and kissed his cheek. "Well, Lansing, I guess I can't ask for more than that."

"What's this all about?"

"That's what I love about you," Margarite said,

laughing. "You're so blissfully ignorant about your own wisdom." She put her head against his chest. "One more question."

"Okay."

"Do you want me in your life?"

Lansing knew the answer. It was simple and it didn't need any flowery embellishment. "Yes."

"I came to the conclusion I want you in mine. Sometimes a woman wants assurance in a relationship. Not commitment, just assurance. She likes to know she's made a wise emotional investment."

"Are you sure you have?"

"One of the things I've learned in the last year or so is that Clifford A. Lansing is an honorable man. He sticks by his friends. When I was shot you got me to the hospital, sat by my bed when I was in a coma, held my hand. I owe you my life.

"The way I figure it, if you consider me a friend and you want me in your life, I can live with that. I don't need to pry words out of you. Your actions speak pretty well for themselves. I just want you to do one thing for me."

"What's that?"

"Call me once in a while. I like to know what's going on."

Lansing laughed. "I guess I can do that."

They kissed. It was a long, lingering kiss that said they were still friends, and more.

35

LANSING AND C.J. WERE OUT OF THE HOUSE before seven o'clock. Margarite left at the same time, heading back to her clinic at Burnt Mesa Pueblo.

"Are we going to eat before we go to Chama Meadows?" C.J. asked as they turned onto the highway toward town.

"Yeah. We have time. We'll pick up Sheriff Fulton, then stop by the diner." It sounded simple, but Lansing was a little concerned. He had called Fulton to tell him they were on their way, but no one answered. Both Bill and Emily Fulton were early risers. He hoped they were simply outside looking at the garden or on the porch having coffee.

In the early seventies Bill Fulton had bought a small acreage east of town, where he and Emily built their own house. It was a single-story ranch with an attached garage. Emily was tired of having to tromp through snow to get to their car in the winter.

Fulton had made plans to eventually add a barn and a toolshed, get some chickens, cows, and horses, and turn the place into an operational ranchette. While he was sheriff he got as far as building a chicken coop. By the time he retired he had lost interest in his ranch idea. Coyotes had decimated his chicken flock, and his ten acres lay fallow. In a way it reminded Lansing of the hundred little projects he wanted to do on his own ranch, but never had time for.

It really hadn't bothered Emily. All she cared about was the small vegetable garden they worked and the attached garage.

Fulton's truck was parked in the driveway when Lansing pulled in. He told C.J. to wait in the Jeep as he stepped out.

Lansing went up to the front door and rang the bell. When there was no answer he rang it a second time and tried to peek through the front curtains to see if there was any movement.

"I'm going to try the back of the house," Lansing yelled to his son.

As he started around the front, he heard the muffled sound of a car engine. He stopped in front of the garage door and listened. The sound was coming from inside the garage. There was also the strong smell of engine exhaust.

Lansing pulled on the door, but it was locked from the inside. He ran around to the side door, but it was locked as well. He stepped back and kicked the door in. A gush of carbon monoxide and engine fumes billowed through the opening, stinging his eyes and choking him.

The garage was dark. He flicked on the light switch next to the door and made a quick scan of the interior. Emily's car was running. It looked as if two people were inside. Across the garage, next to the door leading into the house, was the switch to the garage-door opener.

Burying his face in the crook of his elbow, Lansing ran to the garage-door switch and pushed it. The door began to open. Not waiting for the door to open all the way, he ran to the driver's side of the car. The window was down. He reached inside and switched off the engine.

Bill Fulton sat in the driver's seat. He was slumped sideways, leaning against the still form of his wife.

Lansing felt for a pulse. There was none. Pulling open the door, he dragged Fulton's body from the car and out of the garage.

"C.J.!"

C.J. jumped out of the Jeep. "What's wrong, Dad?"

"Call dispatch! Get the paramedics out here! Now!"

As C.J. got back into the Jeep to make the call, Lansing ran back into the garage to pull Emily into the fresh air. He quickly checked her for a pulse, but found none.

He knelt over the body of Bill Fulton again. Tipping Fulton's head back, Lansing began CPR.

"Dad," C.J. called. "The paramedics are coming! Dispatch wants to know if there's something they can do."

Lansing looked up from his task. "Tell them to get Dr. Tanner out here. We need all the help we can get."

Lansing was still in the process of trying to bring life back to Fulton when he heard the wail of the rescue unit's siren. He kept at his work until Willy Sutter and Carlos Gomez came running up.

"We'll take over, Sheriff," Gomez said. His manner was confident and professional.

Lansing moved out of the way. Gomez knelt and began checking Fulton as Sutter attended to Emily.

"What happened?" Gomez asked.

"I found them in the garage. The car was running and the doors were all closed."

Sutter checked for any signs of life. "How long were they in there?"

Lansing shook his head. "I don't know."

"I'm not getting anything," Sutter complained.

"Me neither," Gomez said. "Check the temp."

Sutter reached inside his emergency-aid bag and pulled out a battery-operated thermometer. He slipped the cone end into Emily's ear and pressed a button for a reading. A few seconds later the mechanism emitted a muffled beep. "I've got eighty-eight degrees. I'm afraid she'd been down awhile."

He popped out the plastic cone and inserted a new one. He handed the device to Gomez, who made the same check on Fulton. "Yep. Eighty-eight."

"Can't you do something?" Lansing asked desperately.

Gomez shook his head. "Sorry, Sheriff. We can bust the sternum and start pounding on their chests, but it ain't going to do no good. They've been dead at least three hours. Maybe more."

"Even if we got the hearts going, they'd be dead upstairs," Sutter added, pointing at his own head. "They died of suffocation. Lack of oxygen to the brain."

Lansing looked down at the bodies. They seemed small, almost shriveled. Las Palmas was small, and he had known the Fultons his entire life. He couldn't equate the two vibrant people he had known with the shells stretched out before him.

"What do you think, Sheriff? Accident?" Gomez asked, breaking Lansing's train of thought.

"It must have been. I was supposed to pick Sheriff Fulton up this morning. He was going to go back up to the Meadows again."

"I wonder where they were headed?" Sutter asked as he packed his gear away. "Mrs. Fulton's in her night-gown, and the sheriff's still in the clothes he had on yesterday."

"I don't know," Lansing said, shaking his head. He glanced up and saw C.J. standing at the corner of the Jeep, keeping his distance. "How about covering them up? Doc Tanner's going to be here in a minute."

36

"How well did you know them, Sheriff?" Tanner asked as he handed the stethoscope back to Gomez.

"Fairly well. Bill was my boss for four years before I replaced him as sheriff. I've known them both since I was a kid."

"How would you have rated their mental health?"

"There wasn't anything wrong with either one of them. I just worked with Bill yesterday. He was going to come out again today." He gave Tanner a questioning look. "You're not saying that they did this intentionally, that they committed suicide."

"It's not unheard of for an elderly couple to commit suicide together, especially if one of them is terminally ill. But I don't think that's the case here. As far as I know, Bill had high blood pressure, but that was it." He paused for a moment, then motioned Lansing aside. He spoke in a low, confidential voice. "I don't think this was a double suicide."

"So it was an accident."

"I'm not saying that either. Take a look at the bodies."

Lansing looked down as Tanner pulled back the plastic sheeting the paramedics had provided. The upper bodies were exposed, but Lansing didn't see anything significant. "What am I looking for?"

"Do you notice their complexions?"

Bill Fulton's face was flushed, with a pink glow. Emily's face was a pale whitish-blue. At first glance Lansing assumed the difference was because Fulton had spent more time out of doors than his wife. "Are you talking about their skin color?"

Tanner nodded. "Bill died from carbon monoxide poisoning. When breathed, carbon monoxide molecules hook up with red blood cells, displacing the regular oxygen atoms and hanging on permanently. If enough carbon monoxide is taken in, the body suffocates. Because the gas is an oxide, all of the blood in the body tends to turn red, giving the body a ruddy complexion."

"What about Emily?"

"My guess is she was dead before the car was ever started."

"How?"

Tanner pointed. "See these purplish marks here in the front of the neck? Watch what happens when I push." He pushed his finger against the throat. As he did, it sank an inch into the flesh. "The larynx has been crushed. She was choked to death by someone with a lot of strength in their fingers."

"I can't believe this was a murder-suicide."

"That's why I was asking about their mental states, Sheriff. Right now that's the most obvious explanation."

"That doesn't make any sense. I saw Bill less than ten hours ago. Everything was fine. They were getting ready to sell this place and move to Corpus Christi."

"Unless you can find something that says differently, you're going to have to go with the obvious explanation."

"Could an autopsy turn up anything?"

"It might, but it's a long shot."

"How soon could you do one?"

"I could do one today, but I'm not board-certified. If you're looking for something other than suicide, I may screw things up. You'd better go with someone with experience."

The thought of asking Margarite Carerra flashed through Lansing's mind. "Okay. I'll see what I can do." He looked at the two paramedics. "I guess you may as well wrap them up and take them to the mortuary."

"Sure thing," Sutter said. "You still going to need us up in the Meadows today?"

"Damn, I forgot all about that," Lansing said. He glanced at his watch. It was seven forty-five. "Yeah, head on up as soon as you can. It doesn't look like I'll be making it."

Gomez went to retrieve two body bags from the rescue unit. They would need Bert Sellers and his van from the mortuary to transport the bodies.

Lansing studied the garage behind him. He was amazed at how clean and orderly Fulton had kept it. All of the tools were arranged on peg boards. Boxes were stacked neatly on built-in shelves. All the doors to the storage cabinets were closed. The floor was swept.

"Have you been inside the house?" Tanner asked.

"No, not yet," Lansing admitted.

"There might be a note. Something that might shed a little light on what went on."

Lansing was starting to feel overwhelmed. He had a search-and-rescue mission running in the mountains. He had a possible murder-suicide to investigate. There were two unsolved murders on the Apache reservation that, technically, weren't his responsibility, but they still had occurred in his county. And he didn't have the slightest inkling what he was supposed to do with his son.

"Sheriff!" Gomez called from behind him. "We might have something here."

Gomez and Sutter were in the process of trying to position Bill Fulton for the body bag. At the moment they had him facedown. Lansing walked over to see what they had.

"What do you think that is?" Gomez was indicating a spot at the base of Fulton's skull.

Lansing knelt for a closer examination. There was a large red mark, slightly raised with swelling. There was also blood.

"It looks like he was hit from behind," Tanner commented over Lansing's shoulder. "The force of the blow was hard enough to break the skin."

"Could he have gotten this accidentally?"

"Yeah, if he had slipped. Or possibly if he stood up real fast and hit it on a drawer or the bottom of a table. At the back of the neck like that, I'll bet he saw some stars."

"Could a blow like that knock him unconscious?"

"Sure, if it was hard enough." Tanner watched as Lansing looked from the bodies to the garage and back again. "Are you thinking someone put both bodies in the car?"

"And started it up to make it look like a suicide," Lansing said, completing the thought. He stood and hurried to the garage. Something slightly out of place had caught his eye.

When he reached the side of the car he got down on his hands and knees for a better look. Yes. There was something there. In a cluttered garage or on a less well-kept floor it would have gone unnoticed. He had to lay on his stomach to reach it. A moment later he was walking out of the garage with his prize.

"What's that?" Tanner asked.

Lansing held up the item for Tanner to see. "An owl's feather."

37

"DISPATCH TO PATROL TWO," LANSING SAID over Marilyn's radio. "Do you read me?"

"Patrol Two here," Gabe Hanna responded a moment later. "Go ahead."

"Gabe, you've just been appointed head of the search-and-rescue teams."

"Say again, Dispatch."

"You're in charge, Deputy. I can't make it today."

"Is there a problem?"

"Yeah." Lansing didn't see a need to broadcast the news about the Fultons. "Who's up there with you?"

"The forestry crew and Mr. Prentiss. I haven't seen Sutter or Gomez yet."

"They're on their way. They'll fill you in on what's going on. I want you to put the teams on entirely new trails today. You need to man the command post in case I have to reach you. I'll make some calls. If nothing turns up today, maybe we can get more help for tomorrow."

"Ten-four," Gabe responded.

Lansing turned off the transmitter and looked across the reception area. Marilyn, normally unflappable, sat alone, her face buried in tissues. She had worked for Fulton for twenty years before Lansing inherited her. She had been close to both Bill and Emily for a long time.

He stepped through the door of the dispatch area and went to her. "Marilyn," he said, kneeling, "if I could spare you I'd let you go home."

"Not a chance, Sheriff," she sniffed. "I'll be all right." She paused to blow her nose. "I want to be in the middle of this."

"Good." He patted her shoulder. "When you're ready I need for you to call all the deputies. I want everyone in the dayroom for a noon briefing."

"Even the night patrols?"

"Even the night patrols. The only exception will be Deputy Hanna. He's tied up with the search-and-rescue teams."

"Don't worry. I'll take care of it." She stood and straightened her dress. "If you would excuse me a moment, I need to go splash some water on my face."

"Go ahead. I'll listen for the radio."

Lansing went into his office. C.J. was sitting there, waiting patiently.

"Dad, I'm sorry about Sheriff Fulton. I wish there was something I could do to help."

At the moment C.J. was only a distraction. If he tried to do anything he would just get in the way. "You still haven't had breakfast. Are you hungry?"

"Maybe a little."

"Why don't you run over to the diner and get something?" He pulled a five-dollar bill from his wallet. "This should be enough."

"What do you want me to do when I'm finished?"

"I guess come back here. We'll figure out what you can do later."

"Okay." C.J. took the money and left.

Lansing studied the owl feather he had found beneath Fulton's car for a full minute. Finally, he picked up the phone and dialed the Thunderchief Motel. Sheridan's phone was busy. It was another five minutes before Lansing could get through.

"Sheridan here."

"Yeah, Agent Sheridan. Sheriff Lansing. I need to meet with you as soon as possible."

"I'm tied up right now trying to get some reports faxed up to the reservation," Sheridan said. "However, I'm meeting Dr. Miles for breakfast at the diner at nine. Would you care to join us?"

Dr. Miles was one of the last people Lansing wanted to see this morning. He felt as though he was going to sound like a fool as it was. "Nine o'clock will be fine."

38

 As Lansing entered the diner C.J. swiveled his counter seat around. C.J.'s face beamed when he asked, "Are we going to have breakfast together?"

"No, I'm sorry, son," Lansing said, patting the boy's shoulder. "I have to meet some people."

"Oh." C.J. had a hard time hiding his disappointment. "Do you still want me to go back to the office when I'm finished?"

"Yeah, that'll be fine."

"Hello, Sheriff," Velma sang as she came out of the kitchen carrying a plate of food. "A cup of coffee?"

"I'll have one in the back."

She set the plate of food on the counter. "You're not eating with C.J.?"

"Sorry, I've got work to do."

"I know," Velma said very seriously. "I heard about poor Sheriff Fulton and his wife." She reached across the counter and patted C.J.'s hand. "And this poor boy had to see everything." She tried to sound secretive. "John told me somebody murdered them. What do you think really happened?"

"Right now I'm not sure about anything." Lansing saw Dr. Miles sitting at a table in the back. She was alone. He would have preferred if Sheridan was there before he joined her, but he wanted to escape Velma's questions. "Excuse me. There's someone I have to talk to."

He approached the table. "Do you mind if I join you?"

"I was waiting for Agent Sheridan." Her tone indicated Lansing was not necessarily welcome.

"I know. I needed to speak to him. He suggested I join you two here at the diner."

"Oh, he did." There was a touch of resignation in her voice. "Then by all means have a seat."

"Thank you." Lansing sat across the table. He wasn't sure why there was still animosity between them after ten years. He assumed it was the same resentment toward white men that seethed in many Native Americans.

Kelly approached with a pot of coffee. She turned Lansing's empty cup over and filled it. "It's just terrible about Bill and Emily Fulton," she said.

"Yeah. Terrible." Lansing tried to indicate he wasn't interested in discussing the issue. He picked up his cup and took a sip. "Thank you, Kelly."

"Do you want to order anything?"

"In a minute."

"Okay, I'll be back."

Lansing sensed the waitress's disappointment. Kelly really wanted to know what was going on. In a little town like Las Palmas the murder of an ex-sheriff was big news. Besides, everyone knew Bill and Emily Fulton. They were neighbors and friends. The community had a right to know what was going on. He just didn't have anything to tell them yet.

"I overheard a couple of people talking," Miles said. "What a tragedy. I understand it was a double suicide."

"We're still piecing things together." At the moment

Lansing didn't have a problem with the suicide rumor. If, indeed, he was dealing with two murders, he didn't want the public to panic. Before the topic could be pushed any further, Agent Sheridan arrived.

"I'm sorry I'm late," Sheridan apologized, seating himself. "Being a one-man field office gets a little hectic. Especially if your evidence is spread out all over the countryside."

Kelly approached with her coffeepot. Sheridan didn't push the conversation any further until she had taken their breakfast orders. He began again once they were alone.

"I know you have something you want to talk about, Sheriff. Before we get started there were a couple of questions I wanted to ask Doctor Miles while they were still fresh in my mind."

"Certainly," Lansing agreed.

"Doctor Miles, what can you tell me about Cuartelejo Management?"

"What do you mean?"

"I guess I don't quite understand how the Jicarilla government works. It's structured somewhat after the federal government, with executive, judicial, and legislative branches."

"Yes."

"And all of the resources belong to the tribe as a whole."

"And that's true."

"Where does something like the Cuartelejo Management Company fit in?"

"The tribal council, the tribal judges, the president, and his staff ensure the laws of the tribe are upheld. They also make sure our resources are managed properly. They look out for the general welfare of the tribe.

"The Jicarilla Cattleman's Association, the Sheepman's Association, and Cuartelejo Management are all privately owned businesses or coops. The tribal council regulates them just the way the federal government regulates AT&T or Delta Airlines."

"What exactly does Cuartelejo manage?"

"Originally it was a land-management company. It was formed about fifteen years ago when the tribe bought Horse Lake Ranch so we could expand the reservation. They were so successful in turning a profit from the ranch that the tribe turned over Stone Lake Lodge for them to manage. Unfortunately, that operation went bust.

"By then it didn't matter. Most of the board members also belonged to the tribal council. Whenever a contract came up for renewal Cuartelejo got the contract. After the mine accident last year, the council decided Cuartelejo could do a better job. So now they manage the mines. I'm sure Baltazar Brothers will lose its drilling concession after the well explosion. It's just the way business has evolved on the reservation over the last forty years."

"Don't the people in your tribe think the politics are a little soiled? The council members award themselves contracts and skim a little off the top before the rest of the tribe sees anything?"

"The Jicarilla Reservation is not the United States in microcosm, Agent Sheridan. There are only three thousand of us. We can't pay professional politicians. The president of the council and the council members all have other jobs. If Hector Velarde is also the president of Cuartelejo Management, that's just the way things have shaken out.

"What does any of this have to do with your investigations?"

"Probably nothing, but you're the only one who has provided me any motive for the murders."

"Me? And what was that?"

"The division between the Olleros and Llaneros. You

made it sound like there is some sort of power struggle going on."

"I think I might have exaggerated the situation. You heard President Velarde say there was nothing like that going on."

"I see." He thought for a moment. "Out of curiosity, where did they come up with the name *Cuartelejo*? As near as I can tell, it translates from Spanish as 'the far lodges.' "

"That's very close. They were 'the people of the far lodges.' They were plains Apaches closely related to the Olleros. Their territory extended into eastern Kansas. Over the centuries the Jicarillas and the Taos people became close friends and allies. When the Spanish reconquered New Mexico after the Pueblo Revolt of 1680, the Taos tribe picked up and moved rather than live under Spanish subjugation. For over twenty years they lived among the plains Apaches. Taos sites have been found as far away as Wichita. The Spanish called the Apaches they lived with 'the people of the far lodges.'

"The Taos, the Cuartelejo, and another branch, the Carlanas, were all driven back to the south by the invading Comanches around 1720. The Cuartelejo and Carlanas disappeared as separate tribes as they were absorbed by the Olleros. The Taos returned to their pueblos, preferring the Spanish whip to the Comanche knife."

"Don't you find it interesting that Velarde and his group chose a name that specifically identifies their management company with the Ollero heritage?"

"Not particularly. I think you're looking for a conspiracy where nothing exists."

"I think Doctor Miles is absolutely right," Lansing interrupted. He'd had enough of history lessons for one day. "Those murders had nothing to do with Jicarilla politics."

"Oh?" Miles looked at Lansing, surprised at the unexpected support.

"I believe our murderer struck again last night." Lansing reached into his pocket, pulled out the feather he had found beneath Fulton's car, and laid it on the table. "And here's his calling card."

39

"A FEATHER?" SHERIDAN ASKED.

"Specifically, an owl's feather. Ned Koteen found one at Esteban Baltazar's place the morning the body was found. There was one laying next to Ned's body behind the liquor store.

"I found Bill Fulton, the former sheriff around here, and his wife dead this morning. They were in a locked garage with their car running. Someone tried to make it look like a double suicide. I found the feather underneath the car."

"Their throats weren't cut?"

Lansing shook his head.

"Then that hardly fits the M.O., Sheriff."

"In general terms it doesn't. But owl feathers don't necessarily show up around here every day. And they don't end up on the floor of a recently swept garage."

"It could have blown in," Sheridan observed.

"It could have, along with grass and leaves. But there weren't any grass clippings or leaves on the floor. Just the feather."

"So what's the significance?"

"I don't know," Lansing admitted. He looked at Dr. Miles. "Do you have any suggestions?"

Miles seemed lost in her own thoughts as she studied the object lying on the table. "I'm sorry. What?"

"I was wondering if you had any idea why an owl feather might be left at the murder scenes."

"The feather can be used as a fetish or totem. When left with a dead person it's to help that person's soul fly to the holy place where all the souls are gathered. But I think you're reaching, Lansing. I agree with Agent Sheridan. Whatever happened to your Sheriff Fulton had nothing to do with the reservation deaths."

"In Apache beliefs isn't the owl associated with death?"

"Sometimes. Sometimes Big Owl is depicted as a clown and a fool as well. A symbol of stupidity."

"What is your opinion?"

"My opinion is you're confusing fairy tales with facts and coincidences. There are two dead men on the reservation. You have two dead people. You want to pretend they have something to do with one another to make your job easier. I don't think you have much of a case."

"I'm afraid she's right, Sheriff," Sheridan said. "I'd like to help you, but a feather under a car isn't much evidence. Do you have anything more substantial?"

"Dr. Tanner, our town physician, examined both bodies this morning. Emily Fulton was strangled to death. Her larynx was crushed. Bill had a knot at the base of his skull. It looked like someone might have knocked him unconscious. I believe whoever did this placed both bodies in the car, then started the engine. It was supposed to look like an accident, or suicide, or murder-suicide."

"If this is the same person why did he go to such lengths to cover his tracks? Why didn't he just cut their throats? And if he was covering his tracks why did he leave a feather behind so he could be linked to the other two murders?" Sheridan asked.

Lansing balled his hand into a fist and squeezed, trying to mask his frustration. "I don't know. Ego. Maybe he's taunting us. Maybe he wants to be caught. I can't read his mind."

Kelly approached with a platter containing the three breakfasts. The table fell silent as she handed out the plates. After refreshing the coffees she quickly left, aware that her presence was not desired.

"Like I said, Sheriff," Sheridan continued, "I wish I could help. I have my hands full with the Jicarilla situation. I don't think my supervisor would appreciate me chasing down a matter that falls under the local-police jurisdiction. I hope you understand."

"Unfortunately, I do." Lansing picked up the feather and stood.

"You're not staying for your meal?" Sheridan asked.

"I wasn't very hungry when I ordered. I have no appetite at all now. Good day."

40

"WHAT'D YOU DO WITH C.J.?" MARILYN ASKED as Lansing entered the offices, noticing his son wasn't in trail.

"I didn't know what to do with him. Velma said she was taking the rest of the day off, so he's riding with her down to Santa Fe. They're going to do some sightseeing and some shopping."

"You sure you want to leave that woman alone with him?"

"I think he's reasonably safe," Lansing said, only half-believing his own statement.

"Maybe it's just as well he'd out of your hair," Marilyn said, handing a piece of paper over her counter. "I think you're going to be busy."

"What's this?"

"I talked to the owner of The Sporting Life this morning like you asked. He gave me two names: Pedro Gomez and Julio Martinez."

"The busser and washer down at Paco's Cantina?" Lansing studied the piece of paper. "Must be. These are local addresses."

"There's more. The most recent things they fenced

with him? Half the stuff had *Prentiss* marked on it
along with I.D. numbers."

"Son of a bitch." Lansing glanced at his watch. It
was nine-thirty. "Marilyn, I need to talk to Judge
Flores and the county prosecutor immediately. I need
a couple of warrants."

Lansing had always prided himself on being able to
handle things pretty much on his own. But there was a
time and a place to play the Lone Ranger, and there
were occasions when it just wasn't smart. Now it
wasn't smart.

He had hoped Sheridan would offer some help from
the FBI to investigate the Fulton murders. When the
offer didn't come, Lansing knew his office couldn't
handle things alone. His resources were being spread
too thin. The State Bureau of Investigation normally
didn't get involved in local murders, but they did
make exceptions if the murder involved the death of a
peace officer. Even a retired one. Lansing needed their
forensics expertise, at least, and wasn't too proud to
ask for it.

With the SBI experts rolling in to help with the
Fulton case, he could direct his attention to two other
cases: the series of camping-equipment thefts and the
two missing girls. All of a sudden, however, those two
cases had become one and the same.

Pedro Gomez and Julio Martinez worked at Paco's
Cantina from four in the afternoon until closing. They
normally didn't get away from work until well after
midnight. Both were in their early twenties and liked
to party until the crack of dawn.

When Lansing's deputies continued to report they
hadn't seen anything unusual during their night
patrols, they had been absolutely right. They had seen
Gomez and Martinez out cruising, but that wasn't
unusual. They were always out cruising.

Judge Flores agreed to issue warrants on both men for possession of stolen property. That gave Lansing the ammunition he needed to drag them in for questioning about the missing girls. He was convinced the girls had no survival equipment, and it had been at least four days since anyone had seen them. Even though the weather had been pleasant, the experience could be rough if they were stuck in the woods with no food or water. He hoped to hell his two thieves could provide answers.

"Pedro Gomez! Julio Martinez! This is the sheriff! I want you to come out with your hands above your head." Lansing had parked his Jeep thirty feet from the trailer the two men shared on the outskirts of town. He was addressing them through the P.A. speaker tied into his radio. He had positioned Jack Rivera on the opposite side of the trailer, just in case their suspects tried to escape.

"I repeat: Pedro Gomez and Julio Martinez! Come out with your hands up!"

Lansing was pretty sure they were in the trailer. Their Bondo-spackled Camaro, the only car they owned, sat outside. He had considered rushing the place, but a trailer didn't provide much room. If one of them was armed, one of his men could get hurt. It was safer just to call them out.

Lansing's radio crackled. "Sheriff, this is Patrol Three."

"Yeah, go ahead, Jack."

"A window just opened on this side. They're dropping out a pair of boots. Yep. Looks like one's climbing out now."

"Can you grab him when he hits the ground?"

"No sweat. I'm on my way."

"This is your last warning," Lansing said again through his P.A., letting them think he was unaware of their planned escape. "You have ten seconds to come out, or I'll have to come in after you." He waited, then began counting over the speaker. "Five. Four. Three. Two."

Before he could finish the two men appeared, walking around the corner of the trailer, prodded by Deputy Rivera. They were dressed in blue jeans with no shirts or shoes. Their hands were cuffed behind their backs.

"This is a mistake, Sheriff," Gomez protested. "We didn't do it, man."

"Didn't do what?" Rivera asked, giving him a little push.

"Whatever it was you think we did! We've been in bed asleep. We didn't do nothin'."

"Jack, you take Martinez in your Jeep. Pedro can ride with me." Lansing took Gomez by the arm and began leading him to his Jeep.

"I need my boots, Sheriff," Gomez protested. "Ouch! Man, there's stickers here."

"Don't worry. You won't find any in my jail."

"Man, I tell you we didn't do nothin'."

"Then why'd you try to sneak out the back of the trailer?"

"The door's stuck. We had to go out the window. Besides, you can't arrest us. I know my rights. You gotta have a warrant."

Lansing produced two pieces of paper from his back pocket. "You mean one of these."

"Oh, man!"

Lansing opened the door to his Jeep and pushed Gomez inside.

41

"MAN, THERE AIN'T NO WAY YOU'RE GOING TO get a confession out of me, cause I didn't do nothin'." Gomez said. He sat in the sheriff's private office with his arms folded in defiance.

From the moment of arrest through the interrogations, Lansing wanted to make sure the two men were separated. He didn't want to give them the opportunity to concoct any cover stories. From the beginning he didn't even want them to know what they had been arrested for.

Jack Rivera leaned against the door to observe the interrogation.

"Pedro, I don't need a confession. You've been stealing camping equipment around the county for the last month and fencing it down in Santa Fe. We have eyewitnesses. We have you on videotape. We have stuff with your fingerprints all over it."

"Then what do we have to talk about?"

"Four nights ago you and Julio were up in the Meadows."

"No, that wasn't us, man."

"Forget the bull. We know you were there. The

equipment you stole had the owner's name and social security number all over it. The owner of The Sporting Life swears you and Julio sold it to him. He has it on his store videotape."

Gomez thought for a moment. "It's no big deal, man. It's not like we really stole it. We kind of found it."

"What do you mean 'found it'?"

"We went up there after work. We go up there all the time, maybe drink some wine, look at the stars. Anyway, there was some high-school punks havin' a beer bust or somethin'. I don't think they saw us when we drove past. They was out of it.

"So *mi compadre* and me, we drive on up and see this little car parked off the road, you know. But, like, there's no one around. So we drive past and park about a hundred yards past the car. We have some wine and think maybe we walk down and take a look.

"So that's what we do. But there ain't no one around. I mean, they got a tent and a Coleman light and a stove. An ice chest. Big Igloo kind, you know.

"We look in the car, but, like, they ain't inside and it's all locked up. So Julio and me, we think maybe they don't like camping. Maybe they go back to town. Maybe they leave the stuff cause they don't want it. So we took it.

"I mean, it's like we found it. It was just laying there. But we didn't steal nothin'."

"What about the two girls?"

"There weren't no girls."

"Yes, there were. There were two of them. That was their camping spot. Those high-school kids saw them earlier."

"There weren't no girls when we were there."

"Are you positive?"

"Sure, I'm positive."

Lansing picked up two photos from his desk and

handed them to Gomez. "Maybe these will jog your memory."

Gomez took the photos, glanced at them, then threw them back on Lansing's desk. "Never seen 'em."

"You know, it's awfully funny, Pedro. These two girls go camping up in the Meadows. These high-school kids see them. One of my deputies finds their car up there. But they're missing and so is all of their camping equipment.

"A couple of days later you show up in Santa Fe with all of their equipment, and you expect us to believe you don't know what happened to the girls?"

"Man, I tell you there wasn't nobody there!" There was a touch of panic in Gomez's voice. "You can ask Julio. We didn't see nobody."

"Did you know your brother's spent the last two days up in the mountains looking for those two young ladies?"

"Man, I don't know what my brother does."

"Don't you think he's going to be a little pissed when he finds out you knew where they were?"

"I don't know where they are! I've never seen them before!"

"Maybe we ought to wait until Carlos gets back down from the Meadows," Rivera suggested. "Since Pedro doesn't want to talk to us, maybe he'd like to talk to his big brother."

"*Mi hermano es hijoputa!*" Gomez spat. "I'll kick his ass!"

Lansing knew that was a hollow threat. Carlos outweighed his brother by thirty pounds and stood a head taller. "I think that's a good idea, Jack. Carlos can deal with him later. Put him in a cell so we can talk to Julio."

Rivera took Gomez by the arm and escorted him out the door. Lansing followed, intending to retrieve a cup of coffee.

"Sheriff," Marilyn called from her reception desk. "I know you're busy, but you have a visitor." She nodded toward the far side of the room.

A boy sat on one of the hard, wooden chairs in the reception area. His feet dangled above the floor. He was dressed in a loose flannel shirt, blue jeans, and tennis shoes. His dark-reddish complexion indicated he was either Mexican or Native American. Lansing guessed he was close to C.J.'s age.

"Yes," Lansing said. "Can I help you?"

The boy stood. "Yes, sir. I was wondering, could I talk to you?" He quickly glanced at Marilyn and then back. "In private?"

Lansing was anxious to get on with his interrogations. "Son, I'm really kind of busy right now. Could you come back later?"

"You're looking for two girls in the mountains," the boy said quickly.

"Yeah. What about them?"

"I can help you find them!"

42

 "I WANT THOSE TWO SEPARATED," LANSING SAID to Rivera. "Put Pedro in the dayroom. Handcuff him to one of the desks." He turned to the boy. "Come in to my office."

Lansing held the door as the boy went in. "Go ahead and sit down," he said, closing the door for their privacy.

The boy sat in the chair recently vacated by Gomez. Lansing sat at his desk. "You look familiar. Did we meet somewhere?"

The boy nodded. "It was at my great-grandfather's house, the morning we found him."

"You're Marcus, John Baltazar's son."

The boy nodded again.

"What are you doing down in Las Palmas? It's a long haul from Dulce."

"I had to talk to you."

"Did your father bring you?"

Marcus shook his head. "He doesn't know I'm here."

"How'd you get down here?"

"I cut over the hills. Then someone gave me a ride when I got to the highway."

By highway it was sixty miles to Dulce from Las Palmas. Even taking a shortcut through the foothills, the boy had traveled over forty miles. "That's not a very smart thing for a young man like you to be doing. There are some dangerous people out on the roads. What time did you leave home?"

"Midnight, I guess."

"You've been up all night?"

"I took a nap for a while."

"You probably haven't eaten anything either, have you?"

"No, sir, but I'm not hungry."

"Don't you think your folks are worried about you?"

"Probably."

Lansing picked up his phone. "Marilyn, ring me the police station on the Jicarilla reservation."

Marcus suddenly jumped up. "No, please. Don't send me back! They're going to send me away. They don't believe anything I tell them. That's why I had to talk to you."

Lansing considered the boy's plea for a moment. "Marilyn, hold off on that call." He returned the phone to the cradle. "Okay, you wanted to talk to me. Let's talk. You said you know something about the two missing girls."

"Yes."

"Did you see them somewhere?"

Marcus hesitated. "Sort of." He turned his head and stared out the window as he looked for the right words. "I have dreams, almost every night. I don't always know what they mean. *Náhánálí* sometimes would help me understand them."

"Who is *Náhánálí*?"

"He was my great-grandfather. He was a very powerful medicine man."

"Yes, I knew your great-grandfather."

"He said I was a Shadowcatcher, because I could see

things that were going to happen. Or because sometimes I can see things that happen far away. But he
can't help me now. So sometimes I have a dream that
I don't understand. And then two or three days later I
hear something that helps me understand it."

"And you had a dream about these girls?"

Marcus nodded. "They were with the Owl."

"Who's the Owl?"

"I don't know. I think it's a man, but I'm not sure. I
can't see his face in my dreams."

"What was the Owl doing in this dream?"

"I could see him flying above the mountains. It
was night. I was in the forest, and whenever he flew
overhead the moon and all the stars would disappear.
But I wasn't afraid, because I knew he wasn't looking
for me.

"Then I heard two women talking in the forest. I
don't think they were very old. But they were next to
a campfire and the fire was going out. One of them
went into the woods to get more wood. She didn't
see that the stars and moon had disappeared. Then she
disappeared.

"The other woman started calling her friend's
name—"

"Do you remember the name she called?" Lansing
asked, interrupting.

Marcus squeezed his eyes shut, trying to concentrate. After a long moment he began whispering words
to himself. "Mary. Mary. Terry. Sh . . . Sh . . . Sheri!"
His eyes popped open. "Sheri!" he said out loud. "The
name she said was 'Sheri!' "

Lansing was surprised at the boy's accuracy, but he
was far from convinced that he was dealing with anything extraordinary. "Okay, go on with your dream."

Marcus had to remember where he had left off.
"Then the Owl flew down from the sky and began
chasing the woman who was calling her friend's name.

She fell down on the ground and the Owl picked her up in his arms."

"The Owl had arms? Did he have any wings?"

"I don't know," Marcus admitted, sounding a little confused. "Maybe his wings changed into arms. I can't remember."

"Go on."

"But he picked her up in his arms and he began running through the woods. He ran for a long time. Then he put the woman down on the ground. She was crying. He put his hand over her mouth and told her not to cry. He laid down on top of her, and after a few minutes he got up. She wasn't crying anymore. It looked like she was asleep.

"Then he picked her up and began running again. After a while he stopped and put her on the ground. This time he put her on the ground next to her friend. They were both asleep. He covered them with branches and then flew away."

Lansing studied Marcus for a few minutes. He remembered Ned Koteen's comment about how much trouble the Baltazars were having with their son. He could understand their concerns after listening to his "dream." "You said you have dreams, but don't know what they mean for a couple of days. What helped you understand this dream?"

"On the radio they said someone was looking for two girls lost in the mountains. They said it was up in Chama Meadows. That's when I knew what my dream meant."

Lansing thought about the short press release his office had put out. It included the names of both girls. That explained how Marcus knew one of the names. The rest of the story Marcus could have concocted after he heard the radio report. Koteen had hinted that the boy suffered from emotional problems. The explosion John Baltazar had survived, the murder of old

Esteban, the emotional pressures Marcus must be experiencing all added up to one screwed-up little kid as far as Lansing was concerned.

"Have you told anyone else this story?"

Marcus shook his head. "Because I didn't think they would believe me."

"Why do you think I would believe you?"

"Because I can prove my dream was true."

"How are you going to do that?"

"I can show you where the Owl laid them down."

43

LANSING SLOWED HIS JEEP AS HE APPROACHED the turnoff for the Meadows. He could see his young companion intently studying the mountains above them.

"No," Marcus said. "Don't turn here."

"This is how we get to the Meadows."

"We need to go north some more."

Lansing was hoping he wasn't chasing his own tail. He had two men locked up in his jail who probably had the answers he was looking for.

There were two reasons he was taking Marcus into the mountains. The first was that Marcus stuck by his story. Lansing tried to trip him up on his tale a half dozen times, but the boy never wavered from the original version. The second was that over his twenty years in law enforcement, Lansing had developed a sixth sense. He had learned that whenever he had a hunch about something, more times than not, the hunch was correct. As bizarre as Marcus's story was, Lansing thought there was some truth to it.

Two miles farther down the highway Marcus pointed at the forest above them. "It's up there."

"The turnoff to the Girl Scout camp is just ahead. We can turn there."

The road leading up to the camp was dirt and gravel, but it was better maintained than the road leading into the Meadows. During the summer months it was used constantly and had to accommodate school buses bringing Girl Scouts from as far away as Las Cruces and Carlsbad.

By road it was five miles from the highway to the main camp. After the first mile the gravel ribbon began to zigzag back and forth because of the steep grade. During the drive Marcus studied the woods on either side of the road, as if he were looking for some specific marker.

"Let me know when it's time to stop," Lansing said.

"Okay," Marcus muttered, concentrating on their surroundings.

It took ten minutes to reach the main camping area from the highway. When they got there Lansing brought his Jeep to a stop. Dozens of girls were spread out around the compound, subdivided into little groups, working on projects that would earn them merit badges. To Lansing it was a misnomer to call the area a campground. There were no tents. Instead, there were twenty little cabins equipped with electricity, a large communal bathhouse with flushing toilets, and a pavilion that doubled as a cafeteria and community center.

"All right, son. Now what?"

Marcus studied the area intently. He focused on the far side of the compound where the sleeping cabins were concentrated. He pointed. "Over there. On the other side of those buildings."

The main "camping" area was blocked to vehicular traffic. Lansing knew that behind the cabins a forestry road descended down the far side of the mountain. It had been built to provide easy access to the forest in case of a fire. Fortunately, it had been seldom used. To get to the road, however, Lansing would have to drive through the middle of the compound.

"How much farther?"

"I'm not sure."

"Can we walk there from here?"

"Yeah, I think so."

Lansing and his guide left the Jeep in the parking area next to a half dozen cars and the camp bus. Halfway across the grounds they were intercepted by one of the camp counselors, an attractive woman in her late twenties, dressed in shorts and a T-shirt sporting the Girl scout emblem.

"Can I help you?" the counselor asked cheerily.

"Uh, no, not really," Lansing said. "We're looking for someone."

"One of our girls?"

"No. There are a couple of campers missing from Chama Meadows. We understand they might have been sighted close to the camp here."

"We haven't seen anyone around here like that. If you want I can ask some of the other counselors."

"That won't be necessary. We were just walking through the camp to get to the forestry road."

"Okay, Sheriff. If there's anything we can do to help let me know. My name is Cindy. I'm the chief counselor here."

"Thanks, Cindy. Hopefully, this won't take very long."

He and Marcus proceeded past the cabins and started down the one-lane road. Every few years the forestry service came along and cleared the brush and saplings from the road to make sure it was usable. Lansing could tell it was time for them to make another visit.

Marcus didn't seem to be in a hurry. He was still

concentrating on the woods around them, studying the undergrowth on either side of their path.

A hundred yards from the compound the boy stopped. He stood motionless, as if he were listening for something. He slowly turned to his left and looked down the mountain. Without a word, he pointed below them.

A shudder ran down Lansing's spine. He looked back at the camp, then down the slope. He had been there before. Years earlier. It was an experience he couldn't forget, as hard as he tried. Even in the security of bright sunlight, he felt an eerie pall envelop him.

"Are you sure?"

Marcus only nodded as he kept his finger pointed toward the forest below them.

"How far?"

Marcus shook his head. He didn't know.

"All right. Let's go."

Lansing stepped off the road and started to descend the steep hillside. He had gone thirty feet when he turned to see how his companion was doing. Marcus still stood on the road.

"What's wrong?"

Marcus shook his head. His mouth was set in a frown and his bright eyes were clouded in fear.

"It's all right, son. There's nothing to be afraid of. I'm right here."

The boy looked as though he were about to turn and head back to the camp.

"Marcus, I can't do this alone. I'm going to need your help. Come on, son."

Marcus hesitated a moment, then took a deep breath and started down the hill behind the sheriff.

The slope was steep, just the way Lansing had remembered it. And even in the daylight it was a trick to walk down the incline without slipping. The line of trees that marked the edge of the forestry road had just disappeared above them when Marcus stopped. "Sheriff, I think they're over there." The boy had lagged behind Lansing twenty to thirty feet during the descent. Lansing looked at Marcus. He was pointing toward a knot of bushes fifty feet away and a little below them.

"Okay. You wait here."

Lansing worked his way along the slope, using trees and saplings to keep from sliding down the hill. When he reached the tangle of bushes he realized they had not grown there. He could tell someone had stacked them recently. The leaves hadn't started shriveling from lack of water or nutrients.

He began pulling the branches off the pile. A wave of fear and horror began to overtake him. He had lived this scene before. It was a nightmare he knew he would never escape, and he was going through it all over again.

He could feel the sweat break out on his forehead like a fever. He worked harder and harder as he tore away at the dead limbs, hoping he would never reach the bottom of the pile.

Sheri Prentiss and her friend, Barbara Good, lay side by side. They were half-naked, stripped below their waists. The pale, soft skin of their faces and legs was scratched and bruised. What clothing there was was soaked in blood. Their throats had been cut.

Lansing turned away and leaned against a tree for support. He buried his face in his hand and squeezed his eyes shut. A deep, primal urge overwhelmed him. He wanted to scream in rage. He knew he wouldn't. He had promised himself years before that he would never let his emotions overtake him again.

He was a lawman. He was the Lone Ranger. There was no room for emotions.

"You bastard!" he swore under his breath. "You bastard! You bastard! You can't be doing this again. You son of a bitch, you're supposed to be dead. Do you hear me? You're dead! You're dead!"

44

DR. MILES UNDERSTOOD WHY THE JICARILLA tribe never had managed to make a go of Stone Lake Lodge. The gravel road winding through the mountains was tortuous. In a few places it was wide enough for only a single vehicle. She suspected that when the summer monsoon season hit it would be nearly impassable.

She was confident that she was wasting her time. In fact, she was embarrassed by the thought that she was even making the drive. She had returned to her sister's house in Dulce after her breakfast meeting with Sheridan and Lansing. She had considered that encounter fruitless.

Sheridan seemed to be chasing shadows. She guessed his previous experience had been investigating white-collar crime, because that's what he wanted to turn the Jicarilla investigation into.

She disliked Lansing on general principles.

With a doctorate in history she had come to understand the inevitability of change. Man was not a stagnant creature, bound by the shackles of instinct and inherited traits. He was a thinking creature, an opportunistic creature. He was curious, and he was driven by more than the mere need to survive.

Miles thought about her own people. At some point in the past, a point shrouded by the mists of time, a group of people collectively known as the Athapaskans crossed a thousand-mile-wide prairie, now called the Bering Strait. They settled in a new land that must have been richer in game or more pleasant in climate than their homeland. For twelve thousand years they lived in the same mountains and valleys as their fathers and their fathers' fathers.

Then came change. It was a change that affected the entire globe. Between 800 and 1200 C.E., entire nations were on the move. It was the time of the great Muslim expansion from North Africa into Europe. It was the era of the Norse conquests. The epoch of the Mongol hordes was about to commence.

In what the white man called the "New World," the Incas were building an empire in South America. The Mayan were building great city-states around the Yucatan Peninsula. The Anasazi, a culture already a thousand years old, began to build the great houses and kivas of Chaco Canyon. And large groups of the Athapaskans, after twelve thousand years, began to leave their "new" homeland.

They came in groups, the Navajo, the Chiricahua, the Mescalero, the Jicarilla. For whatever reason they came, following the great Rocky Mountains southward. Over a period of nearly seven hundred years they drifted into the southwest, settling in the deserts of Mexico and Arizona, the canyons of Utah, and the mountains of New Mexico. They hunted buffalo on the plains. They wove baskets from desert yucca. They learned a new way of life. They changed.

Miles thought it was inane how the revisionists and the politically correct had united to trash Columbus on the five-hundredth anniversary of his crossing the

Atlantic. True, she didn't agree with the terminology *discovery*. But Columbus was no better or worse than any of the other white men who followed. And if he hadn't crossed the Atlantic in 1492, someone would have the next year, or the year after that. There was proof enough that the Norse had visited the continent two hundred years earlier. There was always the possibility they might have returned. It was all part of the inevitability of history.

What she couldn't do, even as a historian, was forgive. Millions of Native Americans died because of the diseases the white man brought. That was an inevitability. But millions also died because of the tyranny and greed of the white man. That was what she couldn't forgive.

The white man took the land, enslaved the natives, and forced his version of civilization on cultures thousands of years old. The white man wrote laws that benefited him and disenfranchised the "lower" races. And any time a law was broken it was only natural to accuse an "Indian"—another term Miles took issue with.

That was the source of Miles's animosity toward Lansing. He not only represented the land-grabbing white man because his family had homesteaded in her country, he was the embodiment of the laws that were used so capriciously against her people.

Her only run-in with Lansing had been ten years earlier. Sheriff Fulton and his chief deputy, Lansing, had accused a friend of hers, a childhood friend, Huero Mundo, of a heinous crime. She ended up spending her entire life savings paying for his legal defense. Although Mundo was acquitted he was returned to prison for other crimes he didn't commit. That's where he died.

She hated Lansing for that.

Before he was taken away Mundo thanked her for

all of the help. He asked her not to write to him. It would cause him too much pain. It would remind him of the freedom he was about to lose. However, he told her that no matter what happened in prison, he would return. When he did he would send her a signal. She asked what kind of signal, but he just shook his head. She would know it when she saw it.

When the news came that Mundo had died in a prison fire, she quit looking for his signal.

Miles was a pragmatist. She only half-believed in an afterlife and was thoroughly convinced divine intervention played no part in the events of human history. She believed in religion, but only as a foundation block of a culture. Religion codified a people's belief system and moral values. It provided a past, explained the present, and promised a future to the people who followed it. To Miles, religion was as necessary to a culture as language. To her, preserving the Jicarilla Apache religion, along with its mythology and archaic supernatural beliefs, meant preserving her culture and her heritage.

But just because she preserved it did not mean she subscribed to it. There were no powers in the world greater than those defined by nature and physics.

Huero Mundo had been dead for nearly eight years. People didn't come back from the grave. Despite her Christian beliefs, she had doubts about the Resurrection.

Now Miles wasn't sure what to believe in.

When Lansing laid the feather on the table that morning, all she could do was stare at it. He said there had been one at Baltazar's cabin and one on the ground next to Koteen.

When Mundo went away he gave her something to remember him by: an owl's feather. The owl had been his totem, his guardian. She couldn't help but wonder: Was this also his signal that he had returned?

Stone Lake was located on the eastern side of the reservation. In the summertime the mountain pastures around the lake were used for grazing sheep. That's where she had spent her summers growing up, helping her grandparents with the flock. That's where she got to know Mundo. They had spent eight consecutive summers together.

Whenever she thought of her youth she thought of the shimmering lake and the mountain breezes. She thought of the games of tag and hide-and-seek she had played with him. She thought of the secret places only the two of them knew about, the places they would go to tell each other their innermost thoughts and desires.

Their youth, unfortunately, came to an end. Miles went away to college. Mundo left the reservation. Nearly twenty years passed before they saw each other again, and then it was with Mundo locked in the jail in Las Palmas.

Miles knew that if, indeed, Mundo had returned he would come back to their place of youth.

She parked in front of the abandoned lodge. It had been built after she went away to college. For ten years the tribe had tried to use it as a hunting and fishing lodge for tourists, but it had been too remote and too expensive to operate. Even the successful Cuartelejo Management Company couldn't make it profitable, so it was closed.

It had been vacant now for years and had fallen into disrepair. However, if Mundo was back he would need a place to stay. The old lodge was as good a place for Miles to look as any.

The weathered boards of the steps creaked under her weight. The veranda that ran across the front of the lodge was awash in pine needles blown in from the nearby forest. The windows on the front doors were cracked. One had a bullet hole through it. From the outside, the interior of the lodge looked dark and uninviting.

Miles hesitated as she reached for the doorknob. This was ridiculous, and she felt like a fool. There was no one here. Still, she had come this far. The least she could do was look inside.

She tried the knob. It wasn't locked. She pushed the door open and walked inside.

The lobby of the lodge looked like a great den. A large stone fireplace took up one wall. The room was paneled with rough-hewn planks, and exposed beams supported the cathedral ceiling. The place was bare, all of the furniture hauled away to be used in other endeavors. It smelled old, musty, and unused.

"Hello?" Miles called, almost hoping there wouldn't be an answer.

"I was hoping you would come, Vicky."

Vicky! She hadn't been called that in years. Not since . . .

She turned to the voice. A man slowly emerged from a dark corner. In the dim light she could see he had long, straight hair that hung below his shoulders. It was all black, except for a single streak of white about an inch wide. As he came closer she could see the scar on the right side of his face. It ran from the shock of white hair to below his collar. Even in the dim light of the lobby his dark eyes flashed as if they were illuminated from within.

"Huero!" she whispered, tears welling in her eyes. "It *is* you!"

45

 VICKY HAD A HUNDRED QUESTIONS SHE WANTED to ask. Before she could, Mundo put his fingers to his lips for her to be silent. He motioned her to follow as he led her through the lodge to the back exit.

Once they were outside he guided her through the woods for another ten minutes. The path was no more than an animal trail, but Mundo seemed familiar with it. After a short time the trail split. The right track went deeper into the forest. The left track, the one that they followed, took them to a secluded cove on the lake. Vicky recognized it immediately. It was one of the secret places of their youth.

Mundo seated himself on a boulder at the edge of the water. "Now we can talk."

"How did you find this place?" Vicky asked. "I had forgotten all about it."

"I looked for it when I came back. I had to find it. It was the memory of this place, and places like it, that kept me alive while I was in prison."

"Prison." Vicky became aware of the fact that they

were in the present. "What happened in prison? They said you died."

"I did, Vicky."

"Wh-what?"

"But don't believe all of those stories about a bright light that guides you to the holy place. Don't believe them when they tell you your loved ones are standing there with open arms, ready to receive you." He picked up a rock and tossed it angrily into the water. "There is a hell. I saw it."

"What are you talking about?"

"How did you hear that I died?"

"They said you were in a prison hospital, after an accident. They said you burned to death in your bed."

Mundo shook his head. "That was later. That was after I had died and come back."

"I don't understand."

"When they sent me back to prison they locked me in solitary confinement. They said I was a risk. That I might escape again. They said they didn't want to take any chances.

"For two years I was locked in a cell that had a bed, a toilet, a sink, and a single light bulb in the ceiling. My only human contacts were the two guards that led me to the exercise yard every day. My hands were in cuffs and my feet were in shackles. I was allowed to shuffle back and forth in a yard twenty feet by forty feet. It was the only time I saw the sun. It was the only time I could breathe the air that told me one day there would be freedom."

"It must have been awful."

"No. Out in the yard, even in shackles, that was the best part. The bad part was in my cell, alone. You have no idea what loneliness can do to a man. It went on for two years. They thought they were going to break me. But I wouldn't let them. I don't know how long I had been there before I realized there was something I could do.

"Old Cesar TeCube had said that in the old days the medicine men had learned how to leave their bodies. It was a combination of prayer and meditation. They would burn tobacco and other leaves in a fire, and the odor would help them concentrate. Of course, I didn't have the luxury of starting a fire in my cell. But I had all the time in the world.

"I began telling myself all the old stories from our childhood. Out loud. As if there were children sitting around me, holding ears of corn to help them remember the stories I was telling them.

"I began with the beginning, how we emerged onto the earth from the inner world. I told the story of how White Painted Woman became pregnant by the sun. I told the story of how her son, Born of Thunder, Slayer-of-Enemies came to life. I told all of his stories. How he defeated the Wind, cut him into pieces, and tossed him to the four corners of the earth.

"In my mind there was a great fire. All the old chiefs were there, and we performed the Bear Dance together.

"And when I had been through all the cycles and all the stories, I began again. And then again."

Vicky sat hypnotized by Mundo and his story. She was transported to her youth, when she would listen to him for hours. He had been a medicine man in training. His grandfather, Cesar TeCube, had been teaching him the ways of the *tsanati* since he was a small child. Mundo would practice on Vicky, repeating all the stories his grandfather had told him. Telling her secrets only the wise men of the tribe knew. Throughout their entire youth his only goal in life had been to become a great medicine man.

"Then came the day of my redemption. I was taken to the yard, as any other day. When they closed the door behind me I just stood there for a moment. The air seemed different. It was still, heavy. So thick you could hardly breathe. I stepped to the center of the yard. I could feel a presence with me.

"That was when I heard someone call my name. I looked up. On the wall of the exercise yard was an owl. He was looking down at me. He blinked once and called my name again.

"Before I could answer him there was a rumble of thunder, then a great flash of light. I could feel a thousand suns burning in my soul. I was transported, not to the holy place, but to a place of darkness. I could see nothing, but I could hear the moans and screams of tortured souls.

"I cried out, 'What is this place?' And a voice told me, it was oblivion. It was an eternal solitary confinement, where there was no light, no sound, no feeling. There was only the soul and all the thoughts and fears and unfulfilled hopes that the soul experienced in life. Plus the knowledge that nothingness would follow, forever.

" 'Is this my reward?' I asked. 'I followed the ancient ways. I prayed the ancient prayers.'

" 'No,' the voice told me. 'Knowledge is born out of pain. Wisdom can spring only from despair.' He told me I would know the joy of the holy place only when I understood the misery that could befall us all.

" 'What is my path?' I asked. 'What is the road to redemption?'

"The voice said three words: *Rebirth, renewal, retribution.*"

"What did they mean?" Vicky asked, oblivious to anything in the world except Mundo and his voice.

"I knew what rebirth meant when I opened my eyes. I was in a bed. A hospital bed. The room was white, antiseptic. I don't know how long I had been there. Weeks. Months maybe. I'm not sure.

"People came into the room, and I closed my eyes so

they wouldn't know I was awake. They were talking about me. One came over to my bed and began touching my face. I realized they were removing a bandage. The tape tore at my skin, but I knew I didn't dare move.

"The one working on my bandage said I had been struck by a bolt of lightning and that I had been in a coma since the accident. That by all rights I should be dead. The doctors were sure I would never recover.

"When they left the room I got up and stumbled to the mirror. That's when I first saw my face. The face you see now. The scar runs from my face, down my body, to the bottom of my foot. But don't feel sorry for me. It is not a scar of disfigurement. It is the symbol of my resurrection, my rebirth.

"I got back into bed. I had to think. What did it mean? I knew I had been reborn. But renewal, retribution. What did they mean?

"For two weeks I pretended I was still in a coma.

"When I was alone I exercised, walked, tried to rebuild my strength. The IV tubes were easy enough to disconnect. Having to leave the catheter in place was almost unbearable, but I couldn't let them know. And all the time I listened, trying to figure out where I was.

"I had been moved. The prison infirmary wasn't equipped to handle a man in my condition. I had been taken to a hospital at a minimum-security facility. They thought I was no longer a threat. They didn't think I could ever escape.

"Soon I was strong enough that I could have walked out of that place. But if I had, they would have come after me and put me back in solitary confinement. I knew I hadn't been given a new life to be imprisoned again.

"I began to explore the hospital. I stole clothes I could wear. I stashed food away. And then I waited. I knew the time would come. I waited for the signal, and finally it came.

"I was on the second floor of the hospital. There were a dozen rooms like mine, all filled with patients that were about to die. A fire started at the nurses' station. The corridor filled with smoke and flames, and I knew it was my time to make my escape.

"I crawled down the hallway until I came to the little storage room where I had hidden my things. I changed clothes, then ran out into the hall. The wing where I had been staying was on fire. There was no way they could have saved me or any of the others.

"I ran to the fire exit and climbed down the stairs. When I got to the ground I began running, and I kept running until daylight. In the confusion no one missed me. A few days later I heard they found a body in the room I had been in. It must have been an orderly trying to get me out.

"I thought it was a great joke on the prison. Three orderlies, prisoners themselves and all trustees, had escaped in the confusion. Of course, they were all recaptured within a couple of days. However, the authorities thought four had gotten away. They're still looking for the one whose body was found in my room, I guess. Meanwhile, I'm dead, buried, and forgotten."

46

VICKY THOUGHT ABOUT MUNDO'S STORY FOR A few moments. "But, Huero, that was eight years ago. Where have you been?"

"Ah," Mundo nodded. "That was the time of renewal. I didn't know what that meant at first. When I was in the hospital all of my energies were concentrated on escaping. Once I was free I had to figure out what renewal meant.

"The minimum-security prison was located near Muskogee, Oklahoma. We have many brothers who live in that part of the state: Cherokee, Choctaw, Seminole. I took a job as a laborer at a ranch owned by a Cherokee elder. My plan had been to earn enough money to return to New Mexico. But while I was working there I was invited to a powwow.

"A great many Cherokee came from all over the United States to attend. They performed their dances and ceremonies, and I was taken back to the time of my youth. Even though many of their songs were in Cherokee, I understood their meaning. I also understood what renewal meant. I had forgotten that I had planned to become a great medicine man. The white man had beaten that dream out of me.

"But when I heard our brothers pray to the Great Spirit who guides us all, when I heard their pledges to never forget the ancient ways, I knew I had to follow my destiny.

"At night, after their dances, I would sit with their elders and listen to their stories. Sometimes I was asked to tell the stories of our people. As we traded the secrets of creation I came to understand that my chosen path to seek the truth would be a long road. Our Cherokee brothers came from a land that bordered the great eastern ocean. They understood things about the great waters that our grandfathers could never know. So I sat and listened and learned their secrets. I was enlightened. I knew that to be the greatest *tsanati* the Jicarilla people have ever known, I would have to seek the wisdom of others. Many others.

"I stayed with the Cherokee for six months. When I felt I had learned all they had to teach, I moved on. First I went north. I talked with the wise men of the Omaha and Winnebago tribes. I spent time with the Brulé and Crow, with the Cheyenne and Sioux. I worked small jobs here and there so that I could dedicate my life to listening to the wisdom of the elders.

"Weeks, months, years, they were all the same. I prayed at Wounded Knee. I fasted for a week in the Black Hills. I saw visions of Crazy Horse and Sitting Bull. They spoke to me. They told me the sacrifices I made then would benefit all the races of red men.

"I hunted buffalo and antelope. I found a race of men in the northwest who spoke our native tongue, or one very close. I caught salmon in their streams and shared their sweat lodges. I had great visions there.

"Vicky, I cannot tell you how all-consuming such a quest can be. I had forgotten there was supposed to be an end to the journey. All that mattered was the journey itself. All I cared about was the search for knowledge. Each time I peered under a new rock or looked around the next tree, I learned something I had never known before. Every time an elder spoke, his words lifted my soul onto another plain of enlightenment."

"It must have been wonderful," Vicky whispered.

"It was," Mundo nodded. "And it wasn't. There is one great truth I came to understand. For every level of joy we experience in life, there is an equal and opposite plane of despair. They go hand in hand. A soul cannot know happiness unless it has experienced sadness as well."

"The Chinese call it the yin and the yang."

"The Lakota say it is *iktomi* and *iya*, wisdom and malevolence. They are brothers, born of the same egg. When I accepted the joy and despair within me, when I finally acknowledged my own good and evil, I knew I was approaching the end of my quest and it was time to return home."

Above the two of them came a rustling of branches. Vicky looked up to see a great horned owl perched on a limb twenty feet above them. The bird was large, larger than any owl Vicky had ever seen before. It looked down at her—almost with disapproval, she thought.

Mundo emitted a low, guttural *ho-o-o*. The great bird spread its wings, then leaned forward and glided to a boulder a few feet from the medicine man. Once the owl landed, it turned to face Vicky, as if it were keeping an eye on her.

Vicky had grown up around animals, both domestic and wild. She did not harbor any fear of them, because she felt she understood them. This owl, however, was different. There was an air of malevolence in its stare.

"The animals speak to me now," Mundo explained. "And I speak to them. *Nascha* and his brothers are my eyes and ears in the forest. They are my lanterns in the darkness. They are the wings for my soul."

47

THE PRESENCE OF *NASCHA* AND HIS OMINOUS stare brought Vicky back to present reality. It was an owl's feather that had led her to Mundo. What's more, an owl's feather was found at each murder scene. She looked from Mundo to the owl and back again.

"Rebirth and renewal," Vicky said. "And now you're having your retribution."

"All I ever wanted in life was to be a medicine man for our tribe. A good medicine man. A *tsanati*, a healer. The white man tried to take that away from me. Nearly twenty years ago they sent me to prison for a crime I didn't commit. That was partially my fault. I never should have left the reservation. But when I escaped and came back to the reservation, I thought I would be safe, protected by my own people. That didn't happen.

"Esteban Baltazar and Ned Koteen turned against me. I had the right, by our people's law, to punish them for what they had done."

"Sheriff Lansing thinks the same person killed the old sheriff, Fulton. He found an owl's feather at his house. That's how I knew to come looking for you."

Mundo thought for a moment. "Lansing. So he does not think Fulton took his own life. That is too bad. It seems it should have been obvious that was what happened."

"You left the feather."

"It should have been nothing to him. A piece of litter. Trash.

"But yes, Fulton too. When Baltazar and Koteen betrayed me they also conspired with Fulton, who said I committed another terrible crime. I know now why they did that. They were afraid of me. They were afraid of the powers I had, the powers that I might gain.

"I could never return here and live in peace if any of them still lived. They had to be punished for what they did."

"What about the old woman, Fulton's wife? Why did she have to die?"

"It's hard for me to explain how much I have learned these past few years, Vicky. To become a great healer, a *tsanati* must also learn about the illnesses that can befall a body. He must be able to look into a person's eyes and see the sickness within.

"I did the Fulton woman a great service. She was dying of a cancer. In a few years it would have racked her frail body with tremendous pain and she would have suffered greatly. I could have let her live, but I took pity on her. It was better that she find peace in death, next to the body of her husband."

Mundo spoke so softly and earnestly that Vicky knew he could be telling her only what he really believed. "You know that the FBI is looking for the man who killed Baltazar and Koteen."

Mundo nodded. "I know. I saw you talking with the agent at Esteban's funeral."

"You were there?"

"I had my respects to pay as well. A true warrior always honors his enemies. But I am not worried about the FBI, or anyone else for that matter. I have learned too much for them to be able to stop me."

"What about me, Huero? The FBI is using me as a consultant. If I should suspect someone of these murders, it's my obligation to tell them."

"There have been no murders. Murder is the unjustified taking of a life. What I have done has been honorable. Honorable in our ancient traditions. Those are the laws and the traditions I hold most dear.

"When a Spaniard or a Comanche took the life of a *diné*, we did not turn the cheek. We did not sit and pray for the Great Spirit to avenge us. We took a life in return.

"I have died once at the hands of these men. I would not let it happen again. Retribution is mine."

"Why have you told me this? What am I supposed to do?"

He walked over to the spot where she was sitting and knelt, taking her hand in his. "Of all the people I have known in the world, you alone, Vicky, I trust. You alone know the true Huero Mundo. You know I speak the truth. I have told you these things because I know you will not betray me. I know you will do nothing."

"How do you know I will do nothing?"

"Because I love you, as much now as when we were children. And because you love me. Our souls were joined as one many years ago. That is why I never took a wife. That is why you never took a husband.

"Now that I have returned we can be together."

She attempted to reach out and touch the scar on his face, but he turned his head so she couldn't. She gently took his chin in her fingers and turned his head back. When he faced her again, she kissed him.

"You're right, Huero," she whispered. "I do love you. And I could never betray you."

"AGENT SHERIDAN, THANK YOU FOR RETURNING my call," Lansing said. "Has your Santa Fe office been in touch with you yet?"

"No," Sheridan responded. There was an edge of impatience to his voice. "I've been out conducting interviews all afternoon. I suppose this is about the Fulton case."

"Not directly, no." Lansing had been pushed to the limits of his own patience. He didn't care if Agent Sheridan thought himself above local police matters. The current problem was under federal jurisdiction. "We have two more murders on our hands."

"What do you mean 'we have'?"

"I found the bodies of two campers in Carson National Forest. The forestry service is sending a couple of investigators, but this is beyond their capabilities. They told me to get in touch with your offices. Director Williams said he would have a team up here tomorrow. In the meantime I was supposed to contact you."

"What specifically for?" Sheridan's voice had softened to a more apologetic tone.

"There's a strong likelihood these two deaths are linked to the Baltazar and Koteen murders. They were two college girls. It appears they were sexually molested, and their throats had been cut, just like the other two."

Sheridan cleared his throat uncomfortably. "Where did you say the bodies were found?"

"Carson National Forest. About five miles from the Jicarilla reservation. I have the crime scene roped off and a deputy keeping an eye on it."

"Where are the bodies now?"

"I had them brought down to the Las Palmas Funeral Home."

"Would it be possible for me to take a look at them?"

"I would appreciate it if you would."

"I'll leave Dulce now," Sheridan said. "I'll meet you at the funeral home in about forty-five minutes."

"Good. I'll see you there."

Lansing's day had started off bad and was getting progressively worse. For the moment he had to step away from the Fulton murders. The forensics team from the State Bureau of Investigation was combing their residence for any clues. He had sent Jack Rivera to interview the Fultons' neighbors, but he knew that was going to be a bust. Their closest neighbor lived nearly a half mile away. They would have heard nothing, probably had seen nothing. In the meantime there was nothing he personally could contribute to the investigation.

In a week, maybe two, he would allow himself the luxury of grieving for the loss of his friends Bill and Emily Fulton and Ned Koteen, as well as for Esteban Baltazar. Maybe he would even have a moment to think about the two young women whose bodies he'd found, have a chance to mourn the wasting of their lives. But he didn't have time now.

He had to step back and look at everything that was going on. He had to forget the fact that he had lost friends. He had to lock his emotions away and play the objective lawman.

It wasn't every day that someone was killed in San Phillipe County. Suddenly, he had six murders in as many days. That wasn't coincidence.

Four of the deaths had resulted from slit throats. That wasn't coincidence. That was a pattern.

Lansing was totally convinced Bill Fulton had been murdered. The bump on the back of his head didn't just get there. The pathologist could second-guess all he wanted: Lansing knew Bill could never do anything to hurt Emily. And the ex-sheriff was still too full of life to commit suicide. That left only one explanation.

He had to admit, trying to use a feather to link the Fulton murders with the Apache murders was flimsy. Sheridan was right. It wasn't the same M.O. He had to come up with something a lot more substantial.

He looked at the clock. It was four-thirty. That would make it five-thirty in Oklahoma. All the state offices would be closed already. He wanted to make a call. He knew it would be a waste of time because he already knew the answer. But he wanted to ask the question anyway. Was Huero Mundo really dead?

He jumped when the phone rang on his desk. "Lansing." He was irritated at himself for being on edge.

"I hope I'm not interrupting anything," Margarite apologized.

"Not right this second." Hearing her voice was the best tonic he could think of for his nerves.

"Sometimes it takes a while for news to reach the pueblo. I just heard about Sheriff Fulton and his wife. I'm awfully sorry, Lansing."

"Yeah, thanks."

"Tough day?"

"And it doesn't look like it's going to let up anytime soon. We found the two girls we had been looking for."

"Were they all right?"

"No. They were dead. Someone killed them."

"Oh, my God, no! Your search teams found them?"

"No—Damn!"

"What's wrong?"

"I forgot about something. I've had someone waiting for me in the lobby for the last hour."

"I think I'm keeping you from more important things. Is there anything I can do?"

"I wish there were."

"Maybe we can talk later?"

"I hope so. I'll call you."

He hung up the phone, regretfully. There was nothing he would rather do at the moment than hide someplace with Margarite and let the rest of the world go to hell. He also knew it wasn't going to happen.

He went to the door of his office and opened it. "How about coming in here? We need to talk, Marcus."

49

IN THE CHAOS OF THE AFTERNOON MARCUS Baltazar had become an afterthought to Lansing. The sheriff had to recall his search parties. The paramedics and Deputy Hanna were instructed to report immediately to the Girl Scout camp. Knowing full well what awaited him, Sheri Prentiss's father had insisted on coming along. In a way, Lansing was grateful for that. One of the worst duties his job entailed was telling a parent or spouse they had just lost a loved one.

When Gabe arrived he still had a few sandwiches that had been prepared that morning. Lansing had given them to Marcus and asked him to stay out of their way while they recovered the bodies.

Marcus obeyed every instruction he was given. When they returned to Las Palmas he sat quietly in the reception lobby and waited for Lansing's next order. He had been waiting for over an hour.

As Lansing ushered the boy into his office he couldn't help but feel a little guilty. He had literally abandoned the poor kid. He had Marcus sit in the chair in front of his desk.

"Were those sandwiches enough? Would you like something else?"

"I'm okay," Marcus said.

Lansing studied the boy for a long moment. "Marcus, I want you to tell me the truth. I promise no one is going to get angry with you about any other stories you've told. But right now I have to know, how did you know where those bodies were?"

"Sheriff, I already told you the truth."

"Son, I know you think you dreamed all that, but I want you to think back. Maybe you were in the woods. Maybe you saw someone carrying the bodies. Or maybe you overheard a conversation. You heard someone say that they had killed those girls and hid them in the woods near the Girl Scout camp.

"Sometimes we hear or see something so terrible we try to block it out of our minds. We try to forget everything about it. But our minds won't let us. So when the memory of that event comes back to us, it doesn't seem real. It seems more like a dream. Couldn't something like that have happened?"

"No," Marcus said with certainty. "I couldn't have been in the woods with the Owl because I've never been to the Girl Scout camp. I didn't know where it was till today. I've only been with my parents and my friends the last few days. None of them even knew about the girls being lost in the woods.

"I told you the truth. I had a dream about the Owl and what he did."

"How did you know where to look for them? There are thousands of acres of forest out there."

"It felt like a campfire when it's cold outside. If you sit sideways the part of your body facing the fire is warm. The other side is cold. That's what it felt like when we drove into the mountains. And the closer we got the hotter I felt."

Lansing shook his head. He had read enough about

ESP to suspect there might be something behind it. But this wasn't just ESP. This was "remote locating." This was a mind tuning in to events miles away involving people Marcus didn't even know. Lansing wasn't willing to accept Marcus's explanation. Not yet, anyway, despite the fact that the boy had led him directly to the spot where the two bodies were hidden.

There was something else bothering him. *Why that spot?* He pushed that question aside for the moment.

"Okay, Marcus. For the time being I'm going to have to accept your explanation. This Owl-man you keep talking about. Do you think you would recognize him if you saw him?"

"I'm not sure. I never saw his face."

"What about the feeling you got? Like when we were looking in the mountains. Do you think you might get it again if you were near him?"

Marcus shrugged. "I don't know."

"Come with me a minute."

Lansing took Marcus to the dayroom, where Pedro Gomez was still handcuffed to one of the desks. Gomez jumped up when the door opened.

"Hey, Sheriff. How much longer you going to chain me up like a dog? I have my rights."

Lansing ignored his prisoner's protest. He turned to Marcus. "Does this man look familiar?"

"Hey, kid, you don't know me! You never saw me nowhere, so don't try to say I did something."

"Ignore him," Lansing instructed.

Marcus only shook his head. "No, that's not him."

"You damned right! You see, Sheriff? You should let me go!"

Lansing closed the door to the room and led the boy to the jail cells. Julio Martinez was stretched out on the metal bed, sound asleep.

"Julio!" Lansing yelled. "Wake up!"

Martinez stretched lazily and sat up. "Is it time to eat?"

"Not yet. Stand up so we can see you."

Martinez stood and stretched again. Lansing brought Marcus closer for a better look.

"What about him?"

Marcus shook his head again. "No. That's not him either."

"All right, Julio. You can go back to sleep."

"When do we eat?" Julio said, yawning. "I'm hungry."

"Later." Lansing closed the door to the cell area and took Marcus back to his office. He didn't think Martinez or Gomez was capable of murder, but Marcus's failure to ID them wasn't enough to absolve them either. He didn't think Marcus would be able to recognize the real murderer in the first place.

"I have one more question for you, Marcus. What in the hell am I supposed to do with you?"

"What do you mean?"

"By law your parents are responsible for you. If for some reason they can't take care of you, you become a ward of the Jicarilla tribe. You're a minor and I'm obligated to return you to your own people."

"If you do they're going to send me away."

"Because of your dreams?"

Marcus nodded. "And because they are afraid. Everyone on the reservation is afraid."

"Do you have a lot of dreams?"

"Yes."

"What else have you dreamed about?"

"I had a dream that the oil well where my father worked would explode. I cried and told my mother. She thought it was just a nightmare, so she called the clinic. They made her bring me in, and they gave me a shot so I would sleep. I didn't want to sleep. I wanted to tell them about the explosion."

"Any others?"

"I had a dream Captain Koteen was going to die. I tried to warn him. I told him to be careful because the Owl was looking for him."

"When did you tell him this?"

"The day of the big funeral. I left a note under his windshield wiper."

Lansing remembered the note and the grim look on Koteen's face when he read it. "You've had other dreams?"

"The night my great-grandfather died. I saw that in my dreams. I wanted to go out to his house that night, but my mother said no. She had just dropped him off and everything was fine. I kept asking to go there, but my parents wouldn't take me. Finally, the next morning they said we could go. But it was too late."

"The dream you had about your great-grandfather, what did you see?"

Marcus paused, almost surprised someone wanted to hear about one of his dreams. He began to describe what he had seen. His eyes focused on some far, unseen horizon as he spoke. As he told the story tears welled up in his eyes and his voice quavered. "*Náhánálí* was walking up the road to his house. His house was dark and it was night out. Just before he got to his porch all the stars and the moon disappeared. He stopped and looked into a tree. He stopped because he heard an owl call his name. Whenever an owl calls your name, that means you're going to die. That's how I knew *Náhánálí* was going to die. And it's because of me that he did."

"It wasn't your fault."

"Yes, it was." Marcus reached inside his shirt and pulled out a small leather pouch. "Before he left my house he gave me this. It's his *jish*. He said I had to wear it, because it would protect me. If he hadn't given it to me he would have been safe. He wouldn't have died."

Marcus was crying now. Lansing reached into one of the drawers of his desk and produced a box of tissues. He handed several to the boy.

Marcus paused to blow his nose and wipe his eyes. "It was my fault that someone killed him, but I couldn't tell anyone. He told me to keep the *jish* close to me and never tell anyone I had it. He said it is very powerful. He said there was evil on the reservation and that the evil should never find it. He said we might not be able to defeat the evil if it has his *jish*."

Lansing had seen the medicine pouch before. It had been years earlier. He wasn't sure it held any particular powers, but he knew Esteban Baltazar believed it did. "Why are you showing it to me now?"

"Because you listened to me. Because I need your help. If my parents send me away I can't stop the evil."

Lansing thought back to the condition of Baltazar's house. It had been torn apart because someone was looking for something. John Baltazar didn't think anything had been taken. Maybe he didn't think about the *jish*. Maybe that's what the assailant was looking for.

"In your dream what happened to your great-grandfather when he went into his house?"

"I don't know. I woke up when the owl called his name. I was yelling for him not to go into his house. Then I heard his voice. He told me it was all right. He said he was doing what he had to do and that he wasn't afraid. He knew he was going to die. I didn't want him to die, but I couldn't stop it."

Lansing was a pragmatic lawman. Everything could be explained, broken down into its essential elements, and analyzed. He wasn't a psychiatrist, so he didn't have a lot of use for dreams and their meanings. But he was beginning to see Marcus's nightmares overlapping with the hard evidence he had seen.

"Do all your dreams have owls in them?"

"No. Not all."

Lansing considered his options: taking the boy into custody, returning him to his parents, or handing him over to the tribal authorities in hopes he wouldn't be sent away. He knew he didn't have the authority for the first option. He was pretty sure the tribal authorities would simply send him home. He was confident his only choice was to hand him over to his parents.

"Marcus, I'm afraid I'm going to have to send you home."

"What?"

"Before I do I'm going to have a talk with your parents. I don't know what's going on up at the reservation. I'm not sure what's going on around here. But you've been a big help to me. I'm going to ask your parents not to send you away. I may need your help again."

"Really?"

"Really." Lansing smiled. "What's your home phone number? I'll give them a call right now."

50

 LANSING HAD DEPUTY BARNS TAKE MARCUS back to the reservation. The Baltazars were at once grateful that they had found their son and perturbed that Lansing hadn't called them sooner. They had been looking for him since that morning, and with the recent deaths around Dulce their worries had been magnified.

Lansing had asked about their intentions to send Marcus away to school. John Baltazar didn't think their family business was any of Lansing's concern; however, it wouldn't be until the end of the summer. Before packing him off for home Lansing reassured Marcus that they both had time to work on changing his parents' minds. A lot could happen in a couple of months.

As Lansing was about to climb into his Jeep to meet Agent Sheridan at the funeral home, Velma pulled into the courthouse parking lot. A beaming C.J. waved from the passenger side. He wore a new ball cap embossed with the Phoenix Suns logo.

"Well, how was it?" Lansing asked as his son jumped from the car.

"It was great!" C.J. spouted. "We saw the demolition derby at the fairgrounds, then we went on a bunch of rides at the carnival. We had pizza and corn dogs. Then we stopped off and got some ice cream on the way back."

"Sounds like you know how to show a girl a good time," Lansing said, laughing.

"It really was fun, Sheriff," Velma said, standing next to the open door of her car. "I haven't had a time like that since I was in high school. C.J. can be my date anytime he wants. He was a perfect gentleman."

"I'm glad to hear that." Lansing noticed his son's blush when Velma mentioned he could be her date again. "Do I owe you anything?" he asked, reaching for his wallet.

Velma waved him off. "Absolutely not! This was my treat. But I've got to run. John's going to pick me up later."

Lansing caught the look on C.J.'s face. It was a combination of surprise and disappointment. Velma saw it too. The look on her own face told Lansing that she didn't know about C.J.'s strong, though adolescent, feelings toward her. She wiggled her index finger at the boy, indicating he should come closer.

When he was close enough she bent over and whispered something in his ear, then gave him a soft, lingering kiss on the cheek. She turned and waved at Lansing. "See you later, Sheriff." Without another word she slid into her car and drove away.

C.J. watched the car leave as he let out a sigh.

"Do you mind me asking what all that was about?"

"Oh, nothing." C.J. had a sheepish grin on his face. "She said I didn't have anything to worry about. She said she and Doctor Tanner are just friends."

"Oh." Lansing hoped Velma had told him that to spare his feelings. She probably knew he would outgrow his infatuation with her. Of course, knowing

Velma, there was always the possibility that she was just keeping her options open. Whatever her motives, Lansing decided he didn't need to be involved. "Are you hungry?"

"Oh, no." C.J. shook his head. "In fact, I think I ate too much. And I'm tired. Could we go home now?"

Lansing looked at his watch. Sheridan would be at the funeral home any minute. It would take Lansing at least thirty minutes to run C.J. down to the ranch and get back to town. The hell with it, he thought. Sheridan hasn't been bending over backward for me.

"Yeah, hop into the Jeep. I'll run you out to the ranch, but I'll have to leave you alone for a while. I've got to come back to work."

"That's okay," C.J. said, yawning. "I think I want to go to bed early anyway."

51

LANSING PULLED UP IN FRONT OF THE FUNERAL home just as Sheridan was coming out. The agent walked over to the patrol Jeep as the sheriff got out.

"I thought you were going to meet me here a half hour ago."

"I had to take care of some personal business," Lansing said. "I didn't think my being here would affect anything. Did you see the bodies?"

Sheridan nodded. "I'm not a forensics expert by any means, but I've reviewed a lot of cases. For what it's worth those girls look like they could have been attacked by Baltazar's and Koteen's killer."

"Where does that put us now?"

"Unless you have some eyewitnesses we're still on square one. The two Apache deaths you can almost lump under a factional or political category. Murders like that are done by someone who's trying to get even with the system. Those two girls? That's an out-and-out sex crime, like the Green River Killer or the Hillside Strangler."

"Can we raid the FBI data base and track down any similar crimes?"

"Sure. That's why we built it."

"I mean now. Tonight."

"Is the issue that pressing?"

"Sheridan, even if you decide you don't want to include Bill and Emily Fulton, I've had four murders in my county in the last week. I don't know when those girls were killed, but Ned Koteen was killed just two nights ago. The murderer is probably still around here and may not be finished yet."

"All right, let's use your office. Do you have an on-line computer system?"

"Yeah, we're tied into the state's Comfax."

"That'll be perfect. We can download files directly from Washington. Lead the way. I'll follow you over in my car."

Deputy Peters seemed overly protective of his equipment as Lansing and Sheridan leaned over his shoulder studying the screen. It would have been easier if Sheridan could have used the keyboard himself, but the Comfax had too many quirky commands for the agent to learn in a short time. That suited Peters. This was his computer and only he was going to touch it.

Sheridan had to get Regional Director Williams to make a call to Washington. The FBI files weren't tied in to the internet, the Comfax, or any other on-line service. One of the file clerks had to be called in to headquarters to call up the information Sheridan needed. That took time. It was eight o'clock at night before the printer started churning out the data, close to a hundred pages of information.

The computer and printer were crammed into the small dispatch/reception office, which was designed to accommodate a maximum of two people. Despite the close quarters Lansing and Sheridan stood at the tray next to Deputy Peters, reading each page as it rolled out of the printer.

"Do you plan on ever taking a break today?"

Lansing looked up from the page he was reading to see Margarite standing at the reception counter. "What are you doing here?"

"I called the ranch. C.J. said you were still at work. I figured if I didn't drag you away from your office for a little while, you'd never get a break. How about a cup of coffee?"

Lansing looked at the paper tray. There were only two more sheets ready to be read. His printer spewed out a page every thirty seconds, and it would be an hour before all of the data would be printed.

"You know, a cup of coffee does sound good." He slipped the page he had been reading into the tray. "Care to join us, Agent Sheridan? You could probably use a break yourself."

"Actually, I'd like to get something to eat."

"We can go in my Jeep. Paco's serves up a good Mexican feast."

Sheridan rubbed his stomach. "I don't think anything spicy tonight."

"Don't worry. You can get a decent steak there. Come on."

Before leaving the office Lansing gave his ranch a call. The phone rang six times before C.J. answered it. He apologized for taking so long. He had fallen asleep on the sofa. Lansing told him he would be working late and that he should go on to bed. C.J. didn't argue with the suggestion.

The cantina was almost empty by the time they got there. It was a week night, and the main dinner crowd had already left. Paco, who normally worked in the kitchen, greeted them at the entrance. He was a short, heavyset man who looked as if he enjoyed his own cooking. He had a thick mustache, thinning hair, and a round face that always had a smile.

"Where's Christine?" Margarite asked, referring to Paco's pretty daughter, who usually served as hostess.

"She's doing dishes," Paco snorted. "Somebody arrested my dishwasher today, along with my busboy."

Margarite glanced at Lansing, who only shrugged. "They got caught with stolen goods, Paco. Wasn't much I could do."

"I know, I know. I always told those boys, stay out of trouble. Do they listen to me? No. No one listens to Paco.

"Three for dinner?" He grabbed three plastic-coated menus from the reception counter.

"Yeah. And we'd like a table in the back, so we can talk."

"This way, please." Paco led them through the darkened interior of the cantina. Mariachi music drifted faintly through the air, loud enough to provide atmosphere without interfering with a quiet conversation.

Paco laid out the menus after they were seated. "Is it true what they say about Sheriff Fulton?" he asked confidentially.

"I don't know," Lansing said. "What have they been saying?"

"I heard that they committed suicide together."

"We can't release a statement until the state coroner takes a look."

"What do you think? You were there."

"I think I want a cup of coffee."

"Me too," Margarite added.

"Make that three," Sheridan said.

Paco took the hint. No more questions.

Lansing had introduced Margarite and Sheridan on the way to his Jeep. While they waited for their coffees Margarite made casual conversation about her work and the pueblo people she dealt with. She really wanted to ask about the Fultons and the two college girls, but knew she would have to wait until they wouldn't be interrupted.

When Paco returned they placed their orders. Sheridan chose the New York strip. Lansing wasn't particularly hungry, but he knew he had to eat sooner or later. He and Margarite decided to split an enchilada platter.

As soon as they were alone again, Margarite looked up from her cup of coffee. "Okay, *hombres*, what's going on? What's this about you arresting all of Paco's help?"

"I'm sorry, Doctor," Sheridan began. "We really shouldn't be discussing ongoing investigations."

"Sheridan, when you're on a case and you need technical advice, do you ever turn to experts?" Lansing asked.

"Certainly."

"Me too. Dr. Carerra happens to be my resident forensics specialist. She's board-certified and has helped me on other cases."

"I'm sorry. I thought she was just your girlfriend or something."

"On occasion she is, when she's not mad at me." He looked at her. "So far we're still friends today, right?"

"So far," Margarite said, smiling. "So you were saying about the dishwasher and busboy."

"We picked them up at about noon today. They were pawning stolen camping equipment down in Santa Fe. The last stuff they delivered belonged to the two girls who were missing from the Meadows."

"Are they the ones who killed the girls?" Margarite asked.

Lansing looked at Sheridan. He hadn't filled in the agent about the arrests. "I don't think so, unless they're the same ones who killed Baltazar and Koteen."

"You have suspects under arrest?"

"I've known these two since they were kids. They didn't kill anyone. But there is a chance they saw someone who did."

"I'd like to talk to them."

"They're locked up in my jail. You can see them any-time you want." He paused for a moment to take a sip of his coffee. "The past couple of days things have been coming at me so fast and furious I haven't had time to step back and look at the whole picture. Things started to come into focus this afternoon when I found the bodies of those two girls. Things started to make sense, and I have a suspect in mind."

"Who?" Sheridan asked.

"A man by the name of Huero Mundo."

"Let's bring him in. Where can we find him?"

"That should be easy enough. He's at the bottom of a grave in some prison yard in Oklahoma."

52

 LANSING COULD TELL FROM HIS COMPANIONS' faces that he needed to do some explaining. "This business started ten years ago. It wasn't long after I came back to San Phillipe County as chief deputy. One night I had to break up a bar fight over in Brazos. The guy who started it was an Apache by the name of Mundo. Huero Mundo.

"At the time I didn't know anything about him except that he was drunk and that he was trying to punch out anyone in his way. It took me and three patrons to tackle and cuff him. Mundo had busted up the place pretty good, and the bar owner wanted to press charges. I had no choice. I had to haul him off to jail.

"I guess I got lucky. He passed out in the back of my Jeep on the way back to Las Palmas. The night clerk and I dragged him back to a cell so he could sleep it off. He didn't have any I.D. on him at the time. I took his prints while he was asleep and ran a standard I.D. check.

"He was from around here originally. The Jicarilla reservation. But he had been gone for years. It turned out he had a rap sheet as long as your arm, plus he had escaped from the Oklahoma State Penitentiary about two weeks earlier. He was serving ten to fifteen for aggravated rape.

"I guess he didn't care for our accommodations either. When we went in there the next morning he was gone. Bill Fulton gave me a supreme butt-chewing for not locking the cell door. To this day I swear it was locked. That's besides the point. Sometime during the night he walked away from our jail.

"We put out a notification over the Teletype that he had been in our custody but somehow escaped. Everyone should be on the lookout. He could be armed. Approach with caution. The standard B.S. that goes along with those bulletins.

"We told the reservation police that we had sighted him. They said they'd cooperate, and that was the last thing anyone heard for about a week.

"Then one night we got a call. It was from one of the counselors at the Girl Scout camp. Three of their girls were missing. The counselor had heard screams and said it didn't sound like the girls were just clowning around. She said she had never heard anything like it before. By the time she reached their cabin, they were gone. Two of the beds were covered with blood. That's when she heard the last screams, further down the mountain.

"She called our office immediately. I was cruising south of town, so it took me a while to get up there. Sheriff Fulton beat me to the camp. He tried taking off after the girls on his own, fell, and nearly broke his leg. By the time I got there he was already on the phone, rousting out a bunch of guys from town.

"There must have been a dozen of us, but it was after midnight before we started down that mountain. Bill put me in charge only because he couldn't walk. I spread the volunteers out about thirty, forty feet apart.

"In the dark, in the woods like that, it was impossible to get a good look at anything. We were all hyped. The adrenaline was pumping. Every two minutes someone was yelling they had found something. It always turned out to be a piece of paper or a rock or some weird shadow made by someone else's flashlight.

"And that mountain was steep. It was tough trying to keep your footing. And there was no sign of anything. I was almost convinced the counselor didn't know what she was talking about.

"I guess we had been looking for about thirty minutes when the guy closest to me yells that he's found something. I was tired and worried. The whole time we were going down that mountain, we hadn't seen or heard a thing. I ran over to where he was standing. I must have fallen a couple of times. My pants were torn in two or three places.

"I got to where he had stopped. He was pointing his flashlight at a big pile of brush. There were some dead branches in the pile, but there were also a lot of green boughs someone had just torn from trees. It looked like somebody was getting ready to start a fire.

"I started pulling the limbs off the pile and tossing them out of the way. The other volunteers came running over. They were all yelling, wanting to know what we had found. I don't remember saying anything. I just kept pulling at those branches.

"The pile must have been three feet high and four feet across, but it couldn't have taken me more than a couple of minutes before we finally saw something. A small piece of cloth was sticking out. It was one of the girls' nightgowns.

"I must have been acting like a madman, because the other guys stayed clear while I dug the rest of the trash off those poor things. I couldn't believe what I had found.

"Their three bodies were lying side by side. They

were covered with leaves and needles from the pile of branches. I brushed the leaves away. They were all dead. Their throats had been slashed wide open.

"I couldn't help myself. I started crying like a baby." He had to stop a moment to take a sip of coffee. "That was the last time I ever let myself get emotional at a crime scene." The last comment was an observation meant as much for himself as for his audience.

He began again as soon as the picture of the three waifs faded from his thoughts. "From the autopsies we found out that all three had been sexually molested. The semen came from someone with O-negative blood. Coincidentally, the same blood type as Huero Mundo, our escaped con who was serving time for a sex crime.

"The Girl Scout camp isn't more than five miles from the Jicarilla reservation. The reservation police hadn't seen any sign of him, but there's a lot of wild country in those mountains. He could have been hiding anywhere.

"With the permission of the tribal council we started looking for Mundo. Two days after we started the manhunt we got a tip from a sheepherder. He had seen someone camped near Stone Lake. Whoever it was took off just before we got there. But they left a bunch of stuff behind, including a big hunting knife. The knife had traces of blood that matched up with the girls who had been killed. It also had Mundo's finger-prints all over it.

"After a week of chasing our own tails we realized the sheriff's office and the reservation police couldn't handle the manhunt alone. We called in the FBI and the state police. At one point we had over three hundred law-enforcement officers scouring the mountains in and around the reservation looking for one man.

"And he was taunting us. We had helicopters. We had trackers. We had dogs. But every time we got even a little close, he'd disappear. Sometimes it seemed like he disappeared into thin air. Of course, you have to remember, he was an experienced woodsman and he knew those mountains. He had grown up there.

"We had been playing cat and mouse for over a month when we finally tracked him to an old cabin that herders used in the winter. It sat on a hill. The nearest tree had to have been a hundred feet away. There were thirty of us. The place was surrounded. We could see smoke coming out of the chimney and you could smell bacon cooking. We had him. We were sure.

"We rushed the place and kicked in the front door. There was bacon in a skillet cooking on the stove. There was a fresh cup of coffee, steam coming off it, sitting on the table. But Mundo? Nothing."

"What happened to him?" Sheridan asked.

Lansing shook his head. "Beats the hell out of me. We checked the rafters. We checked under the house. We looked for an escape tunnel. We couldn't find a thing.

"Of course, the press was having a heyday. Every week Mundo became more famous as we poured more and more time and manpower into the search. He was the topic of conversation at every bar and restaurant in northern New Mexico. And it got worse. As days turned into weeks we looked like a bunch of incompetent idiots, while Mundo was becoming some sort of folk hero. People were calling him the modern-day Cochise.

"There was talk in the papers that the governor was getting ready to declare a state of emergency. He was going to call out the National Guard and take over the manhunt personally."

Paco arrived with the plates of food. "Careful," he warned. "Everything's hot."

"Paco, do you remember the business ten years ago with that Apache, Mundo?" Lansing asked.

"Oh, *sí*. He was a bad man. Sheriff Fulton almost lost the next election because of him."

"That's right," Lansing agreed. "He almost did." He paused with his story long enough to put a portion of the enchilada platter on a separate plate. After a few bites, he resumed.

53

"IT WAS NED KOTEEN WHO FINALLY FIGURED out how we were going to catch him. We'd been at that business for six weeks. Neither one of us had been able to spend time with our families. Never any more than two nights in a row at home.

"It must have been the night after the bacon episode. He and I were licking our wounds and knocking down a few beers at the same time. Ned said the only way Mundo could slip away like he had was by using magic. I thought he was nuts or drunk or both.

"That's when Ned explained Mundo's background. Mundo was Cesar TeCube's grandson. At the time TeCube was considered the chief medicine man on the reservation.

"TeCube raised Mundo from the time he was an infant. He trained the boy to follow in his footsteps and become a medicine man. Mundo was supposed to become the chief medicine man for the tribe one day.

"When Mundo was about twenty, something happened. He and TeCube had a big falling out. No one was really sure what went wrong between them, but TeCube kicked him out of his house and told him to leave the reservation. Mundo went off to live with some distant relatives who had settled in the panhandle of Oklahoma.

"Evidently he did nothing but cause trouble for his relatives, and after a while they ran him off. He drifted back and forth between the reservation and Oklahoma for about ten years. Always getting drunk. Always getting into scrapes. Usually ending up in jail. During one of his drunkfests he broke into a woman's house, beat her up pretty badly, and raped her. That's how he ended up in prison.

"Evidently Ned had contacted the prison authorities to get an insight into what Mundo had been like. The story he got was that while Mundo was in prison he got back into the medicine-man business. He started studying under an old Cherokee medicine man. Ned thought that Mundo probably learned a whole new bag of tricks, like how to make himself invisible.

"That was Ned's theory on how he had escaped from prison. He insisted that's how he walked out of my jail. He made himself invisible. When we opened the cell door to get a better look inside, he just walked out.

"Ned guessed that when we raided the cabin with the bacon cooking, Mundo was in the cabin all the time. We just didn't see him."

"You didn't buy his theory, did you?" Sheridan asked. The question was laced with cynicism.

"No, of course not. I'm sure he had his tricks, but invisibility wasn't one of them. But I never argued with Ned—he was bigger than me.

"Anyway, Ned claimed the only way we were going to catch Mundo was to use stronger magic. I told him I didn't think Sheriff Fulton was much into voodoo. He said his boss wasn't either. He said we'd have to do it on our own.

"I still thought he was nuts, but the next morning I went with him to visit Cesar TeCube. The old man listened to everything Ned had to tell him, but TeCube would have nothing to do with it. I don't know if he didn't want to betray his own grandson or if it was because he was afraid, but TeCube sent us away. He said there was no way he could help us.

"That's when we went to Esteban Baltazar. I guess the medicine men don't belong to a union where they have to follow the head man's lead. Ned explained everything to Baltazar, just like he did to TeCube. Baltazar listened, nodded, said he would help. He said Mundo knew a great deal about the medicine ways, but Mundo was using his knowledge for evil and for his own selfish purposes.

"He told us we had to wait until the full moon, which was going to be in about six days. That's when the dark magic that Mundo used would be at its weakest. Then he took his *jish*—that's the medicine pouch he carried around—and poured powder out of it. I think he called the stuff *hoddentin*. He put the powder in two smaller pouches and handed them to us.

"He told us we had a week to find out where Mundo was holing up. When we found out where he was we had to go alone to arrest him. He told us to put some of the *hoddentin* in our shoes. That way Mundo wouldn't be able to hear us. He said to sprinkle a little powder on our hats. Then Mundo wouldn't be able to see us. We were to keep the rest of the powder in the pouches and wear them from a string around our necks. That way Mundo wouldn't be able to harm us.

"It took us four days to find Mundo's new hiding place. It was a hunter's cabin up in the mountains. I wanted to go in immediately, but Ned insisted we had to wait. So for two days we staked the place out. We saw Mundo go in and out several times, but he never once suspected that we were watching him.

"Finally, on the sixth day Ned said we could make our move. I wanted to go in during broad daylight.

That damned Ned said we had to wait till the moon was up. I went along with what he wanted.

"It was midnight when we sneaked up on the cabin. We knew there was only one door to the place, but there was a back window. He gave me the honor of arresting the son of a bitch. He went around back in case Mundo tried to sneak out the window.

"It was kind of strange. As I walked up to the cabin my footsteps weren't making a sound. Instead of kicking in the door, I gently lifted the latch and pushed the door open. There was nothing but silence.

"The cabin was just one big room, and Mundo was sound asleep on the floor. I had my gun drawn, but for some reason I felt I didn't need it. I put it back in its holster and pulled out my cuffs. I took two quick steps, grabbed Mundo's wrist, twisted it behind his back, and cuffed it. That's when he woke up. I had his neck pinned with my knee. Before he could do anything I twisted his other arm behind him and cuffed it as well.

"I swear he roared like a bull in heat. As soon as he realized what had happened he began arching his back and bucking like a bronco, trying to get me off. I jumped clear. I figured he was cuffed. There wasn't anything he could do.

"In a second he was on his knees. Before I could pull my pistol he dove into the middle of me. He was biting and snarling like some wild animal. I finally managed to kick him off. I rolled out of his way and shut the door so he couldn't get out.

"That's when I got my gun out again. I told him to lie down or I'd shoot. Instead, he got to his feet and dove through the glass of the back window.

"Thank God, Ned was out there waiting. When I got to the window Mundo was trying to get up. Ned walked over and stuck the barrel of his shotgun behind Mundo's ear. Ned said if he made one more move without being told, he'd need a pumpkin if he ever wanted to wear a hat again.

"Well, we got him down the mountain and took him to the San Phillipe County jail. This time Sheriff Fulton wasn't taking any chances. He kept Mundo in a cell under a twenty-four-hour watch. It was a strain on all of us, but it stayed that way for four months, until the trial was over.

"That was the first time I met Doctor Miles. She came up from Albuquerque with a high-priced trial lawyer in tow. She wanted to make sure Mundo got a fair hearing. That was the beginning of the biggest joke in New Mexican history.

"The judge refused a change of venue since none of the victims was from San Phillipe Country. They held the trial right there in the courthouse with twelve impartial jurors from our voter rolls.

"Now, keep something in mind. One third of this county's population is Native American. One third is Hispanic. The rest are Anglos. When the jury selection was over, there was one Anglo on the panel. The other thing to keep in mind is the fact that Huero Mundo had become a real hero to a majority of the people around here. The Sheriff of Nottingham had Robin Hood on trial. That's the way they looked at it.

"Mundo pleaded not guilty, and the defense was, someone else did it. His attorney was good. He shot down everything we threw at him.

"All of the evidence was circumstantial. The semen found on the little girls was O-negative. Mundo's blood type was O-negative. That blood type occurs in less than seven percent of the population.

"However, with twenty thousand people in San Phillipe County at any one time, 1400 had O-negative blood. Why should Mundo be persecuted? There were 1399 other potential suspects. Unfortunately, we didn't have the luxury of DNA analysis back then. Things might have turned out differently.

"The hunting knife we found at Mundo's campsite had the girls' blood on it. It had his fingerprints on it.

"In his deposition to the sheriff Mundo insisted he had found the knife in the woods where someone had dropped it. His lawyer maintained we had no proof that he had possession of the knife prior to the murders.

"There were no eyewitnesses. No one saw Mundo anywhere near the crime scene.

"My testimony about finding the bodies was stricken from the records. The defense maintained that there was no argument that a crime had been committed, but he claimed my testimony and the photos of the crime scene were inflammatory and could prejudice the jury against his client. The judge went along.

"The trial lasted four days. It took the jury less than an hour to deliberate. They found Mundo not guilty."

54

"So you had to turn him loose?" Margarite asked.

"No. Remember? He had escaped from prison in Oklahoma. He still had a sentence to serve there. Prison officials came and hauled him back. He still had four years to go on his original sentence. I heard they tacked on another five years because of his escape."

"But you said he was dead," Sheridan observed.

"Poetic justice, really. If we had convicted him he would have gotten the electric chair. I don't know how long it was after he had been sent back. Two years maybe. He was out in the exercise yard by himself. The story I got was that it was a clear day when literally, out of the blue, he was struck by a bolt of lightning."

"*Vengeance is mine, sayeth the Lord,*" Sheridan said. "Sounds like God finished up something that we couldn't."

"Oh, God wasn't finished with him," Lansing said. "Not yet anyway. The jolt of electricity only knocked him into a coma. They ended up moving him to a hospital at some minimum-security facility. He had been there for about three months when a fire broke out. He and a dozen other prisoners were burned to death in their beds."

"My God," Margarite whispered. "That must have been awful."

"As far as I'm concerned it wasn't awful enough. There's a special place in hell for people like him."

The three sat in silence for a few minutes. Margarite and Sheridan were so engrossed in Lansing's story they had forgotten to eat. Their food was cold.

Sheridan asked Paco if he could warm their plates. While they waited for their food the special agent asked, "Why do you think this Mundo character is our suspect? It sounds to me like he's dead and buried."

"The two girls I found this afternoon were in the exact spot I found the bodies of the three Girl Scouts. Or pretty damned close. There can't be more than a handful of people in the entire world who know where that spot is."

"Coincidence?" Margarite asked.

"Like hell. Two murders, ten years later. The same M.O. They were raped, their throats cut, their bodies put in the same spot, hidden the same way. That wasn't coincidence. That was intentional."

"How do they tie into the reservation murders?" Sheridan asked.

"You said it this afternoon. Baltazar and Koteen were killed by someone trying to get even. Revenge. They were instrumental in capturing him and sending him back to prison."

"And the two college girls?"

"Mundo's such a sick son of a bitch, he can't help himself." Lansing thought for a moment. "Since we don't have any hard evidence for the Fulton murders, how about a strong motive? Bill Fulton was the sheriff when we arrested Mundo. Bill was on his hit list."

"If it is this Mundo, that would make sense," Sheridan agreed.

"There's something else, Lansing," Margarite said, a worried look on her face. "You're the one who actually captured him. It stands to reason he'll be coming after you too."

"Sheriff! Sheriff!" Paco yelled, running out of his kitchen. "You have to go! *Pronto!*"

Lansing automatically jumped up. "What's wrong?"

"Deputy Peters called. Your ranch. It's on fire!"

55

LANSING COULD SEE THE BLAZE AS SOON AS HE passed the last streetlight in town. At first it was only a glow in the distance, but it grew larger and more distinct as he sped down the highway.

Two miles from the turnoff he could see the flashing lights of the fire trucks and other emergency vehicles. He took the turn onto his access road on two wheels, slamming his two passengers into each other and the opposite door of the Jeep.

There had been no conversation since they'd left the cantina. As soon as they were in the Jeep Lansing threw on his lights and siren. Any talk would have been drowned by the noise. Besides, Lansing's full attention was concentrated on the road in front of him and the fire in the distance.

As the Jeep neared the ranch complex Lansing made a quick evaluation of the situation. Only the ranch house was on fire. One water truck had been positioned at the front of the house. The tinder-dry lawn had caught fire. They had contained the grass fire, keeping it from spreading to the surrounding pastures, but the house itself was being consumed. Fire and smoke billowed into the sky. In spots, flames had eaten through the roof, allowing more air to pour through the doors and shattered windows.

A pump truck was positioned between the Rio Questa and the back of the house. Hundreds of gallons of water were being siphoned from the river and pumped onto the house blaze.

Yet a third water truck sat close to the barn. The fire fighters were dousing the barn and other outbuildings to keep them from igniting from the intense heat. Two police cars and a paramedics' unit blocked the end of the access road.

Lansing slammed on his brakes at the last minute, skidding to a halt only inches from the paramedics' unit. As soon as he jumped out he ran to the closest fire fighter.

"Where's C.J.?" he yelled above the deafening sound of the pump truck. "Where's my son?"

The fire fighter pointed at an ear and shook his head. He couldn't hear the question. Lansing ran to one of the men close to the house.

"Where's my son?" he yelled again. "Has anyone seen my son?"

"Haven't seen anyone, Sheriff," the fireman yelled. "The inside was filled with fire by the time we got here."

Lansing turned to face the fire. Five generations of his family had lived in that house. Over a hundred years of history and memories were going up in smoke. That didn't matter to him. All he wanted was his son.

He started toward the house. The flames were intense, and he could feel his skin sear. There was a chance that C.J. was okay. Maybe he had found some small corner where the flames couldn't reach him. Maybe he had covered himself with a blanket so he wouldn't be burned. There was a chance. There was always a chance.

He had nearly reached the back steps when something inside the kitchen blew. The force of the explosion knocked him to the ground. Cinders and sparks peppered his body, burning through his uniform and singing his flesh.

As he scrambled to his feet, hands grabbed him from behind.

"No!" he screamed. "Let me go! I've got to get C.J.!"

"No, Sheriff! It's too late!" Gabe Hanna yelled, pulling at his boss. "I tried already. Come on. Get back."

Another set of hands clamped onto Lansing's arm, and he found himself being dragged away from the flames by his deputy and Special Agent Sheridan.

"He's right, Sheriff!" Sheridan yelled. "It's too late for anyone in there. Get back before you get killed."

As tears from smoke and his own frustration filled his eyes, Lansing watched as the roof began to collapse. Even if he had made it through the door, he wouldn't have lasted more than a couple of seconds inside.

He wished to God he had made it through the door.

56

 THE RANCH COMPLEX SEEMED TO FILL WITH silence when the drone of the pumper truck ceased. The feed from the propane tank had been cut so that gas wouldn't fuel the fire. The electrical lines from the county coop had been disconnected so that even the lights in the barn didn't work.

The beams from strong flashlights swept back and forth across the ground as firemen recovered gear and disconnected hoses to be rolled onto spools. Paramedics Gomez and Sutter attended to burns and abrasions that had been suffered during the catastrophe.

Gabe Hanna's left arm was bandaged from his hand to the elbow. He had been the first one on the scene. Juan Martín had seen the blaze from his house and called 911. The operator relayed the information to the firehouse, then to Deputy Peters. Peters put out the notification to all patrol cars before calling the cantina.

When Gabe had arrived at the ranch the interior of the house was completely ablaze. Peters had told him C.J. was at home alone. Gabe kicked in the back door and tried to make his way down the hallway to the bedrooms. By that time it was too late. The ceiling was beginning to fall, and he had to block a beam with his arm.

The fire trucks were just arriving as he stumbled through the back door to safety.

Lansing sat by himself on the rail of his corral, his head bowed. The horses had been released from the barn in case it should catch fire. Cement Head nuzzled his nose against Lansing's shoulder, trying to lend comfort. Margarite sat a few feet away, wanting to hold the man she loved and knowing at the same time that he needed to be alone with his grief.

"Sheriff," Gabe said, standing a few feet away. "I'm sorry. I should have gotten him out. I tried. I really tried."

Lansing didn't look up. "I'm sure you did, Gabe. Don't blame yourself. He was my son. I should have been here with him." He paused for a moment of reflection. "There are a lot of things I should have done. That I should have done better."

As the firemen switched off their flashlights, the grounds began to glow from the light of the moon. It was a sliver short of being full. To the west came a faint rumble. A flicker of lightning bounced along the horizon.

A front was moving in from the Gulf of California. In a day the parched prairies and the dry forests would get their first taste of rain in months. The dry season would be over.

"In a day," Lansing said to himself. "In a day there will be rain." He glanced at Margarite. "Isn't that just like life? Things always seem to come a day late."

What had been the Lansing homestead was a blackened, charred shell. The stone walls still stood, a monument to the history of the Lansing clan. But to the sheriff it seemed like a hollow tribute. At the moment it represented the end of a line, the end of a heritage he had hoped to pass on to his grandchildren, and to their children. It was a blackened mausoleum holding the remains of his only son.

The fire captain approached, wiping his face with a dirty cloth. "I'm afraid what's left is too hot for us to do any more tonight. I understand your son was at home. I'm awfully sorry." Lansing nodded. "We'll do the recovery in the morning. We'll make it around eight, in case you want to be here."

Lansing sat silently staring at the ground.

"You should know something, Sheriff. This was no accident. The fire was spread out too evenly. There was no hot spot. Somebody poured gasoline or something like it all through the place. We'll have a better idea tomorrow."

"Knowing that makes this a whole lot easier," Lansing growled sarcastically.

There was nothing else the captain could say. He joined his men, and moments later the emergency vehicles began to pull out.

"Lansing," Margarite said softly.

He pulled away from her touch. At the moment there was no room in his life for words.

He jumped from the rail he had been sitting on and began strolling toward the burned-out ruin that had once been his home. The only light came from the nearly full moon hovering above him. He kicked at the dirt, like a bored child looking for something to occupy an idle mind.

A waft of wind stirred the air. It was pungent with the smell of charred timber. Bits and pieces of ash and dust stirred around his feet. And something else.

Lansing bent over and looked. He hesitated for a moment, then grabbed the object.

A feather.

An owl's feather.

He crushed it in his hand, then turned his head to stare the moon in its face.

"Mundo!" he bellowed. "Hear me! I'm coming after you! You son of a bitch! If I have to track you to hell itself, I'm going to get you! And I'm going to kill you with my own two hands!"

On the ridge overlooking the Rio Questa, less than a quarter mile from the Lansing compound, stood a lone figure. The streak of white in his hair shone almost iridescent in the bright moonlight.

Lansing's words carried far into the night. Those close to him couldn't hear the threat without a chill running down their spines.

The figure only frowned. Their business wasn't finished. Not by a long shot. And a question had to be answered.

How did Lansing know?

Mundo bent over and picked up the bundle crumpled at his feet. Slinging the lump over his shoulder, he trotted into the darkness. The night was still young, and now there were other things he needed to take care of.

57

LAS PALMAS WAS A SMALL COMMUNITY. WHAT impacted one household had a domino effect on the rest of the residents. The network of gossip traders and information hounds had shifted into full gear that morning when the news of the Fulton deaths hit the street.

The arrest of Pedro Gomez and Julio Martinez created another thread of news to be woven into the tapestry of gossip. Were they responsible for what had happened to Bill and Emily?

The two bodies found on the mountainside now shaped every conversation. The hues in the picture were turning dark and ominous. People were afraid. Were these all coincidences, inevitabilities that were going to happen anyway? Or were there sinister forces at work, random evils that were ready to spring on the innocent citizens of their town without warning?

Whatever fears they had were multiplied tenfold when the news about the fire at the Lansing ranch began to circulate.

As Lansing drove back into town he passed dozens of parked cars along the highway. The curious, the

fearful, the busybodies had all gathered to watch the
fiery tragedy. They were respectful enough not to come
onto the ranch itself. Most knew they would only get in
the way. But they stayed, even after the fire trucks had
departed.

The word had spread. Cliff Junior had been at the
ranch alone. He had been trapped in the house. He
had burned to death while his father was on a date
with Dr. Carerra. Tragedy upon tragedy was being
heaped on their town, and Lansing was off carousing.

Both sympathizers and accusers averted their eyes
as he drove past. The former didn't want to see his
pain. The others—if the rumors were true—were
ashamed of the man they had elected sheriff.

At the moment Lansing didn't know about the stories that were circulating. And if he had known, he
wouldn't have cared. He was burdened with his own
guilt for all the things he could have done. But he
didn't have time for guilt. There was one person
responsible for everything that had happened. Lansing
had only one mission in life: Destroy Huero Mundo.

As Lansing, Margarite, and Sheridan drove into
town, it looked as if every light in every house was on.
The diner, which normally closed at ten o'clock, was
open. Dozens of people had gathered for coffee, a
piece of pie, or a late meal. There would be no sleep in
their little town that night.

Most of the citizens fully supported their sheriff, no
matter what the rumor mill was grinding out. They
knew he would be up the entire night, trying to deal
with his loss. None of them could rest, knowing what
he was going through.

Dozens of sympathizers were gathered at the courthouse. They knew Lansing would show up there
sooner or later. They wanted him to know they were
there for him.

As he stepped from his Jeep, they parted, giving him

a clear path to the courthouse door. He was peppered with dozens of soft-spoken questions. "Can I help?" "Is there anything I can do?" "I have clothes at home that will fit you. Should I bring them in?" "Do your horses need looking after?" "I have a spare room you can use!"

He stopped at the door and turned to his friends. "Everyone, thank you very much. Please, go on home. There's nothing anyone can do tonight. If I need anything I'll let you know. Right now I have to take care of my own business."

Inside the offices, Marilyn had shooed away anyone who didn't have official business. Her eyes were red and puffy, but her manner was straightforward and businesslike. "Cliff, can I get you a cup of coffee?"

"Yes," Lansing said, trying to hide his own emotions. "Bring it to my office."

Not sure what they should do, Margarite and Sheridan followed Lansing into his private office.

"Lansing," Margarite asked, "do you mind if I stay?"

Lansing had stopped long enough to hang his Stetson and holster belt on his hat rack. He wasn't sure that he had the strength to look her in the eyes, but he tried. "I think we're going to be busy in here tonight."

"I don't care. I'll help where I can. I'd like to stay."

Lansing nodded. "I'd like that too." He looked at the FBI agent. "Sheridan, you want to grab those computer printouts?"

"You sure you want to do this, Lansing? Wouldn't you rather get some rest?"

"I'm not going to get any sleep tonight, no matter what I do. I might as well get some work done, but I'm going to need your help."

"I'm at your disposal." Sheridan stopped before going through the door. "Lansing, how sure are you that all of this business is tied into your Huero Mundo?"

"It doesn't matter if his name is Huero Mundo or Jack the Ripper or Jack Be Nimble. Someone's out there killing people, and it's our job to stop him. And that's exactly what we're going to do."

The San Phillipe Sheriff's Office was not the only place where people ended up working through the entire night. Special Agent Sheridan called Regional Director Williams at home. Williams was angry at being disturbed after midnight, but Sheridan assured him they were working under emergency conditions. Their killer had struck again. Sheriff Lansing's own home had been burned to the ground, killing his twelve-year-old son. In fact, Sheridan was convinced now that the Fulton cases were tied to the Apache murders. The death toll stood at seven. They were dealing with a madman, and they needed to assemble every resource available to stop him.

When Williams finally agreed, Sheridan provided him with a list of what they required.

They had to have a copy of the complete prison files on Huero Mundo from Oklahoma. They needed a detailed account of the hospital fire in which he was allegedly killed. And they needed to have his body exhumed. There was sufficient evidence to support the theory that he might still be alive.

"Anything else?" Williams asked.

"Yes, sir," Sheridan continued. "We need enough manpower to cover every inch of northwestern New Mexico and catch this man before he kills again."

"We'll see what we can do," Williams said.

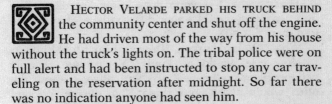 HECTOR VELARDE PARKED HIS TRUCK BEHIND the community center and shut off the engine. He had driven most of the way from his house without the truck's lights on. The tribal police were on full alert and had been instructed to stop any car traveling on the reservation after midnight. So far there was no indication anyone had seen him.

In a spruce tree overlooking the center, the great owl stirred. His night of hunting was being disturbed by the man below him. The owl emitted a low, guttural *ho-o, ho-o*. The warning was clear—if the man chose to heed it.

Velarde only half-heard the threat. His mind was on other things. He was going to use his key to open the back entrance to the building, but the lock had already been broken. He pushed the door open, then turned on the small penlight he normally carried in his glove compartment. He used it to light his way down the corridor to the gymnasium.

"Hello!" he said in a hoarse whisper once he was inside the gym. The only illumination in the cavernous room came from the four EXIT signs and the moonlight pouring through the high windows. "Is there anybody here?"

"Yes, there is."

Huero Mundo stepped from the shadows into a square of moonlight.

"Dammit, Mundo," Velarde blustered. "Didn't I tell you? Never call me at home."

"That was before."

"Before what?" the council president snapped angrily.

"Lansing knows."

"What are you talking about?"

"Lansing knows it was me. He knows I'm back."

"Nobody knows you're back. How could they? Everyone knows you're dead!"

"That's right. Everyone does know I'm dead. The only way they could know differently is if someone told them."

"What?" Velarde asked. "Do you think I told him?"

"How else would he know? You're one of only two people who knew I was still alive. I know the other would never say a thing. That means you said something."

"That's ridiculous. Why would I?"

"Because you have everything you want now. You don't need me anymore."

"What are you talking about? We had an agreement."

"That's what I thought too. For the last year I've done everything you asked. It took me three weeks to cut through the timbers in the mine. The collapse looked like an accident. Just as you wanted. Cuartelejo got control of managing the mines.

"I do admit I enjoyed staging the hunting accidents. But they appeared just the way you wanted them. They were ruled accidents.

"The rig explosion was the trickiest. But you got what you wanted. Baltazar Brothers' is out of business.

"All I ever asked in return was to let me come back to the tribe. Let me come home."

"Yeah—and part of your deal was that you got to destroy anyone who ever got in your way in the past."

"I spent over twelve years in prison, Velarde. Eight more years in exile. I had to suffer the white man's justice. It was payback time. It was my right to take vengeance against those who wronged me. That was all right with you. Just as long as you got what you wanted."

"What *I* wanted? Everything I've done has been on behalf of our people. For over a hundred years it has been the dream of the Ollero to return to the plains, to own a small part of what had been our homeland. It was your grandfather's dream. You grew up hearing him talk about it.

"Every penny Cuartelejo has made will be used to buy land in the panhandles. You know that."

"I know that's what you say."

"I can prove it. I have contracts in my office. We're negotiating to buy three farms in Oklahoma right now. It will be the beginning of the Ollero reservation." He turned and started for the door.

"Stop!" Mundo ordered.

Velarde froze.

Mundo began a slow walk around the council president. His path was a circle that grew smaller as he talked. "I wondered," he began, "as I stood over Koteen's body, how grateful will the people of our tribe be that I have done this? Will they really understand that I had a right—no, an obligation—to seek vengeance against a man who sent me to prison? They will know I am a great medicine man, but will they welcome my medicine? Will they embrace me as their spiritual leader?"

"I told you they would," Velarde snapped. "No one was happy with Esteban. Everyone knows the spiritual strength of our people comes from the Ollero. You are TeCube's grandson. No one would question your right to take his position."

"A murderer, Hector? They would accept a man who murdered another *tsanati*? They would accept a man who killed their chief of police?"

"Why are you asking me? Those are questions you should have asked yourself before you started on your killing spree."

"And you sit back, absolved of any guilt. No one would suspect that the president of the tribal council had anything to do with the mine accident or the rig explosion. You turn me in for the other murders. I die. You get what you want."

"You don't know what you're talking about."

"There's only one thing I didn't tell you, Hector," Mundo said, stopping a few feet in front of him. "I will live in these mountains forever. I will be the spirit who guides our people. They can't kill me. I am *Sekala Ka-amja*. The One Who Never Dies."

"We'll see about that." Velarde pulled a pistol from the pocket of his jacket and pointed it at Mundo's chest. He fired three times, knocking Mundo to the floor.

Velarde stuffed the pistol back into his pocket and knelt next to the body. "So, what do you have to say about your great magic now?"

Mundo's hand struck with the speed of a snake, grabbing Velarde's throat. "It is stronger than you will ever know," Mundo hissed.

Velarde's hands clamped around Mundo's wrist as he tried to tear himself free from the grasp. Mundo stood slowly, bring Velarde to an upright position as he did.

Velarde's struggles became weaker as the flow of oxygen to his brain continued to be cut off. As he started to go limp Mundo released his grip, allowing him to fall to the floor.

"There is magic and there is illusion, Hector," Mundo said, thumping the bulletproof vest he had stolen from Koteen's Jeep. "A *tsanati* uses both."

Velarde didn't hear the remark. He was on his hands and knees coughing and wheezing, trying to catch his breath. Mundo straddled his body from behind and grabbed his hair, pulling his head back to expose his throat.

The blade of the knife glistened in the bright moonlight still pouring through the windows.

The scream echoed through the halls of the community center. The only creature who heard it was the great owl in the spruce tree outside. He spread his wings and soared from his branch. He had fulfilled his duties as prescribed by the ancient laws. It was time to return to the hunt.

59

 LANSING STARED AT THE PHONE ON HIS DESK. He had excused himself from the others twenty minutes earlier. There were calls he needed to make.

The truth was, there was only one call to be made, and he wasn't sure how to do it.

Telling someone they had just lost a loved one was the worst part of his job. Whenever it was a local, he went to the home personally. If it was someone from out of town he would contact their local police department. They would see to it that the notification was delivered in person.

He had to tell Carol their only son was dead. He wasn't about to turn that responsibility over to the Albuquerque Police Department. And with Mundo running loose he couldn't take the time off to drive down and tell her himself.

He also knew he couldn't afford to put it off. The media picked up on tragedies like this. He wasn't about to let Carol find out through a news report.

He noticed his hand was trembling as he picked up the receiver. As the phone rang at the opposite end he tried to remember the words he wanted to say. He had his speech all prepared, but as the moment neared it seemed weak and useless.

No one picked up until the end of the fourth ring.

"Frank! This is Cliff. I need to speak to Carol. . . . Yes, I know it's late. Just put her on. . . ."

60

IT WAS FOUR IN THE MORNING BEFORE THE FIRST report turned up on the Comfax. It was the prison file on Mundo. Thirty minutes later two reports came in regarding the hospital fire: one from the Muskogee fire marshal, the second from the prison hospital.

While Lansing read through those reports, Sheridan was finishing up his analysis of the one hundred-page report they had received earlier in the evening. They had moved their operations into the dayroom, where there was space to spread out.

Sheridan's report summarized all of the unsolved sexual-assault/murder cases in the continental United States dating back twenty-five years. There were over two thousand of them. Because the complete file was still in the computer, he was able to have Deputy Peters winnow down their choices electronically.

He first eliminated all cases east of the Mississippi River. He then restricted potential cases to those where a knife or razor was used as the murder weapon. He went one step further by eliminating all cases that took place during the time of Mundo's known incarceration. His list decreased dramatically. Instead of two thousand possibly related crimes, he had less than fifty.

He moved into the dayroom, where a large map of the United States hung on the wall. Using colored pins, he began marking the locations. Clusters began to form in southern California and Washington state. The rest were spread out fairly randomly.

Sheridan balked when he found Las Palmas listed as one of the sites. He looked at the date. It was ten years earlier. Of course, he thought. The three Girl Scouts. Mundo wasn't convicted, so the crime had to be listed as unsolved.

Lansing looked up from the report he was reading. "What do we have now?"

"A lot less than we started with," Sheridan admitted. "But more than I know what to do with."

Margarite sat at one of the spare desks the deputies used for filling out paperwork. She had been reading through all of the same reports Lansing and Sheridan were using. "Can you eliminate cases with the same dates?"

"Not really," Sheridan said. "Some of the dates they use are when the bodies were found. They could have been dead for days, even weeks before they were discovered. And if a murder happened in Phoenix the same day one happened in Denver, how do we know Mundo—or whoever it was—didn't do one of them?"

"Good point," she agreed.

Lansing studied the map for a moment. "We know for sure when Mundo killed the Girl Scouts. June fifteenth, ten years ago. Eliminate everything on the map before that."

Sheridan nodded and referred to his computer printout. When he was finished there were still twenty pins on the map. Lansing walked up and put a second pin next to Las Palmas.

"What's that for?" Margarite asked.

"The two girls we found yesterday." He stepped back and studied the map a little longer. "What's similar about the murders of the two campers and the Girl Scouts?"

"They were sexually molested," Sheridan said. "Their throats were cut. You said you found them hidden in the exact same spot."

"Yeah," Lansing agreed. "This may sound stupid, but there's one more thing."

Margarite and Sheridan looked at each other, then at Lansing, and shook their heads.

"The month," Lansing said. "The murders all occurred in June." He walked back up to the map and pointed. "The prison hospital is located in Muskogee. We know the fire occurred in December. What's the date for this pin on Kerr Lake?"

Sheridan referred to his printout. "The following June. Two campers, a man and a woman. Both of their throats had been cut. She had been sexually molested."

"He had six months where he could have done a lot more," Lansing said, his eyes darting from one pin to the next. "Let's try something. Mark those spots where the murders took place in June with a different-colored pin."

Sheridan began replacing the white pins he had been using with red pins. In a matter of minutes he was finished, and he stepped back to look at the entire map.

"You know, I've been racking my brain trying to figure out where Mundo's been hiding for the last eight years, and why," Lansing said. "It's starting to make sense."

There were ten red pins in the map. They stretched north from Oklahoma to the Canadian border and west to Washington. Sheridan shook his head. "I don't see any pattern."

"Forget about the two pins in Las Palmas. Eastern Oklahoma, eight years ago. Seven years ago, eastern Nebraska. Six years ago, central South Dakota. Five years ago, North Dakota. Then Montana, Idaho, Washington, back south to Utah. That was last year. Now home.

"Remember I told you Ned Koteen said Mundo had studied under other medicine men while he was in prison? I just read Mundo's prison record. When he was returned to prison he became a real troublemaker. Finally, they had to put him in solitary.

"While he was in solitary he read everything he could get his hands on that had to do with magic, the occult, Native American healing, medicine, shamanism. He's been studying for the last eight years. I'll bet he visited every medicine man and shaman west of the Mississippi. And if you look closely, each one of those pins is located just outside a reservation.

"He's probably the best-educated medicine man in the country. The problem is, he's also one sick son of a bitch."

"But why June?" Margarite asked. "What's the significance of this month?"

"I don't know," Lansing admitted. "But we're not going to wait another year to find out. There's one person besides Mundo who probably knows. Doctor Miles. We can ask her."

Sheridan shook his head. "She called me yesterday afternoon. She said she's withdrawing her services as a consultant."

"Did she give you a reason?"

"There was a song and dance about how the FBI had already taken up too much of her time and that she needed to devote more time to her teaching duties."

"Did you buy that?"

"Lansing, I've gotten nothing but a runaround since the first moment I stepped on that reservation. Somebody somewhere saw something or knows something. But no one's talking. When Miles quit on me I figured that was just par for the course."

"Has she gone back to Albuquerque?"

"No. She said she was going to leave first thing this morning."

"She can't get anywhere without passing through Las Palmas. I think I'll invite her in for a little talk before she leaves the county."

"Unless you have probable cause to stop her," Sheridan warned, "that is tantamount to kidnapping."

Lansing's eyes narrowed to mere slits, and the muscles in his jaw twitched as he clenched his teeth. He spoke in a whisper that sent a chill down Margarite's spine. "Don't quote the law to me, G-man. Because as of this moment I'm the only law in this county. Neither you, the Constitution, nor the laws of God are going to stop me from bringing in, dead or alive, the man who killed my son!"

61

DEPUTY HANNA SPENT THE ENTIRE NIGHT running errands for Sheriff Lansing. After securing the ranch with a roadblock and rounding up volunteers to keep the curious away, he reported to the office. Fortunately, the entire town was on alert, ready to respond to any requests.

The dry clearner opened so Gabe could get the sheriff's clean uniforms. The mercantile opened so it could provide toiletries and underclothing. The diner stayed open to supply a steady stream of sandwiches, soft drinks, and pastries.

Under other circumstances Gabe might have resented his demotion to errand boy. That night there wasn't enough he could do.

One of the toughest moments he had was during one of the trips to the diner. Velma, usually smiling, usually joking, always seductive, worked with a stone-face intensity that made her look old and haggard. She was filling coffee cups and water glasses as fast as she could while patrons tried to make orders or pay for meals.

"I'm sorry to interrupt, Velma," Gabe apologized. "I was supposed to pick up some sandwiches."

"Ernie's making them. You can go back to the kitchen."

Gabe went around the counter and into the kitchen. Ernie, dressed in his usual white T-shirt, apron, and chef's hat, was busy at the grill, scrambling eggs, frying bacon, and flipping pancakes. A cigarette hung out of his mouth. He normally didn't smoke while he was cooking, but this was a night when all the rules could be broken.

Ernie glanced up from his work when he saw Gabe enter. Without a word he motioned his head toward a plate of sandwiches on the counter.

Gabe was looking around for paper towels or plastic wrap to cover the plate with when Velma burst through the door. She grabbed his sleeve and pulled him toward the back door. "Come on," she ordered.

Velma's reputation as a manhandler had always intimidated Gabe. She always acted the coy temptress around him, never doing anything overt. He couldn't believe that tonight of all nights she was going to try and seduce him. At the moment he wasn't even flattered. He was angry.

The screen door slammed shut behind them. Before he could say a word she threw her arms around his neck and buried her face on his shoulder.

"Oh, Gabe," she sobbed. "He was such a neat kid. I spent all day with him. I was like the first date he ever had in his life!"

Gabe put his arms around her and held her tightly. "Yeah, I know," he said, fighting off his own tears. "C.J. was a neat kid. I was supposed to take him for a ride on my motorcycle. We just never got around to it."

Velma's shoulders shook with emotion, and Gabe could feel his shirt soaking up the tears. He relaxed his hug a little and patted her back. He wanted to tell her everything was going to be all right, but that wasn't how he felt. They were allowed to stand there only a couple of minutes. Ernie started pounding on his bell and yelling, "Order up! Order up!"

Velma released her stranglehold on Gabe's neck and gave him a sisterly peck on the cheek. "Thanks, Gabe. I needed that."

Wiping her eyes with her apron, she pulled the screen door open and went inside. A minute later she was back at the counter with an armload of plates, tending to her customers.

Kelly came through the doors with a stack of dirty plates. She saw Gabe wrapping the sandwiches for his office. "What'd you say to her?"

"Nothing," he said. "Why?"

"That's the first time all night I saw her smile, poor kid. I don't know what you did, but thanks."

"Sure." Gabe picked up the plate and headed for the courthouse.

62

DAYLIGHT BROKE TO A SKY OF DARK AND ragged clouds. Thunder rumbled in the mountains, promising a day of rain and general misery.

Lansing emerged from the shower room located next to the jail cells. The shower and shave helped to revitalize him. He hadn't even tried to take a nap. He knew his eyes would never close. All he cared about was getting on with the business at hand.

Pedro Gomez had been moved back to the second jail cell the afternoon before. Lansing didn't care if his prisoners managed to collaborate on a mutually agreeable story. They were no longer his prime suspects.

"Hey, Sheriff!" Gomez said from his cell. "Listen, me and Julio, we might have stole a few things here and there, but we never hurt nobody. We heard what happened down at your ranch last night. We just wanted to let you know, we're really sorry."

"Thanks," Lansing said. He half-expected to hear a protest over their illegal incarceration, but Gomez had said all he wanted to say for the moment. Lansing had to admit he was grateful for that.

It was only seven-thirty, and the waiting area in his office was already crowded—and the chaos was building. The FBI forensics team had assembled. They were in a huddle with Special Agent Sheridan. Deputy Cortez had already been assigned to escort them to the site near the Girl Scout camp, but at the moment he couldn't be found anywhere.

Two representatives from the State Bureau of Investigation wanted to personally brief Sheriff Lansing on what they had found at the Fulton residence. Gabe was trying to head them off. He promised them he would make sure the sheriff saw their findings; however, now was not a good time to see him.

An ambulance driver was trying to get a release form signed so that he could transport the bodies of Bill and Emily Fulton to Santa Fe for autopsies. He stood at the reception counter arguing with Deputy Peters, who didn't have the reputation of being a real "people person."

Behind Peters, Marilyn was fielding an incessant flow of phone calls. Most were messages of condolence. She had to assure the callers that Sheriff Lansing appreciated the sentiments, but was not available to come to the phone. Meanwhile, she was keeping the patrol Jeeps in the field busy. She dispatched one to a traffic accident west of Dulce. The second one was handling a domestic disturbance in Brazos.

Jack Rivera manned the third unit. He was on special assignment. Parked on Highway 15 south of Dulce, it was his job to intercept Dr. Victoria Miles after she left the reservation and bring her in for questioning.

Lansing ducked into the dayroom before anyone spotted him.

"You feel any better?" Margarite asked, nursing a cup of coffee she really didn't want.

"About as good as can be expected. Is the coffee any good?"

"This cup isn't. I put on a new pot, but I'm not making any promises." She tried to take a sip, but had to give up. "Have you figured out what you're going to do yet?"

"They're still waiting on the court order to have the body exhumed at the prison. As far as I'm concerned that's a waste of time. I'm having Mundo's mug photos enlarged. We'll run off copies and distribute them to the U.S. Marshals when they arrive."

"How many are coming in?"

"I don't know. I haven't talked to Sheridan yet. He talked to Director Williams just before I went in to clean up. Williams said he's pulling out all the stops. He claims we'll have more manpower than we'll know what to do with."

"The fire inspector said he was going to be out to your ranch by eight. Don't you want to be there for the recovery?"

"No," Lansing said angrily. "Would you?"

Margarite looked down at her cup of coffee. "No, I suppose not." She had learned there was a dark, harsh side to Lansing that he kept very well hidden. Whenever he was aroused by righteous indignation he would let the mantle of civilized decorum slip a little. He never lost control, but those who crossed him saw a hint of the beast within. She knew he was doing his very best. The rage was contained. She just wondered how much longer he could keep up the facade.

One of the phones in the room rang. Lansing picked it up. "Yes?"

It was Marilyn. "Sheriff, Deputy Rivera's on his way in. He has Doctor Miles with him, and it sounds like she's not very happy."

"That's good," he said. "On both counts. How soon will he get here?"

"He said they should be here in about twenty minutes."

"Thanks." He hung up the phone and turned to Margarite. "You look tired. Why don't you go home and get some rest?"

"I will later. Something tells me you may still need me around." She paused for a moment. "When are Carol and Frank supposed to get here?"

Lansing shook his head. "Later on this morning, I guess." He grabbed his mug from the top of his desk. "Isn't that coffee ready yet?" he grumbled, abruptly changing the subject.

63

 "I ASSURE YOU, DOCTOR MILES, YOU ARE NOT under arrest," Lansing began. "We're just trying to gather as much information as we can."

"I told Agent Sheridan yesterday that I'm withdrawing my services as a consultant."

"I didn't ask you in here to get your professional opinion."

"I wasn't asked," she snapped. "I was forced."

Lansing rubbed his eyes. The pressure of his fingers against his eyelids seemed to relieve some of the tiredness. "All right then. I didn't have you brought here to get your professional opinion. I need to ask you questions about things you have personal knowledge of."

"Like what?"

"Huero Mundo."

Miles seemed shaken at the mention of the name. She recovered her composure quickly. "Huero Mundo's dead. He has been for eight years."

Lansing normally conducted his interviews in his office. He was conducting this one in the dayroom. He had the reports they'd received stacked neatly on a desk in front of Miles. The desk was positioned so that it faced the wall map with the red and white pins.

Margarite and Sheridan sat to one side, listening and observing.

"That's right. He was supposed to have died in prison," Lansing said.

"It was in a hospital," Miles corrected. "A fire broke out. He died in his bed."

"Yeah, we asked about that." He picked up one of the reports from the desk. "This is the summary from the fire marshal. The fire didn't just break out. It was deliberately set, evidently by one of the trustees. I guess it was to cover his escape. They're still looking for him. I hope they catch him, because he's a real sick bastard. You know what he did?"

Miles shook her head. "I have no idea."

"He went into the nonambulatory ward. These are patients hooked to machines, with tubes running in and out of them. Probably people just waiting around to die. Anyway, he goes into this ward and douses a dozen patients with alcohol, then sets fire to them. He wrapped the fire sprinklers in each room with towels to make sure the fires wouldn't be put out.

"All twelve died. Burned beyond recognition. Good thing Mundo was in a coma. He probably didn't feel a thing."

Miles shifted uncomfortably in her seat. "That's a terrible story."

"It's not a story. It's in the report." He dropped it in front of her and picked up a second one. "The problem is, the hospital administration made an assumption. Since all of the patients were bedridden, they didn't bother to do any autopsies. They assumed the bodies in the beds were who they were supposed to be."

"So what are you saying?"

"I'm saying it's possible one of the patients put the

body of the missing trustee, who he probably killed, in his bed, then started the fire to cover his escape."

"Yeah, I suppose anything is possible." Miles did her best to sound bored.

"We will know for sure by the end of the day. After they exhume the body and perform an autopsy."

"I still don't understand what this has to do with me," she protested.

"We've already made the assumption Huero Mundo's still alive. Two bodies were found yesterday. A couple of college girls who had been missing from their campsite. They were found in the exact same spot the three Girl Scouts were found ten years ago."

Miles seemed to be distressed over the new information. "What does that have to do with Huero? He was found innocent of those other crimes."

"He was found not guilty," Lansing observed. "A minor legal issue, I suppose. That's all besides the point. Only I, a half dozen other men in this town, and the murderer knew where that spot was."

"I still don't know what this has to do with Huero. If he did escape from that hospital, where has he been for the last eight years?"

"I can show you. Approximately anyway." Lansing pointed at the map. "See these red pins? Those are unsolved murders. Murders that occurred after sexual assaults. All the victims had their throats slashed. Just like the two girls we found yesterday. Just like the three girls we found ten years ago.

"This one in Oklahoma. That happened six months after the hospital fire. Here in Nebraska. A year later. South Dakota, the year after that. You can follow them all the way to Washington state and back down to here.

"You testified for him during his trial. You said that he was a good man. You said all he wanted to do was become a medicine man, a good medicine man, a great medicine man. The records show that while he was in prison that's exactly what he studied. I think when he escaped he continued to study. I believe he studied under every medicine man in the West. Or at least tried to.

"The trouble with Mundo is that he has a couple of character flaws. The first is, he has absolutely no regard for human life."

"That's not true," Miles protested. "I asked him before his trial if he hurt those little girls. He told me no, that he could never hurt anyone."

"Add a third flaw," Lansing snorted. "He has a penchant for lying. We need to back up though. We hadn't gotten to the second one yet. And this is the one I needed to talk to you about.

"Every one of his sexually motivated murders happened in the month of June. You testified you had known each other since you were children. What was it in his past that drove him to this? And why only that month?"

Before Miles could say anything the phone rang. Lansing scowled at the interruption as Sheridan picked up the receiver.

"Yes?" He paused for a moment. "This is Agent Sheridan. Go ahead and put him through." He waited a second for the connection to be made. "Yeah, I'm here. Go ahead." He listened intently to the report being made. "Standard procedure. Don't touch a thing. We'll be there as soon as we can."

He hung up the phone and looked up. "That was Lieutenant Vicinti. They found Hector Velarde's body at the community center this morning. His throat had been cut."

"Oh, no," Miles whimpered.

"We've got to stop him," Sheridan said wearily. "What's he up to, eight now?"

"Eight?" Miles whispered. The look on her face told

the others she was trying to calculate where all the bodies came from.

"I guess we forgot to mention Sheriff Lansing's son," Sheridan said. "He was burned to death last night when someone set fire to their ranch house."

"No, no, no!" Miles cried. "He told me ... He promised me, he was only hurting those who hurt him!"

"What?" Lansing stormed. He picked Miles up by the shoulders and lifted her out of her seat. "You knew?" He shook her violently. "You knew he was here? You knew he was doing this?"

Margarite and Sheridan rushed to Miles's aid. Sheridan grabbed Lansing from behind, pinning his arms against his sides, while Margarite pulled her out of his reach.

Miles collapsed into her chair. "Not till yesterday afternoon," she sobbed. "I didn't even know he was alive till then. But he told me. He told me it was only Baltazar and Koteen and Fulton. He said those were the ones who'd hurt him. He said it was their fault he had been punished. He said he had a right to punish them.

"But he lied to me. He's been lying to me all these years. He's always lied to me."

Sheridan still held Lansing back. "Where is he?" the agent demanded. "Where can we find him?"

"Stone Lake. The old abandoned lodge. That's where he's been staying."

Lansing pulled free of Sheridan's hug and stomped to the door. Throwing the door open, he yelled, "Deputy Hanna, get in here."

Gabe appeared at the door a second later. "Yes, sir."

"Turn our two jailbirds in the back loose."

"Sir?"

"Turn them loose. We'll know where to find them if we want them. Then I want you to escort Doctor Miles back to one of the cells. She's going to be our guest for a while."

"Yes, sir," Gabe replied, more than a little confused over the turn of events. "Are we booking her?"

"Yes. Aiding and abetting a known criminal."

"Yes, sir."

As soon as Gabe left, Lansing turned to Sheridan. "All right, G-man. Let's get rolling. We have a criminal to catch."

"I think we can hold off, Sheriff."

"What do you mean, 'hold off'?"

"We've got manpower and equipment on the way. Let's wait for backup. Close the trap all at once. If a handful of us go up there we might spook him, scare him off. Then you'll have a repeat of your manhunt from ten years ago."

Lansing shook his head in frustration. "All right. All right. I guess a couple of more hours aren't going to matter. We'll do it your way."

THE FORCES DIRECTOR WILLIAMS HAD promised were beginning to assemble in Las Palmas. Twenty federal marshals had been bussed in along with fifteen additional FBI agents. Two ten-man SWAT teams from the State Bureau of Investigation had been provided to augment the federal units. Two police helicopters equipped with forward-looking infrared cameras were on their way. They were being delayed by the deteriorating weather outside.

Margarite felt in the way. As tired as she was, though, she couldn't bring herself to leave. Assuming it wouldn't cause a problem, she slipped back through the door to the jail cells to check on Lansing's newest prisoner.

Dr. Miles sat on the edge of the metal bunk. Her arms were folded across her chest and her eyes were closed. She rocked forward and back in a steady rhythm, and her lips moved in a silent chant. To Margarite, she looked like a mental patient entangled in a web of dementia.

"Doctor Miles?" Margarite said softly.

64

Miles's eyes opened slowly. She seemed completely aware of herself and the surroundings. "Yes?"

"I'm Doctor Margarite Carerra. I work for the public health service. I was wondering if I could get you anything?"

Miles shook her head and closed her eyes, continuing her rocking motion. Margarite watched her for a couple of minutes before turning toward the door.

"You know, they're true," Miles said.

Margarite turned back. Miles had stopped her rocking and her eyes were open. Her stare, though, was focused on something far away. "What?"

"The stories. They're all true. I didn't realize that until this morning."

"What stories?"

"The ones we historians so callously refer to as myths. The stories that tie a people, their culture, their religion all together.

"When the Great Spirit made the world he also made powerful holy people to help him with his creation. They were the *hactcin*. *Black Hactcin* lived in the lower world and created all the animals and the humans. *White Hactcin* lived in the upper world. He created the sun.

"*Black Hactcin* saw that his creations were not happy in the dark. He helped them build a ladder so they could climb to the outer world and live in the sunlight. He told the people to always follow the laws he had given them and to follow the sun, because the sun would lead them to the center of the world. There they would live in peace and happiness.

"The people who followed the laws and followed the sun were the Jicarilla. But not all the people obeyed. Some people didn't follow the sun. They lost their way and became other tribes. Others refused to follow the law *Black Hactcin* had given.

"The greatest evil they could commit was for a

brother to sleep with his sister, or a father with his daughter. When this happened the women didn't give birth to children. They gave birth to monsters. The monsters roamed the earth, killing the human beings, and there was nothing they could do to stop them.

"The sun, who was also a great spirit, saw what was happening. He selected a bride, White Painted Woman. He came to her in a storm cloud so he would not burn her and impregnated her with a bolt of lightning. She gave birth to a son, who became a great warrior. He has many names: Born of Thunder, Slayer-of-Enemies, The One Who Never Dies.

"This great warrior went out into the world and slew all the monsters, and because of him the human race still exists."

Margarite had heard many of the creation stories told by the different tribes in New Mexico. This was the first time she had heard the Jicarilla Apache version. It was similar in many ways to others she had heard. She didn't understand Miles's insistence that the story was true. "Is there more?" she asked hesitantly.

"The circle is a holy symbol in our religion. It represents the sun, the earth, the cycle of life.

"I learned this story only last night. I had to find out why Huero left the reservation all those years ago. Pinto Velarde, our chief medicine man, told me.

"When Cesar TeCube was young he had a wife he loved very much. She became pregnant and gave birth to twins, a boy and a girl. The birth was very hard on her and she died. Cesar remarried after that. But he never forgot how much he loved his first wife. He treated the twins poorly because he blamed them for their mother's death.

"When the son was old enough to fend for himself— a teenager, I guess—he ran away from home and no one ever heard from him again. About the same time the daughter became pregnant, even though she wasn't married. This angered Cesar very much. When the child was born he took the baby away from her to raise as his own. He made her an outcast of the tribe. She lived alone in the woods and had to fend for herself.

"Her child was Huero. Old Cesar gave him the last name of Mundo, 'child of the world.' He also did this because he didn't want anyone to know his grandson was a bastard.

"I grew up with Huero. All he ever cared about, all he ever talked about, was becoming a great medicine man like his grandfather. And that's exactly what Cesar wanted. He taught Huero everything: the secrets of herbs, the mysteries of animal-speak, the sacred chants that only *tsanati* are allowed to know.

"We grew apart when I went away to college. We still met on occasion in the meadows above Stone Lake. But when I came home from my second year at school, Huero had left the reservation. Old Cesar wouldn't tell me where he'd gone, wouldn't tell my why he'd left. In fact, he wouldn't even let me mention his name.

"Last night Pinto told me what had happened. Huero's mother came down from the mountains. It was the twentieth anniversary of her exile. Huero didn't even know she was alive. I guess the years in the wilderness hadn't been kind to her. She looked old and haggard. People who had seen her in the past called her the old witch in the woods.

"Cesar cursed her for showing her face. She threw his curse right back. She had come to get even for all of his years of cruelty. She had come to wreak vengeance for her exile.

"For all those years she had watched from afar while TeCube doted over his grandson. She'd watched as

Huero was raised to adulthood and taught all the secrets of the *tsanati*. It was now time for Cesar to know the truth. She and her twin had slept together. They wanted to create a monster, just like in the old stories. They wanted to punish TeCube for how they had been treated. Before he could do anything she ran back into the woods and disappeared.

"TeCube was a traditionalist and a true believer. Children of incest were monsters. They were not fit to live with humans. What was worse, TeCube had taught a monster the ways of the *tsanati*. Huero had been standing there the whole time. After the mother's confession TeCube couldn't stand the sight of him. He banished him from his house, from the tribe, from the reservation.

"That was thirty-three years ago. Thirty-three years ago this month. Pinto said the story goes that before Huero left the reservation he went into the woods, found his mother, and killed her. Only a monster could kill its own mother.

"Lansing asked me why June was such a special month. It's an anniversary of sorts. It was the month he ceased to be human. It's the month he became a monster, just like in the myths."

"If you heard this story last night, why didn't you say something to the authorities?"

"Because I didn't want to believe it. And why should I? Why had the story been kept a secret all those years? Pinto claimed it was out of respect for TeCube, our great medicine man. But it wasn't kept a secret out of respect. It was out of shame, if it was true at all.

"That's why I was leaving the reservation today. I didn't want to find out that everything they said about Huero was true. I loved him. From the time I was a child, I loved him.

"I promised him I wouldn't tell anyone that he was

alive. And the only way I could keep that promise was to get clear away."

She was silent for a moment as she reflected on her story. "You see what I mean about the stories being true. We've come full circle. The monsters have returned to the earth, and we can't stop them. Only Born of Thunder, Slayer-of-Enemies can."

65

SHERIDAN HAD COMPLETED BRIEFING HIS UNIT commanders. The plan was to head north to Dulce, then follow the reservation road south to Stone Lake. The trip would take approximately two hours. Once they had reached the ridge overlooking the lodge, the personnel would spread out through the woods and completely surround the target building. While the teams were taking positions, the helicopters would launch from Las Palmas. Weather permitting, they would fly over the mountains and head directly for the lodge. Flight time was estimated at fifteen minutes.

The helicopters and ground teams would be ready to close in on Huero at the same moment. Each of the unit commanders thought this would be a textbook operation. Even with the impending rain they didn't foresee any problems.

"All right, gentlemen," Sheridan announced. "Let's head 'em out."

Lansing fell in step with Sheridan as he started for the door. "I'll follow up in my Jeep."

Sheridan stopped and turned to Lansing. "I'm afraid you're not coming along."

"What?"

"This is a federal operation. You don't have any authority on the reservation."

"That's no problem. Have one of the marshals deputize me."

"You don't understand, Lansing. I don't want you along. I talked this over with Director Williams and he agrees. You're too emotionally involved in this. We can't afford for some hothead to go rushing in and spoil the setup after this much preparation."

"You don't think I can handle this in a professional manner?"

"Frankly, no. From what I've seen of your actions since midnight, I'd say you're out of control. You're tired. You're emotionally distraught. You have no business being near this operation."

"How do you propose to keep me from coming along?"

"I'm giving out orders. If you put one foot on that reservation, other than to pass from one side of your county to the other, you'll be placed under arrest."

"For what?"

"Obstruction of justice, for starters. And I have over fifty armed men at my disposal to make sure my orders are carried out. Are we clear on this?"

"Yeah," Lansing said quietly. "We're clear."

Lansing stood at the window to his office and watched as Sheridan pulled away in his car, followed by two buses and two SWAT vans. Margarite slipped through the door and came up to stand next to him.

"I heard they decided they didn't need your services," she said quietly.

"Yeah. I guess you could say I was uninvited."

"I'm sorry."

"Me too." He paused. "He was right in doing it."

"Sheridan?"

Lansing nodded. "I was out of control. I can't believe I manhandled Doctor Miles like that. I'm a little bit embarrassed and a whole lot ashamed. I can understand why the FBI didn't want me in the middle screwing things up."

"What are you going to do now?"

"Wait."

She wished there was something she could say that could change things. However, she knew there wasn't. "I guess I'd better get out to the pueblo. Will you call me when you hear something?"

"Yeah." Behind them, his phone rang. He walked over to his desk and picked it up. "Lansing."

"Sheriff," Marilyn said, "I'm sorry to bother you. I don't know how they got in the courthouse, but I have that boy Marcus out here. He's with his parents. They said they've been waiting for hours to see you. Should I tell them now's not a good time?"

"No," Lansing said wearily. "I'll talk to them."

He opened the door to his office so that the Baltazars could come in. He shook hands with Marcus and Christina. John's hands were still bandaged, though not as heavily as a few days earlier. He introduced Margarite, then invited them to sit.

"I'm sorry you had to wait. Things have been kind of rough around here the past day or so."

"We know, Sheriff," John said. "That's why we're here."

"What do you mean?"

"Your deputy. When he brought Marcus home last night, he explained that Marcus helped you find the two girls that were missing in the mountains."

"Yes, he did. He led me right to them."

Baltazar looked at the floor, a little ashamed. "Maybe we have done wrong by our son by not listening to him. There is a lot of truth in his dreams. Truth we didn't want to see because we were afraid. You see, we want him to get an education. Go to college. We thought that was the best way he could help our tribe. Maybe he can do that and still study to become a *tsanati*."

"That's good," Lansing nodded, still wondering what the visit was about.

"You helped us see that. That's why we are here. We want to help you."

"How?"

It was Marcus's turn to speak. "Last night I had a dream about the Owl-man again. He was dancing around a great fire, yelling and howling like an animal. He danced for a long time. When he finally stopped, he bent over and picked up this bundle from the ground. It was long and thin like a rug that had been rolled up. He threw the rug over his shoulder and ran into the mountains."

Lansing nodded. A great fire. His house. Marcus had seen his house burning. "Do you know what's supposed to be in this rug he was carrying?"

Marcus shook his head. "I didn't see it. But I heard it. It was somebody crying, yelling for help."

Lansing sat up in his chair. "There was someone in the rug?"

"It sounded like that. Yes."

"You said he ran into the mountains. Do you know where? Was it Stone Lake?"

"No," Marcus shook his head. "Not Stone Lake. It was south of there." He thought for a moment. "He went to the caves. The Caves of the Wind."

"That's Angelina Peak," Lansing said, standing. "That's not even on the reservation."

"That makes sense, Lansing," Margarite said. "If he's hiding out he'd do it where no one would look."

Lansing stepped around his desk and knelt in front of

the boy. "Marcus, you're sure, in your dream there was someone wrapped up in that rug? And they were alive?"

"I think so. I mean, yes. In my dream I heard them crying. They were alive."

"Thank you, son." He put his arms around Marcus and gave him a hug. "That's the best news I've had in a long time."

Lansing stood. "Mr. and Mrs. Baltazar, thank you for coming here. I'm sorry, but I have to leave. I've got business to take care of." He reached for his Stetson and gun belt on the hat stand.

"Sheriff," Marcus said, pulling his great-grandfather's *jish* from beneath his shirt and pulling the strap over his head. "You have to take this with you. It will protect you."

"Your great-grandfather gave it to you. It's for your protection."

"I have my parents. They will protect me. You are fighting the Owl-man. The spirit of my *Náhánálí* will protect you as long as you wear his medicine pouch."

Lansing took the *jish* and slipped the strap over his head. "Thanks, Marcus. I told you I would probably need your help again."

Margarite followed him out the door. "Where are you going?"

"Where do you think? After my son. And Mundo."

"Because of what that boy said in there? What happened to the eternal skeptic?"

"I guess if a man gets desperate enough he'll believe in anything. I've reached that point." He put his hat on as he stepped outside. Margarite was just behind him. "Where do you think you're going?"

"With you."

"I thought you were heading out to the pueblo."

"It'll be there when I get back."

"I think you'd better stay here."

"Like hell!"

66

LANSING BACKED CEMENT HEAD DOWN THE ramp of the trailer and threw the reins over his neck. The summit of Angelina Peak disappeared into the clouds a thousand feet above him. Water ran from the back brim of his Stetson down the canvas poncho he wore for protection. As he swung himself into the saddle, he could see Margarite's face through the rain-streaked window of the Jeep. She wasn't smiling.

"I'll be back before you know it," he yelled. A moment later he had Cement Head pointed up the side of the mountain. They were looking for a trail that would lead them to the north slope and the Caves of the Wind.

The promise of rain had become a guarantee. A steady mist had started as soon as Lansing had reached his ranch. The fire captain and his assistant approached the Jeep when he arrived.

"Sheriff," the captain said, "I may have some good news. We've been through every inch of that mess in there, twice. There's no sign of a body."

"I had a hunch you were going to tell me that," Lansing said, smiling grimly.

"What do you mean?"

"A little bird told me. A thing called a Shadow-catcher. How about giving me a hand? I need to hook up my horse trailer."

The fire captain turned up his collar to the increasingly heavier mist. "I think you're picking the wrong day to go for a pleasure ride, Sheriff."

"I'm not doing this for enjoyment," Lansing said, starting to back his Jeep toward his parked trailer. "At least, not entirely," he mumbled to himself.

After the chaos and confusion of the previous night, Cement Head seemed overjoyed to see his riding partner. He nearly pranced from the stall as Lansing led him out to be saddled. Even his usual stubborn streak was set aside when he was loaded into the trailer, one of his least favorite places.

Margarite sat silently next to Lansing as he followed the narrow, winding gravel road that crawled up the side of Angelina Peak. She had tried all the arguments she could think of, but none of them worked.

"Shouldn't you notify Agent Sheridan that you've located Mundo?"

"Do you think he'd believe me? Especially if I told him my source was a twelve-year-old's dream?"

"Shouldn't you bring one of your deputies along for backup?"

"Only a couple of them know how to ride, and none of them owns a horse. And they wouldn't be able to keep up with me on foot."

"Don't you think you're setting yourself up to get killed?"

"I'm not worried. I'm wearing my medicine pouch. It's worked before."

"I think you're being a damned fool!"

"That makes two of us."

"Lansing, you're one stubborn son of a bitch!"

"Thanks."

After that Margarite folded her arms, refusing to even acknowledge his presence, even though he was driving.

Lansing was lost in his own thoughts. He had been telling himself for nearly twenty years that the only important thing in life was to be the best lawman he could be. It had ruined his marriage. It was a wedge between him and Margarite. His own son was nearly a stranger to him.

Not everything in his life could be fixed. But maybe a few things could. He was being offered another chance. He could still be a damned good lawman and try to be a good father as well.

Angelina Peak was a heavily wooded mountain that sat at the north end of Questa River Canyon Wilderness Area, only three miles from the southeastern boundary of the Jicarilla reservation. The entire area was remote and hard to get to. Only the hardiest of hikers ever got up to that area. Lansing had to admit, Mundo was smart. If he wanted to stay hidden for a long time, this was one of the best places in the state for doing it.

He parked at the highest point the road would take him. The caves were to the northwest, about two miles from the road and five hundred feet higher. The farther up the mountain the road had taken them, the heavier the rains became. By the time they parked they were in a steady downpour.

To the south and west, ominous thunder rumbled over the peaks. Lightning silhouetted the mountaintops with brilliant flashes that grew longer and closer as the storm increased.

Lansing reached inside his glove compartment and pulled out a pistol. He checked to make sure it was loaded, then set the safety. He handed the gun to Margarite.

"What's this for?"

"Just in case."

"What? Just in case I get hungry and an elk stumbles by?"

"If that's what you feel like using it for, sure."

She put her hand on his arm. "Why do you think you always have to be the Lone Ranger?"

"I don't," he said, patting her hand. "Sometimes that's just the way the cards fall."

He gave her a quick kiss on the lips, then pushed his door open. This was no time for a long good-bye.

The first trail Lansing and Cement Head stumbled on looked promising. After a short distance, though, it switched back on itself and pointed them down the slope. They headed straight up the slope until they found a second trail. This one headed them north and took them higher up the mountainside.

The dark, overcast sky did little to help Lansing's sense of direction. He knew he was headed away from his parked Jeep, but he couldn't tell if they were heading north or if they'd already rounded the mountain face to the west.

As the trail took them higher the trees began to thin. Lansing had been on the mountain only a few times, but the terrain was beginning to look familiar. He knew he was getting close to the caves.

He squinted his eyes against the pelting rain, looking for the marker. Above the caves was a sheer cliff face. Water and wind, cold and hot, had gouged away the volcanic ash layer that contained the caves. Over a million years the ash left by Valles Caldera thirty miles to the south had eroded below the cliff, leaving dozens of pockmarks in the mountainside. Some were only a foot or two deep. Others went on for yards, sometimes joining other caves along the cliff face, forming tunnels. The air seemed to continually rush through these passages. Even on a still day the wind howled its way through the corridors. Caves of the Wind was an appropriate name.

A flash of lightning lit the entire world, followed immediately by a deafening crack of thunder. Cement Head reared up on his hind legs, unable to contain his fear.

Lansing reined him in, pulling the bridle down and to the right, so that the horse's head faced away from the storm. "That's all right, horse," Lansing yelled above the rain. "It scared me too."

He got down from the saddle. He was close enough that he could go on foot. A rider on horseback provided too large a target.

He led Cement Head to a line of trees and lashed the reins to a low bush. Lansing looked up as another flash lit the skies.

The cliff face was directly above him. Now all he had to do was find the right cave.

Lansing didn't try to be quiet. He knew he couldn't be heard above the steady din of the rain.

The first cave he came to that could have held two people was deserted. Even in the dim light of the storm he could see to the rear of the depression. That was the story for the next few.

He finally came to a cave that disappeared into darkness. He hesitated before going in. None of the caves was more than four feet high, which meant he had to enter on his hands and knees or crouched in a position where it would be hard to defend himself.

He pulled out his gun, then switched on the flashlight he had brought with him. He half-expected someone to start firing at him. Nothing happened, and the beam of his flashlight bounced against the back wall, fifteen feet away.

He switched off the light and moved to the next opening.

The story was the same for the next half dozen caves he inspected. A little voice kept nagging at him. He was wasting his time. Marcus was wrong. Mundo was nowhere near here. Neither was his son.

"Shut up!" Lansing whispered to himself. "There are plenty more caves to look in."

The next entrance disappeared into darkness. He cautiously turned on the light. This one was a cave-turned-tunnel. The passage curved around to the right. Lansing guessed it tied in with another entrance further along the cliff face. He quickly turned off the light.

If he were Mundo, he thought, he certainly wouldn't pick a cave that had only one entrance. That would leave him trapped. Mundo was too smart to let that happen to him. He would pick a tunnel, like this one.

Lansing crouched and followed the tunnel around, keeping his back to the wall. Every few minutes, it seemed, there came another flash of lightning. That worked to his advantage. Each flash helped him to see a little farther down the passage.

After twenty feet the cave turned, and Lansing realized he could no longer see the entrance he had used. He couldn't see any sign of an exit either. He fought off the anxiety. He also fought off the temptation to turn on his flashlight. Things were going to be fine. All he had to do was keep to the course he had laid out.

There was another flash of lightning. This time it illuminated the walls of the tunnel ahead of him. He was approaching the opposite end of the passage.

He stopped and listened for any sounds. All he could hear was the rain and the constant growl of thunder.

He edged closer to the exit.

Another flash of lightning.

This time Lansing could see the opening. Silhouetted by the flash was the form of a man, squatting in the entrance, guarding against any intruders. At the same moment his foot hit something soft and yielding.

He carefully reached down and touched something. It was cloth. He pushed with the palm of his hand and felt a leg. When he did, he could hear a muffled whimper.

He quickly bent close to the sound. "Shh," he said as softly as he could. "It's your dad. Be quiet. I'll get you out of here."

There was another flash of lightning. Lansing looked at the entrance for fear he might have been heard.

Mundo was gone.

Lansing switched on the flashlight. He'd been discovered. Stealth didn't matter anymore. What did matter was getting C.J. out of there.

C.J.'s mouth was covered with duct tape. In fact, his hands and feet had been wrapped with it several times.

Lansing stuffed his gun back into the holster and pulled out his knife. A few seconds later his son was free.

C.J. threw his arms around his father's neck. "I knew you would come," he whimpered hoarsely. "I knew you would."

Lansing returned the hug. He had thought he'd never be able to do that again. "Come on," he said, pulling C.J. to his feet. "Let's get out of here."

C.J. tried to take a step, but fell. The circulation to his feet had been cut off for hours. It would be several minutes before he would be able to walk again.

Lansing half-dragged him to the opening where Mundo had been squatting minutes before. There was no sign of the Apache.

Lansing picked his son up in his arms and began walking as fast as he could toward the tree line. Suddenly a heavy force fell upon his back as Mundo let out a war cry in his ear.

He had no choice but to drop his son as he twisted

to fight his assailant. Mundo's knife blade flashed as it reflected another bolt of lightning. Lansing grabbed Mundo's wrist, at the same time trying to clamp down on his throat.

Mundo pushed Lansing's hand away from his throat. The two lost balance and began to roll down the slope. The knife went flying from the Apache's grip. Almost at the same moment Lansing's gun slipped out of its holster.

Their roll stopped with Lansing on top. He had both hands around Mundo's throat. "What were you going to do with my son?"

"I was saving him," Mundo rasped. "I wanted to see the look on your face when you saw that he was alive and then had to watch while I killed him in front of you."

"That won't happen now," Lansing growled.

"You can't stop me," Mundo choked. "No man on earth can stop me!"

With every bit of strength he could muster, Mundo tore Lansing's fingers from his throat. Arching his back, he caused the white man to lose balance. Writhing like a snake, he slipped from underneath Lansing, then gave him a kick in the ribs.

Lansing lunged for Mundo as he scrambled up the slope. He caught the cuff of his pants, but Mundo managed to kick free.

Before Lansing could stop him Mundo had his hands on Lansing's gun. Mundo whipped around, holding the pistol with both hands. Barely ten feet separated them as Mundo began firing. He squeezed off three quick rounds.

Lansing clamped his eyes shut, knowing the worst was about to happen. Nothing did. Not a single bullet hit its mark.

"Ah-h-g!" Mundo screamed in frustration, throwing

the pistol at his enemy. He jumped to his feet and scrambled farther up the slope.

Lansing dove for his gun, amazed that Mundo could miss him at such close range. When he turned back, the Apache had found what he had been looking for.

Mundo stood, his knife in hand. With the weapon raised high above his head he screamed, *"Sekala Ka-amja!"*

Lansing drew a bead on the madman, but before he could fire, the bolt of lightning streaked from the sky. The flash was blinding. The immediate explosion of thunder threw him backward. He was dazed and deafened for several long seconds.

As he began to recover he found his son kneeling over him. "Dad," C.J. pleaded. "Are you okay?"

Lansing sat up, trying to remember what had just happened.

"I thought he shot you!"

Lansing reached under his poncho and felt his chest. He could feel the *jish* Marcus had given him, and his fingers closed around it. "No. He never hit me." He suddenly glanced up the slope. "Mundo! What happened to Mundo?"

"I don't know," C.J. said, looking up the slope to where the Apache had been standing only minutes before. "There was the lightning. When I opened my eyes he was gone."

Lansing got to his feet and scrambled to where the Apache had just been. The ground was charred. Blackened streaks radiated in a star-burst pattern around the spot.

A few feet away was Mundo's knife. The blade was warped, curled at the end, as if it had been exposed to a thousand-degree furnace.

Lansing tried to pick it up, but it was still too hot. He left it where it lay. They could get it later when they came back for Mundo's body. Then he realized: There was no body to recover. It had been vaporized by a million volts of electricity.

If there were indeed Apache gods, Lansing thought, they had just corrected the mistake they had let loose on the world.

C.J. came up the slope and handed him his gun. As he holstered it Lansing looked up in the sky. Something was different. The storm was breaking up. The lightning had stopped. There was still thunder, but it was far away. And the rain was no longer coming down in torrents. It was soft and gentle.

He knelt and put his arms around his son. "C.J., I think it's time we went away for a while. Just the two of us."

"What about your job?"

"It'll be there when I come back. But sometimes there are more important things in life than being sheriff."

"Like what?"

"Like just being your dad."

As they started down the slope the idea flashed through Lansing's mind that he wouldn't mind having C.J. as his chief deputy. He pushed the thought aside. For the time being, he was satisfied with them just being father and son.